Reviews of
Don Johnston Novels

The Dar Lumbre Chronicles

"A clever extrapolation of today's sociopolitical pathologies to the next century . . . Ingenious narrative . . ."

— *Kirkus Reviews*

The Alamogordo Connection

"First contact is an intriguing hook, made more effective through believable details of carrying out scientific research and rainforest trekking, bolstered by Johnston's background in biology, chemistry, and jungle survival."

— *Kirkus Reviews*

By Means of Peace

Don Johnston

ISBN: 979-8-9856454-4-6 (paperback)

ISBN: 979-8-9856454-5-3 (epub)

By Means of Peace is political fiction describing how groupthink will destroy America.

Publishing and Design Services: MelindaMartin.me

Dedication and Special Thanks

This novel is dedicated to my family and friends.

My special thanks to Janice Stewart
for her proofreading and editing help.

CHAPTER 1

D arien Segura linked his iTab to the docking station on his desk. Before he could touch the keyboard or give a voice command, the iTab pinged, and the words, *Incoming Message,* appeared onscreen. The message morphed into an icon of a navy-blue book with *Little Horn Literary Agency* emblazoned in gold on the cover. Darien's heart skipped a beat, and he dared to hope the message was an acceptance letter. Holding his breath, he touched the icon, and it opened to reveal a stark message:

> *Dear Mr. Segura:*
>
> *The Little Horn Literary Agency no longer represents unpublished authors; however, we wish you every success in finding an agency or publisher willing to work with you.*
>
> *Regards, I. Horn*

Darien muttered under his breath and let out a long sigh. He realized that selling a debut novel was considerably more complicated than initially anticipated. Six months ago, he finished his first novel, *The Photosynthesis Gene,* which Kirkus Reviews called *"A clever extrapolation of today's sociopolitical pathologies to the next century . . . an ingenious narrative."* With such a glowing review, he'd expected some literary agent to jump at the chance to market his novel, but it didn't happen.

After a flurry of rejections from literary agents, he sent his work to several dozen imprints represented by the Big Five publishing houses in New York. Like the agents, the publishers gave a pat answer: *We don't accept manuscripts from authors not represented by an agent.* The publishing industry's modus operandi reminded him of the old riddle, *Which came first, the chicken or the egg?*

Further muddling the picture, Amazon had acquired New York's Big Five publishing companies: Hachette, Macmillan, Penguin Random House, HarperCollins, and Simon and Schuster. Purchasing these companies gave Amazon a stranglehold on the industry, but they hadn't changed the way the Big Five conducted business. All of them continued to deal primarily with literary agents, and newcomers without an agent were virtually always given the cold shoulder, an arrangement that seemed designed to maintain the status quo forever.

It was common for authors who didn't have agents to self-publish their work, but Darien hated the idea of becoming an *indie author*–an independent author. To be successful, he would have to be his own publicity agent. He'd researched methods for getting followers via social media–the process of *building a platform*–but hadn't tried it yet. Such an approach was time-consuming and would interfere with his writing.

Darien reread his query letter and tried to think of something eye-popping to say before sending another round. The template he'd chosen from the internet was worthless. It had yet to draw a second look. After a moment of deep thought, he put both hands atop his head, swiveled around, and surveyed his condo.

The unit was about 600 square feet and consisted of a living/sleeping/kitchen area and a bathroom. Since Darien spent so much time writing, he'd set up the living area as a well-organized office with an ergonomic desk and chair, a bookcase, small end tables with lamps, and a love seat with matching chairs. Other than the office, the unit was a mundane, no-frills, one-occupant residence assigned to him by HUD, the *Housing and Urban Development* branch of NatGov.

Even with his monthly rent subsidy, Darien couldn't afford a bigger unit. However, when he sold his novel, he might be financially able to request an upgrade from HUD in his current housing complex, The George Washington. The unit was near the Houston Mediplex, a popular location. His twin sister, Rachel, lived here, as did his best friends, Alden and Justin Thibideaux. The two sets of siblings had been close friends for years, and Justin was Rachel's assistant at Vi-Tech, where both worked as virologists. The quartet was virtually inseparable; however, the possibility existed that Rachel would move when—*or if*—she and Steven got married.

Darien's iTab chimed *Over the Rainbow*, Rachel's ringtone.

It had happened again—less than five seconds ago, Rachel crossed his mind. Now, she was calling him. Over the years, that sequence of events had happened too many times to count. Although extensive psychological tests hadn't confirmed it, Darien felt that he and Rachel occasionally demonstrated ESP, the psi phenomenon that made some of their ancestors famous.

"Hey, Rachel, what's up?"

"I called to remind you about the Citizenship Meeting. You wouldn't want to miss two in a row."

"I know," Darien said. "I'm getting ready to head that way. What's on the program tonight?"

"I think it's another video."

"Probably one we've seen a half-dozen times."

"If so, I'll catch a nap," Rachel said. "I stayed up late last night studying."

"Come by my condo, and I'll walk you to the auditorium."

"Okay, see you in ten minutes."

The *Citizenship Meeting* was a concession residents of HUD-sponsored housing had to make to get rental assistance. The meetings occurred monthly, and a roll call was conducted by retina scan and facial recognition software. Residents were required to attend 75% of the meetings unless they could prove they were out of town on business, which Darien never was.

Housing complexes like The George Washington and its neighbor, The Abraham Lincoln, were required to follow a tedious list of NatGov rules and regulations. The most carefully scrutinized regulation was the *Citizenship Distribution Mandate*, an addendum to Constitutional Amendment Number 127. The amendment required all housing complexes within incorporated cities to balance their resident population proportionate to the city's racial makeup. DNA tests determined ethnicity. Surnames were meaningless, as shown by the name *Segura,* which was Hispanic, though the family's genetic makeup was predominately Scandinavian and British.

When congress enacted the Citizenship Distribution Mandate, inner-city slum neighborhoods didn't disappear as NatGov promised. Instead, they moved to new zip codes. Slum landlords forced out of cities built low-priced, low-quality housing for those without HUD assistance. While NatGov continued to amend existing regulations and pass others, few citizens were satisfied with their efforts. Making everybody equal had proved to be beyond the government's capability. Many people Darien's age thought it was time for new leadership in Washington. And, for the first time in his life, he was tinkering with the idea of getting more involved in the political process.

Darien's doorbell rang, and he stepped into the hallway to join Rachel and a group of other residents walking toward a wide doorway at the end of the hall. The door led to a balcony above the main auditorium where residents of the housing unit gathered for Citizenship Meetings.

"How're things going at Vi-Tech?" Darien asked as he fell in step with Rachel.

"Still slow," Rachel said, "but we got a small order from the NIH today—some work on the Phoenix-75 virus. Dr. Truman thinks it will lead to something bigger."

After a short discussion about jobs and the economy, Darien changed the subject. "Did you get Mom's text this afternoon?"

Rachel nodded. "I did. It will be a special treat to celebrate Papa's 96th birthday with him."

Papa was also named Darien Segura, and the young twins walking along the hallway were two of his grandchildren. Moreover, they were the third set of semi-identical twins born into the Segura family over the past 125 years. The unusual twins had occurred every other generation since the birth of the original Darien and Rachel over a century ago. In each case, the Segura family re-used the original names. Darien, twenty-seven years old, knew that the original Darien was Darien I, Papa was

Darien II, and he, himself, was Darien III. So far, no Darien had used the numerical suffixes, and he didn't intend to either.

The biggest oddity about the Segura twins was that all three sets were semi-identical, the opposite sex, a highly-improbable genetic anomaly that occurs when one twin gets a Y chromosome from his father and nearly all other chromosomes from his mother. The Y results in that twin being a male. The female twin has only X chromosomes, most of them from her mother. Medical records documented less than a dozen pairs of such twins born over the last century, and all except the Seguras had severe congenital disabilities.

Rather than a disability, the Segura twins had an oddity that set them apart. In each set, the females–the *Rachels*–had one blue and one brown eye–a condition known as *heterochromia*. This unusual situation had become a trademark for the female twins, and academics deemed it a sign of high intelligence. In Darien's opinion, Rachel was proof enough the academics were correct.

Darien I and Rachel I were members of the team who decoded an extraterrestrial message. To the astonishment of scientists worldwide, ESP was the primary tool used to decipher the message. The accomplishments of the high-achieving Seguras were TNTC–*too numerous to count*, including their participation in the terraforming of Mars, where a large colony was now thriving.

And the family legend didn't stop there.

The next Darien–Darien II or Papa–was renowned for a phenomenal achievement, the discovery of *iso-lithium*.

Nearly sixty years ago, Papa discovered a way to produce an isotope of lithium known as iso-lithium. Batteries made from the isotope lasted ten times longer than regular lithium batteries. Consequently, automobiles powered by them were cheaper to operate than those powered by hydrocarbons and were virtually pollution free. A few years after the discovery, all industrialized nations, in conjunction with the UN, banned the use of fossil fuels for privately owned vehicles. Papa won a Nobel Prize for his achievement, and environmentalists praised him as the single most significant contributor to reducing man-made carbon dioxide.

Yet, Papa's remarkable discovery was not without detractors. Proponents of fossil fuels quickly pointed out the ban would cripple the economy of many OPEC nations. Moreover, their dire predictions came to pass. Today, most Mideast countries were struggling to avoid returning to their pre-oil status. They had brought the problem before the UN several times, but no one had proposed a workable solution.

Based on the scientific achievements of their ancestors, the Segura family had expected both Darien and Rachel to be STEM proponents. Nothing could be further from the truth in Darien's case. While he admired his predecessors, he didn't plan to follow their king-sized footsteps through the world of science. His degree from Baylor University was in journalism, and he was writing science fiction as a career. He'd never considered anything else. Shunning science for science fiction turned him into the family's *black sheep* for a while. However, most of his relatives eventually realized that having a fiction writer in the family wasn't a total disgrace. Some of them read sci-fi regularly, just as he did. And, although they didn't know it, he'd used some of their unusual character traits to build fictional characters, including both heroes and villains.

Upon entering the balcony, Darien and Rachel looked toward the back of the room—the *catnap section* as some called it. They were too late. Their favorite seats were occupied. While part of the price for rental assistance was attendance at 75% of the Citizenship Meetings, nothing compelled the attendees to listen, and many didn't. Consequently, when HUD repeated a video, snoring sometimes emanated from the rear of the balcony.

"We'll have to go down front," Darien said.

"I saw a new family moving in a couple of days ago," Rachel said as they started down the steps. "We should be able to spot them from up here."

"Maybe we'll get the chance to meet them after the meeting."

Rachel sat down, and Darien stood momentarily to survey the crowd below him. He knew all long-term residents by sight and most by name. So far, he hadn't seen anybody he didn't recognize but kept looking around in anticipation of locating the newcomers.

As the lights dimmed gradually, three strangers hurried into the auditorium through a side door. Two of them were women in their twenties, along with an older woman about the right age to be their mother. Darien watched them pick their way to a row of vacant seats near the back of the auditorium. As they were about to sit down, the tallest of the three, dark-haired and slender, glanced toward Darien but turned away quickly. Though the light was dim, Darien was sure they'd made eye contact. He'd never seen the woman before, but there was something eerily familiar about her, and he kept his eyes fixed on her. A moment later, she turned and looked directly at him as the lights faded to black.

The IMAX screen came to life with a kaleidoscope of colors that coalesced into an image of the American flag waving atop the White House. News banners began to scroll across the screen in bold letters:

PHOENIX-75 ATTACKS GRAIN CROPS

FOOD SHORTAGES PROBABLE NEXT YEAR

OPEC REPEATS REQUEST FOR
UN TO APPEAL FOSSIL FUEL BAN

NEW POLITICAL PARTY PROMISES TO
BRING EQUALITY TO ALL

The news banners were part of the long-standing *Public Information Mandate* requiring regular news updates at Citizenship Meetings in HUD–subsidized housing. Currently, the Alphabet News Network supplied most of the public information broadcasts. Alphabet was closely affiliated with a political party, the RADS–the *Republican and Democratic Society*. The current President, Isaac Ford, was a member of the RADS; therefore, Alphabet News presented the news via a template praising everything the RADS did and criticizing everything done by Independents, the other key political party. It seemed like the Independents were in an excellent position to win next year's presidential election. If so, they would take control of the news media. Darien seldom paid much attention to the news banners preceding the citizenship program, but in this case, he perked up when the headline scrolled by announcing the formation of a new political party. Apparently, the social media was right this time.

The brief news presentation ended, and the citizenship video began with the title, *Peace Through Equality*.

The title was new, but when the video started, Darien recognized it as a collage of previous lectures they'd seen several times. About two minutes into the presentation, he glanced at his sister. Her head was tilted to one side, and her eyelids were nearly closed.

The film droned on for thirty minutes. When it ended, the auditorium lights came on, and Darien nudged Rachel with his elbow. "Look down there," he said, pointing toward the three newcomers.

"Those are the people I told you about!"

"I'm going to run downstairs and meet them," Darien said.

With Rachel close behind, he sprinted down the stairs, burst into the hallway, and looked around. The three women weren't near the exit door where Darien anticipated they would be. Quickly, he looked down the hall and spotted them in the distance. The women were walking away at a fast clip, apparently in a hurry.

Darien took several steps down the hall and then squelched the urge to run after them. As he watched, they went through a hallway door and disappeared.

When Darien returned to his condo, his thoughts remained fixed on the woman who'd hurried away without a backward glance. She bore a strong resemblance to someone from his past—Lorelei Welker.

The thought of Lorelei brought a flood of memories to Darien. He and Rachel had grown up with her in Freeport, Texas. They attended the same schools from kindergarten through high school and graduated nine years ago from Brazosport

High–*B-Port High*–as students called it. Lorelei was the daughter of B-Port's basketball coach, and during his last two years, Darien was the best player in the school. Coach Welker and his wife were very fond of him and, seemingly, picked him as their future son-in-law when he was only a freshman.

The Welkers' over-eager matchmaking was the main factor contributing to the rocky relationship between Darien and Lorelei. They'd fallen in and out of love a half-dozen times and had gone steady, semi-steady, and not-nearly-steady for six or seven years, including their college days. After graduating from college, they'd called it quits by mutual agreement–*no harm, no foul.* Nevertheless, Darien still thought of Lorelei frequently. No woman he'd dated since the breakup had dimmed his memory of her.

The thought of a Lorelei redux intrigued him.

CHAPTER 2

Marisa Da Rosa entered the condo ahead of her sister and mother. She looked toward the kitchen, where her grandmother was stirring a pot on the stove. "Hey, Zina, what's for dinner?"

Zina looked around. "Black bean stew and rice—it's ready."

"Great," Marisa said. "Everybody's hungry."

"Tell me about the meeting," Zina said.

Marisa shrugged. "There's nothing worth telling."

"Yes, there is," Marisa's sister, Izzy, chimed in. "Marisa and some guy made eyes at each other until the lights went out."

"Little Sister, you talk too much," Marisa said. The twinkle in her eyes belied her mock anger.

"What did he look like?" Zina asked.

"He was tall, dark, and handsome," Izzy said.

"So, what happened?" Zina said.

"Marisa ducked out through a side door, dragging us behind her," Izzy said. "I started to wait for him myself."

Amused, Zina looked at Marisa. "Why didn't you want to meet him?"

"For one thing, he was with a woman."

With an amused smile, Zina motioned toward the dining table. "The food's getting cold," she said. "We can continue this discussion while eating."

The three generations of women had lived together longer than Marisa could remember. She'd given her sister and grandmother their nicknames when she was so young she couldn't recall the incidents. Frieda–her mother–had told the stories countless times. When her sister was born, Marisa was less than three years old and couldn't say the baby's name, *Izabel*. Instead, she said *Izzy*, and it became her name. In like manner, Marisa coined her grandmother's name, as the first grandchild usually does. Zina, whose name was Constance, wanted her grandchildren to call her *Azozinha*, the Portuguese equivalent of *Granny*, but the first time Marisa said the word, it came out *Zina*. The name stuck.

"I forgot the lemonade," Zina said. "Would you pour it, Frieda?"

Frieda retrieved the pitcher from the kitchen and carefully filled each glass around the circular table. Zina transferred the stew to a bowl and put it on the table which already held a steaming bowl of rice, a fruit salad, and a platter of plantain empanadas. Everyone sat down except Zina, who remained standing and plated the food with style and efficiency gained over many years as hostess of a TV cooking show in Rio de Janeiro.

"Zina," Izzy said, "now we're American Citizens, so you could get a job with one of the Food Network Channels."

"I retired from the cooking show to cook for my family," Zina said.

Marisa was happy that her grandmother had retired. Having her stay home and manage the household was an excellent plan. Marisa and Frieda worked for the Houston office of the Consulate General of Brazil, and they would cover all expenses related to housing and food. Izzy was attending the University of Houston and had no income, but the family was okay financially without Zina getting a job. The arrangement seemed ideal.

As they ate, the conversation revolved around what it meant to be newly-minted American citizens, a thought that intrigued Marisa. They'd been put on a fast track to U.S. citizenship while many other Brazilians were going through a time-consuming process. She didn't understand why–her family wasn't rich or famous. Maybe it was serendipity, a trait Zina exhibited occasionally, although her early life had been complicated.

"What languages do they speak around here?" Zina asked.

"Mostly English and Spanish," Frieda said, "and a good bit of Mandarin."

"No Portuguese?" Zina asked.

"So far, I haven't heard anybody speaking it except us," Frieda said.

"Maybe we should switch to English," Izzy said, looking toward Marisa.

"I like that idea," Marisa said emphatically. Her college minor was English Composition, and she prided herself in writing and speaking the language well. Moreover, with a major in World History, the move to Houston would allow her to utilize her education to the fullest extent. Long before entering college, Marisa had dreamed of living in the United States and working in a consulate or embassy. Now, her dream had come true.

"Tomorrow is Carnival Tuesday," Frieda said. "The Consulate is closed, so Marisa and I have the day off. Maybe we could do something to celebrate our new citizenship."

"Carnival Tuesday is called *Mardi Gras* around here," Izzy said, "and it's not a U.S. holiday, so I have to go to school."

"I thought you were doing your classes online," Marisa said.

"Not any of the labs," Izzy said, "and I have an important one tomorrow–infectious diseases."

"I'm thinking about going to the Museum of Fine Arts," Zina said. "It's nearby, and the Metro runs in front of it. Anyone care to join me?"

"Sure, why not?" Frieda said with a shrug. "That sounds like fun."

"I wish I could go," Izzy said wistfully.

"What about you, Marisa?" Zina asked.

After considering it briefly, Marisa said, "No, I don't think so. I'd rather sleep late and spend the afternoon exploring the shops near the housing complex."

"Maybe you'll run into that tall, handsome guy," Izzy said. "If you do, don't run away from him again."

Marisa scowled. "Give it a rest."

***

That night, Marisa lay in bed reliving the day's events. She and Izzy shared a bedroom, as did their mother and grandmother. The two-bedroom unit was a comfortable place for four people to live. Marisa was impressed by the way HUD managed NatGov-subsidized housing. The U.S. seemed to be working hard to promote equality among all citizens. Moreover, the Citizenship Meeting video indicated that a more substantial effort was about to be launched by a newly-created political party.

Though the move from Brazil had gone well, Marisa knew she would get homesick for her native land after the newness of America wore off. She had many good friends in Rio and was already missing them. Several had attempted to get on the fast track to U.S. citizenship, but none had been able to do so.

And there was another matter—Octavio, her (estranged?) boyfriend. Octavio was an artist—a *starving artist*, to be exact—with numerous eccentricities typical of creative types. His current project was closely tied to Rio. He was producing holograms of the famous statue, Christ the Redeemer, by putting lead-pencil dots on matte paper. Since he could get the desired 3D effect only by looking at the statue while making the drawings, he'd decided to stay in Rio a while longer. At first, Marisa thought he was suffering from emigration phobia. Now, it seemed like nothing more than procrastination. Whatever the reason, he didn't apply for U.S. citizenship under the exchange program when he had the chance. Now, he was trying to work his way through a maze of digital red tape and was texting daily, telling her about his passport problems.

Marisa and Octavio had a long history together, having met in middle school and becoming best friends in high school. Upon entering college together, the friendship blossomed into romance. They'd been in a relationship for seven years, the last few of which had been rather rocky, especially when Octavio went on a creative binge and ignored everybody and everything except his art. As Marisa saw it, he had two distinct personalities—*an ordinary guy* and *a creative artist.* She'd attempted to deal with both but hadn't succeeded very well.

Marisa knew it would please her family if Octavio didn't move to the U.S. They'd never liked him much anyway. And, from the discussion at dinner, it was apparent they were already looking for someone to replace him ASAP. Still, despite some bumps in the road, she and Octavio had made a long journey together, much of which was worth the effort. So she wasn't ready to give up on him yet.

As Izzy shifted around in the adjoining bed, Marisa pushed aside the thoughts of Octavio. Her mind traveled backward past the happenings of the day, the events of recent years, and focused on her earliest memories–those beginning with Zina and Mom.

One thing troubled Marisa about her mother and grandmother–neither had lived with a husband as far back as she could remember. As much as Zina loved to talk, she'd never told Marisa and Izzy anything about their maternal grandfather. Her entire story about him consisted of one short, stark sentence, *"He deserted me before Frieda was born."* That was all Zina had revealed to anyone, Frieda included. Moreover, she didn't have a single picture of him, which added to the mystery. Whatever the rest of the story was, it seemed that Zina planned to take it to her grave. Marisa respected the commandment, *Honor your father and your mother,* and by extrapolation, *your grandmother,* so she'd put very little pressure on Zina to tell more. Still, curiosity about her grandfather lingered in the recesses of her mind, and she hoped the time would come when Zina would tell the entire story.

Marisa and Izzy knew a little more about their father. Mom had told them a few stories about him and had uploaded pictures to the iCloud, all showing the dashing young Raymundo as a doppelganger of Indiana Jones. According to Mom's brief account, his outward appearance mirrored his adventure-seeking mindset, which he lived to the fullest. Expecting to strike it rich, Raymundo and two cousins trekked to the headwaters of an Amazon tributary to search for an emerald mine. Sadly, they never returned.

Months later, based on information obtained from missionaries residing in a nearby village, the three men were officially declared dead. Unfortunately, that was all Marisa and Izzy knew about their father.

Upon Raymundo's death, Frieda, Marisa, and Izzy moved in with Zina, and they became inseparable. Through hard work, Zina and Frieda provided everything Marisa and Izzy needed and a few things they thought they needed. Some might have deemed it a no-frills life in the lower quartile of middle-income families, but they were happy living together. In retrospect, the story was amazing. Marisa continued to replay it in her mind.

When Zina graduated from high school in Rio, her parents were financially unable to send her to college, so she worked at fast food restaurants for several years while attempting to get a job in an upscale restaurant or club. Eventually, in what seemed like a miracle, she got a job as a sous chef in a popular restaurant, although she had no formal culinary training. A few years later, fortune smiled on her again, and a local TV station hired her as a cooking show hostess.

Another serendipitous event happened right after Frieda graduated from high school. She'd hoped to enter college, but Zina didn't have sufficient funds to send her. While they were trying to figure out some way for Frieda to start her journey to a higher education, Zina won $200,000 in the lottery. Incredibly, someone had given her the lottery ticket as a birthday present. The proceeds went into Frieda's college fund, enabling her to enroll immediately. Three years later, with a degree in HR, Frieda went to work for the Brazilian government in Rio.

So, after a rocky start, Zina beat the odds repeatedly. Her biography would make a great plot for a novel.

Shortly past midnight, Izzy quit threshing around, the room fell silent, and Marisa went to sleep.

CHAPTER 3

Anxious to complete the brief Phoenix-75 project, Rachel entered the laboratory to find Justin already at work. If all went as expected, they would finish before noon. From day one, she'd been obsessed with both speed and accuracy. Moreover, the nature of the work suggested it was a precursor to a much larger project, precisely what Vi-Tech needed to get back on track. The possibility of layoffs had become a daily talking point among the company's workforce; however, the current study offered a glimmer of hope. Rachel suspected the identical project had been farmed out to other biotech companies to compare their capabilities. Believing the work she and Justin were completing would set the curve, she welcomed the comparison.

The project had been authorized by Dr. Ignacio Allende, Director of the NIAID—the *National Institute of Allergy and Infectious Diseases*. NIAID was one of the branches of NIH, the *National Institute of Health*. In addition to being its Director, Dr. Allende was Chief Medical Advisor to the President, a position he'd held for over twenty years. The struggle against Phoenix-75 kept the Director in the public eye, making him one of NatGov's busiest and most-recognized officials, and it was apparent he relished the spotlight.

Like its mythological counterpart, the persistent virus had risen from the dead again. Now, it was attacking plants, especially grain crops. Such a crossover from animals to plants was previously unknown in virology. The transition occurred first in Asian countries near the origin of the initial Phoenix outbreak.

After last year's harvest, the United States shipped surplus grain to stricken areas until the supply was nearly depleted. At that point, Congress passed a bill requiring the U.S. to keep the rest in reserve. With the new growing season about to start, fast action was needed to avert a worldwide famine.

NIAID had ordered some tailor-made viruses known as *chimeras* to study the animal-to-plant crossover. Rachel had done similar work in graduate school, and her master's thesis was the main reason Vi-Tech hired her. The current project required some unorthodox creativity, a character trait demonstrated in abundance by several of Rachel's ancestors and by her as well. She'd already performed several RNA/DNA-splicing feats previously thought impossible by her coworkers and was regarded as a genetic artist in the Vi-Tech community.

Though Rachel hadn't been told as much, she was sure the chimeras she and Justin were producing would be submitted to other companies as templates for developing vaccines, immunotherapy agents, or additional Phoenix variants. Proud of the work, she'd requested permission to track the Vi-Tech chimeras as they progressed through subsequent steps. To her surprise, Dr. Allende denied the request. For some reason, NIAID operated on a strict *need-to-know* basis. Such a secretive approach didn't make sense to Rachel; however, they needed the work, so there was little she could do about it.

After greeting Justin, she sat down at her desk and pulled up the original data on Phoenix-75. The files were scant. Several Vi-Tech biologists, including Rachel and Justin, had worked a small amount on the virus, but a lot more study was needed to learn anything worthwhile. Unfortunately, President Ford was never able to obtain legislative backing to fund the research, so the study had faltered for years. As a result, another crisis was in the making.

"I've finished preparing slides of the new chimeras," Justin said. "Do you want to evaluate them now?"

"Yes," she said, standing. They were well within NIAID's allotted time frame for completing the project, but with Dr. Allende, ASAP was always the order of the day.

Rachel started toward the other wing of the lab, and Justin fell in behind her. They had produced the chimeras by combining two completely different viruses. The new entity was unlike either of its parents. NIAID's current order, based on subtracting protein spikes from the wall of the virus, seemed like a logical approach.

They reached the viewing room and sat down before a large 3D monitor set into the wall. Inactive, the monitor resembled an aquarium filled with swirling fog. Rachel raised her right hand, palm outward, toward the monitor. A remote sensor read her handprint, and the fog changed into a kaleidoscope of colored shards forming Vi-Tech's logo—a highly stylized virus, sky blue in color with multicolored protein spikes. The spiked structure multiplied as it drifted across the screen.

"I always think of porcupines when I see this logo," Justin said.

Rachel gave another hand signal, and Vi-Tech's logo turned into a cluster of real viruses floating in 3D space, the tailor-made chimeras ordered by NIAID. She motioned again, and the magnification increased until the chimeras were the size of marbles. Then, after lining up in columns, they flashed across the screen in a blur. A moment later, numbers appeared at the bottom of the screen as an electron microscope counted the spikes on each unit.

"This first batch will be a keeper," Justin said. "I could tell when I was preparing the slides."

The original Phoenix virus had 75 protein spikes, thus its numerical suffix. NIAID had ordered three new chimera variants, one with 70 spikes, another with 65, and another with 60. Rachel had studied viruses for almost ten years and had developed a unique ability to modify them. RNA-based viruses, such as Phoenix-75, were far more unstable than their DNA counterparts, so her ability as a genetic artist was invaluable. The technique she employed was beyond anything taught in universities; however, under her tutelage, Justin was developing the skill, albeit somewhat slowly.

When the count was complete, it showed the first batch of chimeras to be perfect—over 99% of the viruses had 70 spikes. The subsequent two batches were also excellent—65 and 60 spikes, respectively. To Rachel's satisfaction, they'd met their speed and accuracy goals.

She leaned toward Justin, and they exchanged high-fives.

"We're off to a good start," Justin said. "Maybe we don't need to prepare duplicate batches every time."

"Better safe than sorry," Rachel said, signaling the monitor to shut down.

"That's an old-fashioned saying."

"I picked it up from Dr. Truman."

"Speaking of Dr. Truman," Justin said, "do you think he'll retire now that he's sixty-five?"

Rachel shrugged. "I haven't heard him mention it."

"I'd hate to see him go," Justin said. "He's a good man."

"When he retires, the board will find a suitable replacement. So things won't change much around here."

"They should consider you for the job."

"Thanks for the vote of confidence," Rachel said, smiling, "but I'm a twenty-something without a doctorate. So I won't be on the board's list of candidates."

Though working on her Ph.D. at the University of Houston, Rachel had yet to give much thought to an upward climb into management. She loved laboratory work and preferred a hands-on approach rather than supervising others. Even so, she realized that she would have to take on more management responsibilities someday in order to earn a higher salary. The Peter Principle remained alive and well in the twenty-second century. Apparently, it was a law of the universe as absolute as the speed of light.

When all loose ends of the project were tied up to Rachel's satisfaction, she glanced at the clock and said, "Let's grab lunch before we ship the cultures."

"How about one of the new restaurants in the food court down the street?"

"That's fine with me."

They draped their lab jackets on a hanger beside the monitor and left the lab. Once in the hallway, they joined a group of fellow scientists heading toward the exit. A few of them wore backpacks, and many thumbed their iTabs. Most lab personnel wore nondescript jeans and tops–clothing too drab for Rachel, who was wearing navy blue slacks and a yellow blouse. As they walked along, she overheard snippets of conversation, much of it regarding ongoing projects. When they reached the security exit, facial recognition cameras identified each person in the hallway and noted their departure from the building.

They stepped onto the sidewalk in front of the MD Anderson Cancer Center, one of the busiest locations in the Mediplex at this time of day. The walk was crowded, and a stream of people filed in and out of MD Anderson. Robo-cabs and Metro busses at the curb discharged passengers, many utilizing wheelchairs or walkers. Some wore face masks, even though the mandate had been lifted. Rachel's heart went out to them, and she wondered if any of her work in virology might have application in the field of oncology.

Rachel and Justin joined a group of pedestrians heading toward the crosswalk. A short distance from the hospital entrance, the background noise devolved into separate components—polyglottic conversation, the soft hum of electric vehicles, shoes scuffing on pavement, and sirens wailing in the distance. This lunch-break scene played out daily at multiple locations throughout the area.

As they approached the food court, Rachel asked, "Which restaurant were you talking about?"

"The one called *The Gryphon.*"

"What's their specialty?"

"Greek, I think."

"I should have known by the name," Rachel said. "Greek mythology is in vogue again—Phoenix, Chimera, Gryphon. I wonder what's next."

The locale had much to offer despite the constant hustle and bustle bordering on chaos. The George Washington was nearby, and her parents lived an hour away. Several popular restaurants and shops were located near the intersection of Holcombe and South Main Street. Theaters—both movie and drama—were within walking distance. According to Darien's sci-fi description, the area was *a pocket universe revolving around a bright central star, the Houston Mediplex.*

It was a great place to live and work, yet one thing kept it from being perfect. Rachel's boyfriend, Steven Harrison, wouldn't return to Houston for almost a year. Steve, a captain in the USAF, was currently serving on the International Space Station. In addition, he was talking about taking a trip to Mars and had asked her to consider going as well.

Though a trip into space had its appeal, Rachel knew she had more to offer in the battle against Phoenix-75, and the battlefield was Earth, not Mars. So she needed to stay in Houston for the time being.

Still, she and Steve needed to work out a plan for their future, or they wouldn't have a future together.

CHAPTER 4

While seated at his dinette table with a glass of chocolate milk in front of him, Darien picked up his iTab and clicked on the *ConspiraciesRevealed* icon. The featured article appeared with the title in orange flames, and the story unfolded below it.

CORRESPONDENT DIES IN HELICOPTER CRASH WHILE INVESTIGATING A NEWLY-DISCOVERED JUNTA

Correspondent Juan Piedra was killed last week in a helicopter crash near Barcelona. Foul play–possibly a drone–is suspected, and Spanish authorities are investigating the incident. According to preliminary findings, Mr. Piedra was tracking the activity of an underground political organization that has operated for more than twenty years without being detected. Little is known about this secret society except that it is well concealed and has a large membership. This junta is thought to be planning a move soon–perhaps a coup attempt in conjunction with the upcoming presidential election. A split-second before the fatal crash, Mr. Piedra said a garbled sentence in Spanish referring to the organization as "Los Ignotos," Spanish for "the unknowns" or "the unidentified suspects." Pending the discovery of more details about this consortium, ConspiraciesRevealed will continue referring to it as "Los Ignotos." Additional information will be forthcoming when available.

ConspiraciesRevealed launched during Darien's senior year in high school and grabbed his attention immediately. He remembered the debut issue well. It was primarily a listing of popular conspiracy theories which had been around for years, i.e., the Apollo moon landings were faked, 9/11 was an inside job, the CIA assassinated Kennedy, the earth is flat, pharmaceutical companies are hiding cancer cures, etc. Even so, the publication had built a following quickly.

He didn't believe every claim the periodical made, yet many of them had turned out to be true over the years. With the chaos in the world today, maybe Los Ignotos was poised to make a move, as the article claimed. In any case, it would be a great topic to discuss with Alden. One of his uncles, Zach Thibideaux, was a freelance reporter living in Europe and might have access to information not reported in the magazine. Zach lived in Beaumont during Darien's college years, and they'd had numerous discussions about science fiction and conspiracies. Darien counted him as a good friend, though they hadn't communicated with each other in quite a while.

After mulling over the article, Darien's mind returned to the news posted prior to the citizenship meeting. It seemed odd that Alphabet News was so blasé when announcing the formation of a new political party. Alphabet was closely aligned with the RADS, and Darien would have expected them to denounce the new party. But, for some reason, they didn't. Maybe the Peace Party was an offspring of the RADS, something like a Trojan Horse or a puppet. Stranger things had happened. Though he'd voted every year since turning eighteen, Darien didn't understand the complex world of politics. Even so, he was ready to get more involved in the upcoming election.

Wondering if the new party really offered something different, he googled *The Peace Party* on his iTab, and a simple website appeared. A millisecond later, a pop-up materialized with the words, *We hold these truths to be self-evident, that all men are created equal.*

Darien was shocked. He'd expected something new, not Thomas Jefferson's well-known phrase. The Jeffersonian statement was bold in its day and had been the mantra of practically every political movement since the Declaration of Independence. With his curiosity mounting, Darien clicked the *Home* button, and a table of contents appeared: *About, Contact, Sign In, Join,* and *Donate.* He explored the website. Except for touting a relationship between equality and peace, its content was similar to other political sites he'd seen, including those maintained by the RADS and the Independents.

While exploring the site, his iTab began to vibrate with incoming texts. Darien realized they were linked to the Peace Party's web page, indicating that social media participants were posting comments. He touched the first link, and a text appeared: *Reuben Rogov will be the Peace Party's presidential candidate.* Darien clicked on the next link, and another message popped up. It also mentioned Rogov, along with some other possible choices. Quickly, he opened several more messages. While not identical, the consensus was clear—most of those posting comments believed that Reuben Rogov would be the new party's candidate.

But, that didn't make sense. Rogov was Secretary General of the United Nations and came from a foreign country.

Hastily, Darien googled *Reuben Rogov,* and found a short biographical sketch. To his surprise, Rogov was born in New

York City, so he was an American citizen after all. Upon graduating from the City College of New York, Rogov moved to Guatemala, obtained citizenship there, and became an options trader in the Guatemalan Stock Exchange. He was married to a Guatemalan socialite, but they lived apart and had no children. Two years ago, he moved back to New York and established residency. Though a dual citizen, Rogov met all requirements for a U.S. presidential bid.

Darien glanced at the clock on his iTab. It was 11:00 p.m., and he still needed to spend two or three hours on his part-time job, grading papers for an English professor at the University of Houston. His sleep-wake cycle differed from that of his friends. He got up shortly after 10:00 a.m. and went to bed around 3:00 a.m. His breakfast consisted of nothing but black coffee. After wiling away the afternoon, he felt an energy burst about nightfall and produced his best fiction after 8:00 p.m. It was an eccentric schedule, but he'd been on it since moving out of his parents' condo. At 3:30 a.m., he finished grading the papers and went to bed.

***

At noon the next day, Darien left the George Washington and joined the crowd waiting for the traffic light at Morningside Drive and Dorrington Street. It was a spectacularly beautiful February day, with temperatures hovering near 65° F. Above the sidewalk, the balconies of the multi-floored housing complex seemed to touch the sky. Metro buses crept along the street, weaving in and out of a covey of robo-cabs that materialized at the stroke of noon. Further down the sidewalk near the Abraham Lincoln, a group of people dressed in hospital scrubs waited at the Metro stop. Across the street, lines formed in front of the take-out restaurants, and pedestrians strolled along the sidewalk. The housing units were near the medical behemoth, The Houston Mediplex, one of the busiest locations in the city.

The busy street seemed to belie recent predictions of an impending economic meltdown, but Darien realized the outward appearance was deceiving. Rachel's talk of possible budget cuts at Vi-Tech indicated as much. Moreover, he'd heard that other local companies were facing the same situation, although it had yet to become obvious in the streets of the Mediplex area.

When the traffic light flashed *Walk*, Darien stepped out of the walkway and sprinted across the street, passing a gaggle of slow-moving pedestrians. He headed toward his destination, The Cherry Tree. It was one of his favorite eateries, with good food and a variety of coffees. Craving calories and caffeine, Darien had already decided to have a Country Breakfast Special and a large espresso.

He reached the curb and started toward the row of restaurants. Today, over half of the U.S. workforce performed their jobs from home and never went to an office. As a result, sidewalk food courts had sprung up near most HUD–subsidized housing complexes. Darien passed the Log Cabin Coffee Shop, The Emancipation Bar & Grill, The Valley Forge Deli, and entered The Cherry Tree Diner.

The restaurant was filled with people, most of whom Darien knew. He joined a short line at the counter and surveyed the gathering crowd. As usual, the restaurant waitstaff wore silver jumpsuits appliquéd with red cherries. In sharp contrast, many of the customers, including Darien, wore faded jeans and T-shirts or other equally dull apparel. The clothing industry had been on life support long before the Phoenix-75 pandemic and was currently approaching code blue status.

The front desk was attended by Alden Thibideaux, The Cherry Tree owner's right-hand man and Darien's best friend. Alden had a remarkable gift for remembering names and always met new residents as soon as possible. After an initial meeting, he could call everyone by name the next time he saw them. He was a bona fide *people person* and had probably already met the newly-arrived women whom Darien saw at the Citizenship Meeting.

"Have you met the new family who moved in a couple of days ago?" Darien asked.

"Do you mean the Da Rosas?"

"I don't know their names. That's why I'm asking you."

"Their names are Marisa and Izzy Da Rosa," Alden said, smiling deviously.

"Okay," Darien said. "I'll play your little game. What else do you know about them?"

"They're from Brazil."

"Hmm, very interesting. Anything else?"

"They're pretty."

"I already know that. Tell me something I don't know."

Alden motioned with his thumb. "They're in the back room right now."

Darien's eyes widened. "No way!"

"Would I kid you?"

"Send a Country Breakfast back there for me–and a large espresso."

"Will do," Alden said, tapping the monitor in front of him. "By the way, the tall one's name is Marisa."

"Thanks for the info," Darien said. "See you later." His iTab pinged, and the *Pay Now* icon popped up. He touched it and headed toward the back room, which was full of chattering people. He glanced around and spotted the two women. Marisa was seated at a small table, and Izzy was standing as if preparing to leave.

Darien approached the table and said, "Hello, ladies. Welcome to my world."

Izzy looked at Darien and laughed softly. "That's the corniest pick-up line I've ever heard."

"I know," Darien said, "but it was all I could think of on the spur-of-the-moment."

"Are you stalking us?" Marisa asked.

"Not exactly," Darien said, "but I'd like to meet you. I'm Darien Segura."

Izzy flashed a broad smile. "I'm Izzy Da Rosa, and this is my sister, Marisa."

"Pleased to meet you," Darien said.

"I was about to leave," Izzy said. "Take my chair."

Marisa frowned. "Izzy!"

"Just trying to help you make new friends," Izzy said.

Darien glanced toward the empty chair. "May I?"

Marisa shrugged.

"Is that a *yes* or a *no?*"

Marisa motioned toward the chair, and Darien sat down.

"See you tonight," Izzy said, turning to leave. "Have fun."

Darien looked at Marisa, and she returned his gaze. She had light olive skin and blue-violet eyes; however, close up, she didn't resemble Lorelei as much as he'd initially thought. Though it wasn't precisely déjà vu, it was somewhat surreal.

"Thanks for sharing your table with me," Darien said, sensing that Marisa was ill at ease.

"Why are you following me?"

"I wanted to meet you," Darien said. "What's wrong with that?"

"Plenty, if you have a girlfriend."

"What are you talking about?"

"I saw you with a woman last night."

Darien chuckled. "She's my sister—my twin sister."

"Really?"

"Absolutely. Now can we start this conversation over?"

"I guess so," Marisa said with a faint smile. "Where do you want to start?"

"Anywhere," Darien said. "I know you're from Brazil, but that's all I know."

"How did you know we were from Brazil?"

"Alden told me—the guy at the front desk."

"He has a funny accent."

"He's Cajun and talks a lot," Darien said. "So what brought the Da Rosa family to Texas?"

"Izzy has been here for a year," Marisa said. "She's studying biology at the University of Houston. My mother and I arrived last week to work for the Brazilian Consulate. My grandmother came too."

Darien was puzzled. "How did you get housing at The George Washington so quickly?"

"We applied and were accepted, just like everybody else."

Darien was *double-puzzled*. "I thought HUD-assisted housing was only for American Citizens."

"We're American Citizens," Marisa said emphatically. "Brand new ones."

"How can that be? You've only been here a few days."

"We had a stroke of good fortune," Marisa said. "Early this year, the United Nations initiated a pilot program similar to student-exchange programs. Only a few countries participated in the initial tests. Instead of exchanging students, they exchanged citizens. We were the first Brazilians to participate in the program."

"I've never heard of such a program," Darien said. "What happened after you were chosen?"

"We underwent six weeks of intense study in Rio and took the standard U.S. Citizenship test. All four of us passed with flying colors, so here we are."

"I thought Izzy was already here."

"She was here as an exchange student. Now she's here as an American citizen."

"Let me get this straight," Darien said, still unable to believe what he was hearing. "Are you telling me that, except for Izzy, the rest of your family became U.S. citizens six weeks before arriving here?"

Marisa nodded vigorously. "That's right."

As Darien pondered Marisa's story, a petite blonde carrying a tray approached the table. "Hi, Darien," she said. "Here's your order."

"Thanks, Heidi."

The waitress placed the tray in front of Darien, topped up Marisa's cup with hot coffee, and retreated.

Marisa said, "Now, tell me a little about yourself."

Darien lowered his cup and said, "I'm from Freeport."

"The Bahamas?"

"No. Freeport, Texas. It's about sixty miles south of here."

"What's it like?"

"It's pretty much a gigantic chemical plant," Darien said. "It was founded in the early 1900s by the Freeport Sulphur Company but didn't incorporate until Dow Chemical Company chose it as their U.S. Gulf Coast site. Several other companies built chemical plants in the area after Dow's plant opened. Believe it or not–it has streets named Chlorine, Glycol, Benzene, and other chemical names."

"Wow! What's it like to grow up in a chemical plant?"

"It was all we knew," Darien said. "We never thought anything about it."

During the next few minutes, he told Marisa about playing basketball and attending Baylor on a scholarship. In turn, she told him about her high school and college years in Rio, living with her mother and grandmother, and never knowing a father or grandfather. The conversation flowed easily except for one area–romantic relationships. Darien was tip-toeing around that area of his life and could tell Marisa was doing the same thing. Eventually, he decided to try the *nothing-ventured-nothing-gained* approach.

"Could I ask you a personal question?" he asked.

Marisa shrugged. "I guess so, but I probably won't answer it."

"Do you have a boyfriend in Rio?"

"That's none of your business."

"I know, but I'm curious to find out."

Marisa looked directly at Darien for a moment before speaking. "I'll tell you what," she said. "First, tell me about your love life. Then, I might answer your question."

"Fair enough," Darien said. Briefly, he summarized his rocky relationship with Lorelei, including their mutual agreement to call it quits forever. Then he added, "You look a lot like her."

"I knew something was wrong. You've been acting weird."

"I was surprised. That's all. Now, will you answer my question?"

"I have a boyfriend in Brazil," Marisa said, "but he's working on a project that might keep him there for a while."

"What kind of work does he do?"

"He's an artist," Marisa said, "and self-centered like all creative people."

Darien flinched. "Ouch!"

"Did I hit a nerve?"

"I'm a writer."

"Really?" Marisa said, raising her eyebrows. "English composition was my minor in college."

"Then, we have something in common. Maybe we can collaborate on a science fiction novel."

"Not likely," Marisa said. "I studied English because I planned to move to the U.S., and the only writing I've done is for a newsletter."

"My offer to collaborate is still on the table."

"I don't even like science fiction."

"Okay, let's change the subject," Darien said. "What are you doing this afternoon?"

"Are you asking me for a date?"

"I guess you would call it that."

"I've told you about Octavio."

Darien shrugged. "I know, but he's in Brazil."

Marisa stood. "I'm going to the museum with my mother and grandmother this afternoon."

Darien watched as Marisa picked her way between the tables. She wore jeans, sandals, and a blue T-shirt with the

Brazilian flag embroidered on the back. An iTab case slung across her shoulder on a long strap swung gently back and forth as she walked away.

When Marisa disappeared around the corner, Darien returned to his Country Breakfast, which was getting cold. While eating, he decided to look up some information on the citizen-exchange program. He lay his iTab on the table and searched the U.S. Immigration and Naturalization Service website and its counterpart in Brazil. There was not a single reference to the program. Determined to uncover something, he searched the United Nations website. Again, nothing.

Apparently, the citizen-exchange program that brought the Da Rosas to the United States no longer existed, and every trace of it had been eliminated from official websites. It reminded him of an old novel, *Counter-Clock World,* where the government operated an *Eradication Council.* Maybe NatGov was doing the same thing.

After giving up on the official sites, Darien googled *How Long Does It Take To Become A U.S. Citizen.* A Wikipedia chart popped up, showing five steps from (1) *Processing the application* to (5) *Taking the oath of allegiance and receiving a certificate of naturalization.*

The average time was listed as 1.5 years.

CHAPTER 5

The Metro bus eased to a stop at a kiosk on Bissonnet Street across from the Museum of Fine Arts. The passengers stood in unison and lined up to exit. Marisa grasped the handrail and waited behind her mother and grandmother as they stepped off the bus.

The instant her foot touched the pavement, she saw a sign reading *The Cullen Sculpture Garden*. Behind the sign, rows of statues were lined up on each side of a broad corridor. The scene triggered a replay of recent events in her mind. Only a week ago, she and Octavio had gone to the Sculpture Gallery in Rio de Janeiro to discuss their future before she came to the United States. Regretfully, the conversation had not gone well.

It wasn't as if Marisa had ever misled Octavio about her career plans and where they might take her. Upon choosing English composition as her minor, she'd made it clear that she intended to move to the U.S. permanently as soon as possible after completing college. He'd said he would do the same. However, due to the all-encompassing nature of his Christ the Redeemer art project, he didn't get his act together in time to participate in the Citizen Exchange program before it ended. Now, he was stuck in Rio, and it was anybody's guess when he would get a passport.

The trio of women moved out of the way of other passengers getting off the bus. Marisa stepped to the edge of the curb and said, "Let's cut across the street."

Frieda stood her ground. "We wouldn't want to get a jay-walking ticket our first week in Houston."

"Aw, Mom," Marisa said. "These Texans wouldn't give us a ticket."

"They might," Zina said. "Let's go to the crosswalk."

Marisa turned to join Frieda, Zina, and a group of other people from the Metro bus as they headed toward the traffic signal at the corner.

"Look at that!" Marisa said when they approached the museum entrance. "They're featuring works by Tarsila do Amaral."

They stopped before the marquee, which featured a reproduction of the artist's famous self-portrait. The promotional information below the portrait read:

> *Tarsila do Amaral defined the first distinctly Brazilian approach to art by adapting western themes to Brazilian contexts. She was the first Latin American artist to present nationalist expression in a modern style. Houston's Museum of Art is fortunate to have several of Tarsila's works on loan, including "The Moon," "The Lake," "Familia," and several of her lesser-known works.*

They entered the museum. Marisa and Zina waited while Frieda joined a short line to buy tickets. When her turn came, Frieda extended her iTab toward the attendant behind the counter.

"You can download The Houston Museum App to avoid lines on future visits," the attendant said as she scanned Frieda's PayPal App.

Three tickets appeared on Frieda's tablet, along with a map of the museum campus and a description of each building's contents. She studied the screen briefly and said, "Tarsila's paintings are down that hallway. Let's look at them first."

Over the next two hours, the three women worked their way through a series of rooms containing art collections. Some paintings were spectacular, others less so, even though most were famous. By a wide margin, Marisa's favorite painting was *Joan of Arc* by Jules Bastien–Lepage. The artist had captured Joan's expression upon realizing she had been called to lead France as they struggled to overthrow English domination. Bastien–Lepage's painting remained on her mind as they moved to other rooms. She tried to imagine how Joan felt when she stepped forward in a world dominated by men, knowing the cost might be her life. For some inexplicable reason, Marisa wondered what she would do if suddenly thrust into a Joan of Arc situation. The thought was disquieting.

They passed through the final room of the self-guided art tour and arrived at a small food court. In unison, they veered toward a row of kiosks, each with a serving counter and a row of stools. Tables, only a few of them occupied, were clumped together in the center of the court.

"Let's get something to drink before we leave," Marisa said, sensing that Zina was getting tired.

They stopped at the first kiosk, made their drink selections, and moved to an empty table. While sipping their drinks and discussing the artwork they'd seen, Marisa's iTab sounded Izzy's ringtone.

"Hey, Iz. What's up?"

"I'm taking a break from lab," Izzy said. "What are you doing?"

"I'm at the art museum with Mom and Zina."

"Really?" Izzy said. "I left the restaurant early so you could spend some time with that good-looking stalker."

"Not so. You were already leaving when he showed up."

"What did you think of him?"

"He's nice," Marisa said, "but he's a struggling science fiction writer, and that's a strike against him."

"He might get rich someday," Izzy said. "A few writers do, you know. Rich and handsome make a nice combination."

"We just met," Marisa said, not surprised at Izzy's attempt to throw Octavio under the bus as soon as possible. "You're overanalyzing the situation."

"You better grab him before somebody else does," Izzy said. "Maybe me."

"You're hopeless."

"I've got to go," Izzy said. "The lab instructor is giving me the evil eye."

"Okay, see you tonight."

The women finished their drinks. After deciding they'd seen the museum's best offerings, they left the food court and joined a small group of pedestrians at the Metro kiosk.

Immediately, the walls of the open-fronted hut grabbed Marisa's attention. They bore multiple TV monitors displaying state-of-the-art advertising designed to draw a quick look from Metro riders and pedestrians. Though colorful, many of the ads didn't make a discernable point. However, one of them—a Hi-Caff Beverage ad—stood out from the rest. It showed two little green men landing a spaceship on a red planet. The console between them held two empty soft drink bottles, and a caption, *Hi-Caff Lite–Now Available on Mars,* scrolled across the bottom of the screen.

The ad replayed several times, after which the video morphed into a photograph of a widely-recognized public figure–Reuben Rogov, the UN Secretary-General. The reddish–brown photo resembled an antique portrait from a museum–a unique twist in a world of brightly-colored, fast-moving 3D images. Intrigued, Marisa stared at the picture.

A moment later, sensing she was blocking Frieda's view, Marisa stepped aside to make room for her mother to see the picture. When she moved, Rogov's dark eyes appeared to follow her. The man in the photo was dark complexioned with heavy brows and an aquiline nose. He wasn't handsome but possessed a powerful persona. Even in the still picture, he seemed to be someone Marisa knew in person rather than a remote political figure. Though she didn't understand how the image of a man she'd never seen could make her feel that way, her first impression was that Mr. Rogov could be trusted. He possessed extraordinary charisma, and she felt drawn into the picture.

Three lines of text appeared on the screen:

THE PEACE PARTY PRESENTS REUBEN ROGOV

HE WILL SPEAK AT AMAZON PARK ON MARCH 1, 2148

ADMISSION FREE–DONATIONS ACCEPTED

"He's probably going to announce his presidential bid at the meeting," Marisa said.

"No doubt," Frieda said. "That's all the social media has been talking about lately."

Marisa tapped at her iTab. "I'm going to find out where Amazon Park is located. Maybe we can go hear him."

"His speech will be on TV."

"I know, but I'd like to hear him in person," Marisa said. She studied her iTab screen and added, "Amazon Park is in downtown Houston. It's the home of the Houston Astros baseball team."

"Sounds like you're anxious to get involved in American politics," Frieda said.

Marisa nodded vigorously. "I am. We're U.S. citizens now, and it's our civic duty."

"I agree. We'll register when we get home this evening."

Marisa looked toward Zina. Her grandmother had turned away from the political ad and was idly watching pedestrians strolling along the sidewalk. "What about you, Zina?" Marisa asked. "Are you going to register to vote in the U.S. elections?"

Zina shook her head. "No, I gave up on politics a long time ago."

"Mr. Rogov seems to be a different kind of politician," Marisa said.

"I gave up on politicians too."

***

That night, as Marisa lay in bed, her thoughts drifted back to her conversation with Darien before the art museum visit. After a couple of missteps, she'd found it easy to talk to him, especially about similar childhood experiences they had while growing up in different countries. To her surprise, they had more in common than she expected.

One thing bothered her, though–she felt like she'd talked too much. She told Darien everything about her life as far back as she could remember, even about never knowing a father or grandfather. After some thought, it was easy to understand why it happened. Unlike her friends in Rio, Darien didn't already know everything about her, so he listened attentively when she talked. Sure, he'd pried a little, but a little was all it took to get her to blurt out her entire life story. Oh, well . . . what could be wrong with that?

Marisa sighed, fluffed her pillow, and tried to push the thoughts aside so she could fall asleep.

It didn't work. Instead of falling asleep, she began to compare Darien to Octavio.

CHAPTER 6

Trying to figure out a catchy sentence to begin the next chapter of his novel, Darien paced back and forth in his tiny condo. Unable to conjure up anything worth putting in writing, his thoughts drifted to the upcoming visit with Papa. One thing was sure—they would talk about politics, especially the upcoming presidential election. Though Reuben Rogov had yet to enter the race officially, Alphabet News polls showed he had an excellent chance to win. If he won while remaining Secretary General of the UN, he would fit Papa's model of a powerful leader poised to set up a world government.

Papa was the most brilliant person Darien had ever known. Like Darien, he was a conspiracy theory buff, but their favorite theories differed considerably. Darien's favorites were stolen elections, political coups, lab-produced diseases, and the like. On the other hand, Papa had only one primary theory—a deep state organization was attempting to establish a one-world government. For as long as he could remember, Papa had talked about the *Illuminati*, the *Trilateral Commission*, or some other shadowy group trying to institute a new world order. Maybe he would add *Los Ignotos* to his list. The newly-discovered junta was gaining popularity in the news media.

Like the rest of the Seguras, Darien always voted for Independent Party candidates, no matter what office they were seeking. As far as he knew, no Segura had ever supported the RADS, the party which formed when the Republicans and Democrats merged over a hundred years ago. Whether Rogov won or not, his entry into the race should force the other two principal parties to examine their modus operandi, which would be a good thing. Voters in Darien's age group were beginning to realize that maintaining the status quo was not an effective means of governance.

While pondering the political situation, he glanced toward the small bookcase beside his desk. Again, it reminded him of his grandfather. Darien, like Papa, had a collection of books printed on genuine paper; however, their book collections were as different as their conspiracy theories. Except for the Bible, most of Papa's books were advanced STEM subjects, several of which he'd written himself. Darien's books consisted of science fiction novels and short story collections, none of which he'd written.

Printing books on paper was rare. It was costly and required a special permit from NatGov, along with the payment of a hefty *tree destruction tax*. Consequently, the paperbacks in his small bookcase had soared in price. Though Darien was always short on cash, he'd never considered selling them. Like his car, paper books were one of the frills he afforded himself.

He was constantly on the lookout for works by his favorite old masters, Philip K. Dick, Kurt Vonnegut, and Ray Bradbury. He also had two books by the little-known author, Don Johnston, who wrote his first novel around 2020 when he was over eighty years old.

It was Darien's dream to put a novel he'd written in the bookcase beside the works of the sci-fi legends. It would be incredible to see *The Photosynthesis Gene* between *The Zap Gun* and *Fahrenheit 451*. But, of course, he would have to get it published first, and doing so was proving difficult.

His iTab pinged, and a crawfish icon popped up. Upon touching it, Alden's picture appeared.

"Hey, buddy," Darien said. "What's going on?"

"How'd you like to go out with Marisa and Izzy?"

"What are you talking about?"

"Just what I said. They asked us to go out with them."

"What's the catch?" Darien asked. He didn't believe for a second the invitation was for him and Alden only.

Alden chuckled. "There's no catch. They invited us to Reuben Rogov's rally at Amazon Field."

"How many others did they invite?"

"Everybody living in the George Washington," Alden said. "Since I know them all, Marisa enlisted me to spread the word."

"What kind of response are you getting?"

"Better than anticipated," Alden said. "I've contacted nearly everyone, and it looks like we'll have a busload or more, mostly people about our age."

"When is the rally?"

"Next Friday."

"That sounds good. Put me on the list."

"I already have," Alden said, smiling broadly.

"Have you asked Rachel?"

"Uh-huh, and she wasn't interested."

"I'm not surprised. What about Justin?"

"He can't go," Alden said. "He has a date that night with a girl who moved into the Abraham Lincoln last week."

"I didn't know Justin had a new girlfriend."

Alden shrugged. "He says they're just talking."

"Maybe he'd like to take her to the rally."

"Not likely. He probably won't vote."

After talking a few more minutes, Alden said, "I have to get back to work."

"First, I need something from you."

"Name it."

"I'd like Marisa's telephone number," Darien said. "I know you have it."

Alden frowned and hesitated a few seconds. "She told me to be careful about who I give it to."

"Then give it to me carefully."

They laughed, and Alden texted the number to Darien.

CHAPTER 7

M arisa and her recruits got off the Metro at the Crawford Street kiosk near Amazon Park. The thermometer above the stadium entrance read 66.6° F, pleasant for early March. However, since she was accustomed to 85° F in Rio, Marisa wore a sweater, though most of her companions were wearing short sleeves.

Staying together in a loosely-organized group, they picked their way along the busy sidewalk toward the main entrance. Alden had divided the collection of budding politicos into groups of four to six members, each with a leader, a system akin to the old-fashioned buddy system. He'd put Marisa, Izzy, Darien, and himself in the same group. Marisa liked the arrangement because it would allow her to get to know Darien better without it being obvious she was observing him.

Anticipating that the George Washington residents would scatter once the convention ended, the leaders had assumed responsibility for getting their groups on a bus for the return trip. Of course, not everyone would return at the same time. Most, including Marisa, planned to explore downtown Houston after the meeting. She was looking forward to learning more about her newly-adopted city while in the company of others who knew it. From the Metro bus, she'd seen a row of restaurants and clubs near Amazon field, including one called *Brazil de Houston*. Oddly, Brazil connections seemed to be everywhere. Maybe she was unconsciously looking for them.

The Peace Party's rally in Houston was receiving worldwide press coverage, as evidenced by the line of news-media minivans parked along Crawford Street and overflowing into several cross streets. Reporters and photographers milled around talking into head-mounted microphones, taking photos, and filming videos. Speculation was running rampant in the news media concerning Reuben Rogov's selection of Houston as the city to launch his campaign. The choice was a boon to Texas, but Alphabet News felt that New York would have been better. After all, NYC was Mr. Rogov's home, as well as the home of Alphabet News, the dominant news network in the world. For unknown reasons, the soon-to-be presidential candidate seemed to have a fond spot in his heart for Houston. Marisa was glad. She was excited about the opportunity to see the unique politician in person, and the gathering crowd showed that many others shared her enthusiasm.

She glanced at the massive clock above the doors; it read 6:30 p.m. Though it was thirty minutes before the doors were scheduled to open, a throng of people stood in front of the massive sports complex. Many were waving signs and banners proclaiming Reuben Rogov's presidential bid before his formal announcement. The content of the signs covered the gamut, but three popular ones stood out:

REUBEN ROGOV FOR PRESIDENT

PEACE THROUGH EQUALITY

IT'S TIME FOR CHANGE IN WASHINGTON

Police cruisers and motorcycles eased along Crawford Street, keeping a watchful eye on the excited crowd. Marisa was amazed by the unified demeanor of those waiting for the doors to open. The large gathering was a love-fest coalescing around one man, the charismatic Reuben Rogov, who'd already garnered abundant political capital as UN Secretary-General. Clearly, the crowd waiting in front of the stadium believed Rogov was the man who could lead the United States toward peace and equality. Marisa wondered if the Peace Party had formed with him in mind or at his behest. Probably the latter. Rogov was an unusual leader, a man with whom ordinary people could identify and to whom high-ranking politicians would listen.

"Look!" Izzy said, her voice rising. "They're opening the doors. Let's go." Marisa's group surged forward, as did everyone else on the sidewalk.

Fifteen minutes later, the stadium was crowded with people milling around looking for seats. A large stage surrounded by folding chairs occupied the centerfield area. Bordered by a sturdy railing, the stage held a speaker's podium and a row of plush chairs. At the back of the stage, a small orchestra played *America The Beautiful*, barely audible above the discordant background noise. Atop the outfield fence, a giant TV monitor displayed a gently-waving American flag.

After a brief search, Marisa's foursome found seats on the second row in front of the podium.

"This is perfect," she said, selecting a chair near the middle aisle.

"We'll be eyeball to eyeball with Mr. Rogov," Darien said, taking the chair at Marisa's left as Izzy sat down on her right with Alden beside her.

Expecting it would be a few minutes until the program started, Marisa touched the Alphabet News App on her iTab.

The monitor sprang to life, showing a fashionably-dressed, generic blonde seated at a small desk with the stadium scene at her back. Marisa looked around until she located the broadcast booth in a brightly-lit suite above the outfield seats.

The reporter began, "People throughout the country and from all over the world have turned out tonight to see Reuben Rogov announce his presidential bid. Hand-held signs and placards throughout the stadium indicate that the phrase, *Peace through equality*, has resonated with many Americans, particularly those in their twenties and thirties. They seem excited that the Peace Party has promised to bring equality to everyone regardless of race, creed, color, or social status. Of course, this has been promised repeatedly but never achieved."

As the reporter paused to take a breath, a TV camera swept back and forth over the stadium, pausing briefly to focus on the seating area in front of the stage. For a few seconds, Marisa's group was visible. She nudged Darien with her elbow and pointed to her iTab screen.

"Smile, everyone," Darien said. "We're on the evening news."

"Let me see," Izzy said.

As Marisa held the iTab toward Izzy, cymbals clanged in the orchestra. A second later, a five-person cadre emerged from a door in the outfield wall and marched with color-guard precision toward the podium. When they realized Reuben Rogov was the leader of the quintet, everyone in the stadium stood and erupted into thunderous applause accompanied by shouts and whistles.

Mr. Rogov led his contingent to the chairs near the podium and sat down, as did three of his escorts—two women and a man. The fourth person was Dalton Clayton, Chairman of the Peace

Party National Committee. He stepped to the podium and held up his hands for silence. The cheering continued for a few minutes, followed by chants of, "We want Reuben, we want Reuben."

Like the other officers, Chairman Clayton had been virtually invisible the past few weeks. Marisa assumed they had purposely avoided the spotlight to let it shine on Reuben Rogov, which it had done in abundance. Rogov was the party's logo and, for all practical purposes, the party itself. Marisa was eager to hear him speak. Hopefully, Clayton's remarks would be brief.

The Chairman held up his hands until the chants faded, and the excited audience retook their seats. "Good evening, ladies and gentlemen," he said. "Thank you for that warm Texas welcome. Tonight is a long-awaited occasion for the Peace Party.

"Our great nation has already begun the presidential election process. As you know, Isaac Ford will be the RADS candidate, and the Independents will hold Super Tuesday primaries in twenty-five states next month. At that point, both major parties will have their slates set for the November election.

"Although they have a head start on us, we are ready to challenge them. This evening, we will kick off our presidential campaign and enter the political arena with the RADS and the Independents. I know you came to hear Reuben Rogov speak, but before we turn the microphone over to him, please allow me to introduce the officers of The Peace Party National Committee."

Clayton introduced himself and the three officers seated beside the presidential candidate. Upon being introduced, each officer stepped to the podium and spoke briefly. Clayton pointed out that all of them had once been Independents or

RADS. The introductions and opening remarks droned on until the crowd became restless and resumed shouting, "We want Reuben. We want Reuben."

Clayton smiled good-naturedly and waited for the outburst to run its course.

"Thank you," he said when the chants abated. "During Isaac Ford's three years in office, he's done absolutely nothing to deserve another term, and the Independent candidates who've tossed their hats into the ring are clones of Mr. Ford. They have nothing to offer either. The Peace Party's only presidential candidate, Mr. Reuben Rogov, will launch his campaign tonight. This has been—"

"We want Reuben. We want Reuben."

This time, when the chanting died away, Clayton said, "Okay, I get your point. You didn't come to hear me or the other officers speak. You came to hear Mr. Rogov. That being the case, we'll skip the rest of the preliminaries and turn the podium over to the next President of the United States, Mr. Reuben Rogov."

Everyone jumped to their feet and cheered. Rogov stood and walked toward Clayton. The two men shook hands, and Clayton went to the chair vacated by Rogov.

The presidential candidate stepped to the podium and faced the cheering crowd. A moment later, amid thunderous applause, he moved to the rail surrounding the stage. Most people in the front row had left their seats and were gathering at the rail. As Rogov approached, they lifted their hands toward him. With a smile, he stooped over and brushed his hand across the upraised hands in a group handshake.

On an unreflective urge, Marisa pushed past Darien and worked her way along the row of chairs until she reached the aisle. Once there, she turned and signaled for her companions to follow. To her dismay, all three held their ground. Darien and Alden shook their heads, and Izzy motioned toward the stage, signaling Marisa to go on alone.

With some difficulty, Marisa squeezed through the excited crowd until she reached the rail. Like those around her, she raised a hand toward Reuben Rogov. At that moment, the stage lights shifted, giving Rogov's face an angelic glow. To Marisa's surprise, he looked directly at her and extended his hand. When their hands touched, Mr. Rogov paused his group handshake routine and held Marisa's hand for a few seconds, after which he turned away and went back to the podium. In shock from being singled out, Marisa picked her way back to her seat as the crowd continued to cheer passionately.

Rogov held up his hands for silence. Over the next few minutes, the cheering decreased gradually until the stadium was quiet.

"Good evening, my fellow Americans," Rogov began. "Thank you for that extraordinary welcome. Tonight, the Peace Party is launching a campaign to bring equality to everyone in our great nation. Equality has been promised many times in the past but never delivered. That must change, and when elected President, I will do so. In addition, I will strive to bring peace to the entire world by promoting equality around the globe."

"Peace through equality, peace through equality," the crowd shouted.

Rogov waited until the cheers subsided and continued, "Everyone knows Thomas Jefferson's words, '*We hold these truths to be self-evident, that all men are created equal, that they are endowed by their creator with certain unalienable rights, that among these are life, liberty, and pursuit of happiness.'* This is a beautifully poetic statement, and many politicians quote it. Incredibly, when Jefferson wrote these words, he owned slaves, as did his cohorts. So, from the early days until the present time, *Do as I say, not as I do* has been the standard operating procedure utilized by most of America's political leaders."

Rogov paused, and the crowd resumed the chant, "Peace through equality, peace through equality."

"In the past," Rogov resumed, "those who imposed taxes on you served you poorly. Moreover, they used your money to set themselves up as the ruling elite with you as their subjects. I assure you, most politicians holding office today are committed to maintaining this system forever, though they deny it.

"Our electoral process makes it incredibly difficult for anyone other than a RADS or Independent Party candidate to win a national office. True democracy will never be achieved under a system that requires you to join one of the two approved parties to obtain your constitutional rights. This is not equality, and it is a farce to call it a democracy.

"It is time to make everybody equal," Rogov continued. "If we do not, the flimsy house of cards that NatGov has cobbled together will fall under its own weight. We have a choice—either a government that makes every American equal to every other American or one that will lead to anarchy.

"The power brokers in both major parties talk of equality and freedom, but while doing so, they attempt to censor anyone who disagrees with them. Equality cannot be squelched any longer. Equality is your birthright. It is the foundation on which both peace and freedom stand. Without equality, peace and freedom are only high-sounding words tossed around by politicians to get elected.

"In addition to the presidential election, Peace Party candidates are entering every open race for the US House and Senate. Recent polls show that we have an excellent chance to take control of both legislative chambers. These candidates need your support, just as I do. Elect them and elect me to lead them. Together we will bring equality to this great country."

Following another round of cheers, Mr. Rogov mesmerized the crowd for fifteen additional minutes by pointing out various things he hoped to accomplish during his first one hundred days in office. Then, with everyone still on the edge of their seats waiting to hear more, he concluded, "Thank you for attending this event. God bless you, and God bless America."

Another deafening applause exploded throughout the stadium. As the cheering continued, thousands of multi-colored balloons appeared from hidden locations, floated upward through the grid of overhead beams, and disappeared into the night sky above the open roof. The ovation continued as news banners scrolled across the TV screen above the outfield:

ALPHABET NEWS INSTANT POLLS:

REUBEN ROGOV'S APPROVAL RATE AT 49%

Darien leaned toward Marisa. "Mr. Rogov is getting off to a good start."

"Maybe he'll get over 50% of the electoral votes and avoid a runoff," she said.

"How does that work with three or more candidates?"

"If no candidate gets a majority of the votes, congress decides between them—one vote per state."

"So, a candidate could get 49.9% of the votes and lose to someone with fewer votes."

Marisa nodded. "That's right." She felt her iTab vibrate, flashing a message which also materialized on the outfield TV monitor:

All stadium exits will have an attendant handing out Peace Party armbands. Please take one and wear it daily to show your support for Reuben Rogov. In addition, you'll have the opportunity to join the party by scanning the barcode on the armband. We urge you to do so tonight and get involved in the fight to bring peace through equality.

An unusual feeling came over Marisa after shaking hands with the Peace Party candidate. Their hand contact formed a person-to-person link with Mr. Rogov, and she was ready to embrace his connection between equality and peace.

After chatting briefly with some of the young politicos near them, Marisa's quartet left the seating area. Moments later, they reached the nearest exit, where exuberant attendants handed out armbands and urged everyone to join the Peace Party before leaving the stadium. Virtually everyone accepted the lime green armbands embossed with bold black letters, *EQUALITY = PEACE*. Eagerly, Marisa grasped the band, swung her iTab into position, and scanned the barcode. A sharp ping sounded, and a message popped up, *Thank you for your support, Marisa Da Rosa. You are now a member of The Peace Party.*

She wrapped the band around her left arm and stared at the trio behind her. "Well, are you going to join?"

Simultaneously, Izzy and Alden gave affirmative nods, donned the armbands, and scanned the barcode. After pausing briefly, Darien scanned the barcode and stuffed the armband into his hip pocket.

Concerned, Marisa looked at him. "Are you having second thoughts?"

"This is a tough decision," Darien said. "As I've told you, all of my relatives are Independents."

Marisa understood why Darien might want to tell his family about joining the Peace Party before becoming an avant-garde member wearing an armband. She usually thought that way herself and was shocked that she'd taken the lead in a political movement, something she'd never done before. Even so, she was pleased by her quick response to the party's invitation and eager to get more involved in the presidential campaign.

They left the stadium. The temperature had dropped slightly since their arrival, so Marisa buttoned her sweater and pulled it around her neck. As they walked toward the intersection, she mentioned seeing the Brazil de Houston Restaurant and suggested it as a possible choice for dinner.

"That place is too expensive," Alden said, shaking his head.

"Anyway, it's not like the food in Rio," Izzy said.

"You've eaten there?" Marisa asked.

Izzy nodded. "Uh-huh, a couple of times. The food is okay but not authentic. It's Texas' version of Brazilian dishes—I call it Tex-Braz."

"Any other ideas?" Marisa asked.

Following a short discussion about possible dining choices, Alden suggested an Italian restaurant, *La Cucina Roma,* three blocks from the stadium. "The night manager is a friend of mine," he added. "He'll let us have a booth, and we can stay as long as we like."

Everyone liked Alden's suggestion, and they walked to the restaurant. A few minutes after their arrival, the Maître d seated them. Without waiting for menus, they ordered two sampler platters and a bottle of wine.

While snacking and sipping wine, the foursome lingered in the restaurant until midnight. Nearly all of the conversation was about the political rally and the upcoming presidential election. They hashed over the possibility of the Peace Party winning the House, Senate, and presidency, something no other party had done in a long time. Marisa overheard similar conversations from nearby tables, making it apparent that Mr. Rogov's words had resonated with the local populace, as they had with her. By closing time, most diners in La Cucina Roma were wearing Peace Party armbands.

One notable exception was Darien. His armband remained in his hip pocket.

CHAPTER 8

The autopilot eased the red Apple GT-3.5Y into a parking space marked *Compact Cars Only*, and a computer voice announced, "You have arrived at your destination, Amazon Senior Living No. 3 in Sugar Land, Texas."

Darien pointed to a sign reading *Reserved for Future Residents*. "I hope my car doesn't get towed," he said as he opened the door and slid out.

"Nobody knows whether we're future residents or not," Rachel said, joining Darien on the sidewalk.

"Even if we are, this car is not a compact."

"You should sell it," Rachel said. "Public transportation is cheaper than owning a car."

Darien nodded. "I know, but I love my car too much to part with it."

Rachel motioned toward the building. "Mom and Dad just went inside. It's impossible to beat them anywhere."

"I'm looking forward to seeing Papa," Darien said.

"Please don't get into another political argument with him."

"He and Dr. Throxmire argue about politics all the time. Papa loves it."

Darien and Rachel entered the nursing home. Their parents, Mark and Kendra, were waiting for them in the foyer, which smelled like a mixture of jasmine and mothballs—perhaps sanitary but far from fragrant.

"Phew!" Rachel said, rolling her eyes.

"At least it's clean," Kendra said.

They approached the reception desk and greeted the head nurse, Olivia Torres. The Segura family had gotten to know Olivia well over the last five years. She had a demanding job, but in the midst of it, she always took time to discover Papa's needs and keep the family informed. In addition, the family had a good relationship with Dr. Woody Throxmire, the unit's primary care physician. More importantly, Papa trusted the facility's medical staff enough to predict that he would live to be a hundred. And, at the moment, it seemed quite possible.

Kendra took a Starbucks gift card out of her purse and handed it to Olivia.

"Thank you," Olivia said with an appreciative smile. "Dr. Segura is expecting you."

"Is he taking his nap?" Mark asked.

"He was asleep the last time I checked," Olivia said, "but before he dozed off, he told me to wake him when you arrive."

They followed Olivia down a hallway toward a group of elderly residents. Several people spoke to the Seguras as they picked their way through the human obstacle course. At the far end of the hall, a man wearing a gray suit and matching hat stared at Kendra and Rachel as they approached.

"Good afternoon, ladies," he said, tipping his hat when they were directly in front of him. They returned the greeting, and he smiled broadly as they passed by.

"Mr. Latham considers himself a ladies' man," Olivia said. "He's asked every woman living here to marry him."

"How many accepted?" Kendra asked.

"Most of them."

Darien shook his head in disbelief. If this weren't Papa's residence, he wouldn't be here. He was having difficulty grasping the peculiarities related to aging and senility. Still, after Nana's death, there'd been little choice for Papa other than assisted living.

Nana died from Phoenix five years ago. Sadly, the virus had yet to be defeated, and another pandemic was in the making. Since the new variant was attacking both people and plants, something previously unknown, many believed a secret entity was manipulating it. Darien was inclined to buy into the idea; it was his type of conspiracy theory. Still, regardless of how the virus originated, he blamed Nana's death on NatGov for moving at a snail's pace during the early days of the pandemic.

Darien believed the early success of the Peace Party indicated a change was in the air. Even so, he hadn't told his parents about joining the party and was waiting for the right time to do so. Rachel knew but wouldn't mention it to them without his okay. Maybe he would get the opportunity to broach the subject today.

They approached Papa's unit. The door was closed except for a small crack. Olivia knocked lightly and pushed it open. As expected, Papa was in bed. They stepped inside and were greeted by the sound of gentle snoring. A covey of monitors occupied shelves along the walls, their dully-glowing screens an ever-changing pattern of dots, dashes, and lines. Thanks to Bluetooth technology, Papa didn't have a single wire attached to him and could move around his quarters as he saw fit.

Olivia glanced at the monitors. "His vital signs are perfect, and his color is great. Let me know if you need anything."

When she left the room, the family moved to the bedside in unison. Papa was lying with his arms forming an X atop the sheets covering his chest. He looked at peace, and his thin lips showed a faint smile. Even while asleep, Papa had a subtle aura about him that seemed to speak of the remarkable things he'd seen and done. It was hard to believe he was 96 years old.

As was usually the case, a pile of books lay on the bedside table—genuine paper books, most with hard backs. Although Papa kept thousands of e-books on his iTab and pored over them regularly, he refused to read some books on a tablet. Several such books were at his side—*Advanced Inorganic Chemistry, Organic Synthesis, The Handbook of Chemistry and Physics,* and a few non-science books, including the *Holy Bible.*

Rachel leaned toward Darien and whispered, "I wonder what his first words will be when he wakes up?"

"Something about how he met Nana, of course."

Darien and Rachel leaned closer and said, "Happy birthday, Papa."

Papa's gaunt face showed signs of waking. His eyelids twitched, and he inhaled deeply. Letting the breath out slowly, he looked like a marble statue coming to life. Momentarily, he opened his eyes and looked at the faces above him.

Darien and Rachel repeated their birthday greeting. This time, their parents joined them.

Papa's parchment-like lips formed a barely-audible sentence. "We had some difficulties at first, but we overcame them."

"Papa! You're dreaming," Rachel said.

"Oh, hello, everyone," Papa said, yawning and stretching his arms. He rubbed his eyes and was fully awake a moment later. "Yes, I was dreaming," he said, strength returning to his voice. "Raise my head, and I'll tell you about the dream."

Kendra touched a button on the rail. The head of the bed raised to a comfortable angle, and everyone waited for Papa's dream story to unfold. This routine had taken place numerous times over the past five years.

"I had one of my favorite dreams again," Papa said. "It was about meeting your grandmother in an astronomy class." He threw his sheets aside and swung his feet to the floor as a man half his age might have done. Standing cautiously, he hitched up his blue-striped pajamas.

Mark moved closer. "Let me help you."

"I don't need any help to take two steps," Papa said with a dismissive wave. With Mark flanking him, he shuffled to a chair beside the bed, pivoted, and fell backward into it in one move.

"Nice pirouette," Rachel said, giving a thumbs up. "You look like a ballet dancer."

Kendra took a card from her purse and extended it toward the nonagenarian. "This is from all of us. Happy birthday."

"Thank you," Papa said, reaching for the card. "But you should have sent an e-card to avoid the outrageous tax on paper goods."

"You've always said that some things are worth the tax," Kendra said, nodding toward the books beside Papa's bed.

"Those books are worth it," Papa said.

Kendra and Rachel sat down in the chairs near Papa. Mark and Darien remained standing.

"What have you been reading lately?" Mark said.

"The Book of Daniel–the prophetic parts."

"What are you trying to figure out?" Mark said.

"Nothing specifically, but I'm intrigued by the passages describing the rise and fall of kingdoms."

"Do they refer to kingdoms, past, present, or future?" Mark said.

"All of them."

A moment later, when a brief pause in the conversation occurred, Darien asked, "Papa, what do you think will happen now that three electable candidates have entered the race for president?" He glanced at his sister and mother and could read mild disapproval in their eyes. Neither of them would be likely to join the conversation until the political skirmish ran its course.

"I hate to admit it," Papa said, "but I believe the Peace Party has a good chance to win the election."

Darien was stunned. "Really?"

"What makes you think that?" Mark asked, incredulity lacing his voice.

"Their slogan, *Peace Through Equality*, is gaining traction with people who've never voted before," Papa said, "especially young people."

Darien was pleased. The conversation was going his way. One question had been enough to launch it.

"That slogan is a code word for a *one-world government,*" Papa said emphatically.

"The idea has been tried repeatedly," Mark said, "and has always failed. A majority of Americans will never accept it."

"No other similar party had a presidential candidate like Reuben Rogov," Papa said.

Darien was surprised at Papa's words but agreed with his statement. He'd just listened to one of Rogov's campaign speeches. The man was Napoleonic in stature yet a giant in oratorial skills.

"How did the Peace Party launch so quickly?" Darien asked, suspecting he already knew the gist of Papa's answer.

"Some deep state operation formed the Peace Party," Papa said, "and they're going all in to get Rogov elected President. If it happens, he'll be running both NatGov and the United Nations, and a new world order will emerge just as they've planned for years."

"How did you arrive at that conclusion?" Mark said.

"By detecting clues other people miss, and putting them together like pieces of a jigsaw puzzle."

"Besides his move back to the U.S., what other clues have you discovered about Mr. Rogov?" Darien asked.

"A significant one—he formed the United Nations Peace Committee two years ago," Papa said.

"That committee attempts to bring peace to warring nations," Mark said.

"The concept sounds good," Papa said, "but when I looked at the list of nations on the committee, I got suspicious."

"It's bringing peace," Mark said. "What could be wrong with that?"

"The committee structure suggests they intend to promote a one-world government," Papa said.

"I don't think I'm following you," Mark said, a puzzled look on his face.

"The UN Peace Committee is a ten-country federation," Papa said. "In addition, seven other nations have pledged their support to the committee's efforts. If Reuben Rogov becomes President of the United States, all of the pieces will be in place to move ahead with their plan."

"Papa, I've listened to several of Mr. Rogov's speeches," Darien said. "He always speaks of peace. I don't see how peace can be evil."

"If it's enforced by taking away other people's rights, it's evil," Papa said, "and I fear that's what Reuben Rogov will eventually do if elected President."

"The Peace Party stresses equality as a means of obtaining peace," Darien said, struggling to understand Papa's reasoning.

"*All men are created equal* doesn't mean the same thing now as when Thomas Jefferson penned it," Papa said. "*Equality* has morphed into a buzzword. Today, opposing groups use the word as a lever to pry concessions from each other."

Darien was beginning to understand Papa's reasoning but didn't agree with him.

"What's your *one-world ruler* concept based on?" he asked, leaning toward Papa.

"Primarily on a passage in the Book of Daniel."

"What does it say?"

"By means of peace, he shall destroy many."

CHAPTER 9

S hortly after ten o'clock on Friday morning, Darien went to The Fossil, a tiny bookstore near the Mediplex. It was his go-to spot for inspiration when suffering from writer's block. The store, as its name proclaimed, was a fossil. Only a handful of such stores still existed in the country today. All were dedicated to one thing–preserving books printed on real paper. The little shop, and others like it, existed because bibliophiles kept them open as a hobby, not as a means of earning a living. The owner of The Fossil had shared her story with Darien. Upon receiving a small monthly allowance from her grandfather's trust, she changed her name to *Ima Bookworm* and opened The Fossil. Now, she devoted all of her time to buying, selling, trading, and reading books.

For the last month, Darien's creativity had waxed and waned. He was currently trying to write a fantasy scene, something more difficult for him than writing science fiction. He'd looked at dozens of e-books and found one he liked called *Angry Candy.* It was by an old master, Harlan Ellison. If he could find an affordable paper copy, he'd buy it. Flipping through a paperback usually released his creative muse. Unfortunately, doing the same thing on an iTab didn't produce the desired effect. Apparently, Marisa was right about creative people being eccentric.

Darien, the only customer in the store, browsed along the center aisle. The Fossil's interior didn't resemble the enormous bookstores in old movies. Ima's books were locked in glass-topped display cases. Many of them were in mint condition and priced far beyond his budget. Her system was simple. If a book was on display, she had copies for sale in the storeroom at the back of the shop. The condition of the books ranged from *like new* to *acceptable*, the latter meaning worn and dog-eared. Prices varied accordingly. Ima always gave Darien a small friendship discount and was open to an occasional trade, especially if he had a book she was trying to locate for another customer.

He heard a shuffling sound and saw Ima emerging from the storeroom wearing a black sweatshirt with her name scrawled across the front in red letters. She was thumbing her iTab and hadn't noticed him.

"Hey, Ima," he said, "you've got a customer."

She looked up. "Oh, hello, Darien. You're sure here early."

"I'm looking for something to jump-start my creativity."

"Anything in particular?" Ima asked as she approached Darien.

He told Ima what he was looking for and added, "I looked at the E section and didn't see anything by Ellison."

"Are you looking for *"Paladin of the Lost Hour"*?"

"How did you know?"

"It's the best story in the book," Ima said. "At the moment, I don't have a collection with that story, but I do have one with *"Repent Harlequin Said the Ticktockman."*

"What condition and what price?"

"Poor condition, but a good price."

"Let me take a look at it."

"Follow me," Ima said. She did an about-face and retraced her steps toward the storeroom with Darien at her heels. The back of her shirt featured a red heart with the words, *I Love*

Books, printed on it. Front and back, Ima was a walking advertisement for the cause she loved. She was the most avid reader Darien knew and claimed that she'd read more than 3000 novels in the last twenty years. Science fiction was one of her favorite genres, and they'd had many lively discussions about it.

Ima entered the storeroom and closed the door behind her. As Darien waited, the top half of the door swung inward, leaving them separated by the lower half. Ima lifted a panel into place, forming a small counter atop the lower half of the door. Such was Ima's method of negotiating book deals. She wouldn't let anybody into her storeroom, not even Darien.

Ima turned away and, moments later, came back with a tattered book. She lay it on the counter, and Darien picked it up gingerly. Several pages had separated from the spine, but a quick examination indicated none were missing.

"How much?"

"It's falling apart," Ima said. "I'll loan it to you."

"Well, thanks," Darien said, "but you can't make any money that way."

Ima shrugged and slipped the ragged book into a clear plastic bag. After handing it to Darien, she left the storeroom and joined him as he perused the display cases while drifting slowly toward the exit.

"I've heard NatGov is working up a list of books to be banned," Ima said. "Have you heard anything about it?"

Surprised, Darien shook his head. "That doesn't seem likely with the presidential election campaign in progress. Where did you hear it?"

"It's been circulating among bookstore owners like me," Ima said. "You know how much we fear that kind of government interference."

"Writers fear it too," Darien said, opening the exit door, "but I don't believe it will happen at the national level anytime soon. Some more states may do it—but not NatGov."

"I hope you're right, but my friends think it's more than a rumor."

As Darien stepped onto the sidewalk, his iTab pinged and flashed an icon—a Brazilian flag with *Marisa* written across it.

Somewhat surprised, he touched the icon. "Hi, Marisa. What's up?"

"I'd like to run an idea by you."

"Go ahead—I'm listening."

"I'm working on a new project," Marisa said, excitement showing in her voice. "It involves writing a travel guide about the Houston area, and I need a co-writer. Would you be interested?"

Hardly able to believe his ears, Darien said, "I certainly would."

"Could you come to the consulate this afternoon?" Marisa asked. "The Consul General will have to approve my choice for this job."

"What time?"

Darien heard a muffled conversation in Portuguese, after which Marisa said, "How about three o'clock."

"That's fine. I'll see you then."

He started down the sidewalk toward the housing unit, amazed at what he'd done but somewhat annoyed at what he'd neglected to do. He didn't ask how long the job would last or how much the salary would be. Hopefully, it would last long enough for him to quit his tedious job of grading English papers.

Whatever the case, the thought of working with Marisa was thrilling.

***

At two forty-five, Darien got off the Metro at a kiosk on Westheimer Street, a half-block from a trendy high-rise housing the Brazilian Consulate. The plate glass structure housed numerous offices, including those occupied by consulates from several Central and South American countries. Once inside, he consulted the directory and took the elevator to the fifth floor. He entered the office and approached the receptionist's station, attended by a woman about his age. A nameplate on the counter identified her as *Belmira,* which Darien thought meant *beautiful woman* in Portuguese. If so, the name fit the olive-skinned brunette very well.

"May I help you?" Belmira asked pleasantly.

"Darien Segura to see Marisa Da Rosa."

Belmira tapped her iTab and studied the screen. "She's expecting you. I'll let her know you're here."

"Thank you."

"Wait in that small conference room over there," Belmira said, pointing. "They'll join you in a minute."

Noticing that Belmira said *they* instead of *she,* Darien went to the room and sat down at a table surrounded by a half-dozen chairs. One of the walls had a large window overlooking an office with cubicles along one side and a line of chairs along another. A sign above the chairs read *Passaportes e Vistos,* and several people were engaged in a lively discussion next to one of the cubicles.

As Darien watched, a door opened at the far end of the office, and Marisa stepped out accompanied by her mother. Apparently, the duo was what Belmira meant when she said *they*. The arrangement wasn't what he expected, but he wasn't put off by it. He'd had a couple of short conversations with Mrs. Da Rosa, and she was quite friendly. Surely, he could work with the mother-daughter duo approaching him.

Darien stood as the women entered the room. After exchanging hellos, he said, "Nice to see you, Mrs. Da Rosa."

"Please call me Frieda."

"Let me explain what's going on," Marisa said as they sat down. "As you know, I'm in HR. Currently, everything is stable in that department, so I'm on loan to the Publicity Department, which consists of my mother and a part-time assistant. The Consul General has given us an unusual writing assignment. Normally, a Brazilian Consulate would publicize information about Brazil to the host country. In this case, however, we will reverse that approach and publish information about our host city, Houston. The target audience will be Central and South Americans who have recently obtained U.S. citizenship and moved to this area."

A dozen questions popped into Darien's mind, and he asked the first one. "Are you doing the publication in Portuguese?"

Marisa shook her head. "No, we're doing it in English, but I will probably translate it into Portuguese and Spanish later."

"That's good," Darien said, "because I wouldn't be any help otherwise. Tell me some more about the project."

Marisa tapped at her iTab momentarily and slid it across the table to Darien. The screen showed a booklet entitled *Top Ten Sites in Rio De Janeiro*. A picture of the statue, *Christ The*

Redeemer, adorned the front cover. A list below it read: *Beaches, Historic Sites, Clubs and Restaurants, Hotels, Suggested Itineraries, Museums and Galleries, Other.*

"We'll use this as a template for the Houston area," Marisa said, "and we'll visit the locations before we write about them. I'll take pictures at each site or find good ones online. You'll be the lead writer, and I'll help as much as possible. We'll report to Mom and keep her updated. She won't be helping us, but she'll approve or disapprove each section as we go along. How does that sound?"

"It sounds like a tremendous amount of fun," Darien said, struggling to control his excitement. "But I do have a couple of questions. How long will this project last? And what is the salary?"

With a hand motion, Marisa deferred to her mother.

"We expect it to last about four months," Frieda said, "and the salary will be roughly equivalent to a beginning school teacher. It will be paid as a monthly stipend, not based on hours worked. Does that sound satisfactory?"

"Yes, it does," Darien said. "When do we start?"

"Before we get to that, Mr. Profeto, the Consul General, has to approve you," Frieda said. She touched her iTab screen and added, "He'll be here shortly."

A moment later, the door at the far end of the office opened again. A man emerged and walked toward the conference room. Surprisingly, the man had white hair and appeared to be in his sixties, much older than Darien expected. Even so, he strode past the cubicles with a lively step as if marching to the beat of a drum and bugle corps. He was dressed in a tan suit suggesting a military uniform and had a chain-of-command aura about him.

Darien and the two women stood when the man entered the room. Frieda moved to Darien's side and made the introductions.

Profeto extended his hand and said, "Thanks for coming."

The men shook hands, and Profeto motioned toward the chairs. After they were seated, he looked toward Darien and said, "I'm sure Frieda and Marisa have explained the project in considerable detail. Do you have any questions for me?"

"No questions, Mr. Profeto," Darien said. Though he wondered why the booklet would be published in English, he wasn't going to mention it for fear of putting his foot in his mouth.

"When would you be available?" Profeto asked.

"Any time Marisa wants to start," Darien said, trying not to sound overly anxious.

"The funding will be in place in about two weeks," Profeto said, "so that's our target date to begin."

"That works fine for me."

Profeto asked Darien about some of his favorite sites in and around Houston, and they struck up a dialogue while the women listened. To Darien's surprise, the Consul General was much easier to talk to than his military bearing suggested.

A few minutes later, Profeto stood, signaling the end of the conversation. "I came in here to meet you rather than to conduct a job interview," he said. "So, if you're Frieda and Marisa's choice, the job is yours."

"Thank you, Mr. Profeto."

Profeto started toward the door. Before exiting, he turned toward Darien and said, "Have you registered to vote?"

"Yes, Sir. I have."

"Which party?"

"The Peace Party."

"Good," Profeto said. "The party appreciates your support." With that, he did an about-face and marched briskly toward his office.

When the Consul General was out of earshot, Darien said, "What was that all about?"

Looking slightly chagrinned, Frieda said, "I forgot to mention something important. One of Homero Profeto's cousins is Saul Profeto, the man Reuben Rogov is expected to pick as his running mate."

CHAPTER 10

While walking through the lobby of the George Washington, Marisa passed several small clumps of people wearing Peace Party armbands, as she was. The bands had caused a stir nationwide, and Alphabet News had coined a phrase for Rogov supporters wearing them—*Rogovites.* The term was rising in popularity with the media, as well as with the wearers. She liked the term because it conveyed the idea of allegiance to a person rather than a political party.

Nearly everyone greeted Marisa, and many called her by name. She felt completely at home in the Houston Mediplex area, and residents of the housing unit had welcomed the Da Rosa family upon their arrival. She suspected part of the collective friendliness of the tenants was attributable to Alden, whose outgoing personality permeated the entire unit.

She exited the building. Though it was a sunny day in May, a cool breeze greeted her when she stepped onto the sidewalk. Across the street, the Saturday early-lunch-bunch was gathering at the food court. Again, as in the lobby, armbands were prominent. Marisa turned toward the crosswalk and saw Darien walking toward her carrying a large coffee. They smiled as they approached each other.

"Hello there," he said as he did an about-face and fell in step with her.

"You're following me again," Marisa said, laughing softly and adjusting her stride to match his.

They reached the crosswalk. As they waited for the light, Darien said, "I have a great day trip for us to kick off our Houston project. It's not on our original list, but it's perfect."

"Tell me about it," Marisa said, raising her eyebrows. The traffic light changed, and they joined other pedestrians crossing the street.

"It was Alden's idea," Darien said. "He suggested a trip to Beaumont for a crawfish boil."

"Crawfish! I know what they are."

"Do you eat them in Brazil?"

"Of course," Marisa said enthusiastically. "We call them *pitu* or *langostim*. I love them, but why do we have to go to Beaumont to get them?"

"There're two good reasons," Darien said. "First, Beaumont is called *The Cajun Capital of Texas*. Second, after the Thibideaux family left Freeport, they lived there for several years before Alden and Justin moved to Houston. Their parents still live there. We go back every year for a crawfish boil and some Cajun music. It's a fantastic day trip."

"I'm sure Alden plans to go with us," Marisa said.

"Of course he does, and he's already invited Izzy."

"That sounds like a great idea. Can you get Alden to set it up?"

"He'd like nothing better," Darien said. "By the way, where are you headed?"

"To the Log Cabin," Marisa said. "Izzy is joining me for coffee, and we're going shopping afterward."

Darien raised his cup. "I have my coffee, so I'll tag along."

Marisa didn't respond but was pleased. As a creative person, Darien hadn't shown the self-centered tendencies she'd expected him to. Moreover, she enjoyed his company enough to make her see the possibility of an Octavio-Darien problem developing, especially if Octavio didn't get to the U.S. soon. She was ready to get on with life in her newly-adopted country. If Octavio wanted to share it with her as he claimed he did, he needed to do something other than send daily text messages about trying to get his passport.

***

Two weeks later, Darien and Alden met Marisa and Izzy at the exit of the housing unit. It was ten o'clock, the sky was clear blue, and the temperature was hovering around 72°F, perfect for a day trip or anything else.

"I'll get a minivan," Alden said, thumbing the Transportation App on his iTab. "It'll take about an hour and a half to get there, so we want to be comfortable."

Moments later, a small gray van pulled to the curb, and the doors slid open. The eager foursome got in and sat down. When the robo-pilot sensed that everyone had buckled their seat belts, it asked, "Destination, please?"

"Beaumont, Texas," Alden said. "Ford Park."

"Drive time, one hour and thirty-five minutes," the robo-pilot said as the van pulled away from the curb.

Immediately, Alden struck up a conversation about Brazil, zeroing in on the famous beaches, Copacabana, Ipanema, and Leblon. To Marisa's surprise, he talked about Rio like he'd been there. She could tell he'd done a lot of research on her native country in preparation for today's trip.

After the Brazil discussion ran its course, the conversation switched to Beaumont and Houston. Izzy asked several questions about each city, primarily about restaurants, night-clubs, and shopping. Amused, Marisa leaned back in her seat and listened, surprised at how much Izzy and Alden were alike in their social tendencies. They'd already developed a strong friendship, and she saw the possibility of romance—unless both of them talking so much prevented it.

Noticing Darien tapping at his iTab, Marisa asked, "Are you going to put this discussion in our travel guide?"

"Not all, "Darien said, chuckling. "Only the best parts."

Eventually, Izzy ran out of questions, and Alden said, "We missed something important about Beaumont."

"What?"

"Spindletop."

Izzy bumped her forehead with her palm. "Oh, yes—the big gusher."

"That discovery in the early 1900s made petroleum eco-nomical as a fuel," Alden said, "and put Beaumont on the map. After that, it was considered an oil town for many years, just like Houston."

"We had a lesson about the oil industry while studying for our American Citizenship test," Izzy said. "Oil was an import-ant part of Brazil's economy until the move to electric cars."

"Until Darien's grandfather invented iso-lithium," Alden said.

"The world was already heading that direction before Papa's discovery," Darien said. "He just speeded up the process."

The discussion about the decline of big oil continued for several minutes. Marisa saw it as a *yin and yang* situation. While environmentalists praised Dr. Segura for saving the planet, he was a *persona non grata* among OPEC nations in the Mideast. No doubt, iso-lithium had destroyed their way of life. She'd heard stories of once-wealthy Arabs regressing to the state of Bedouin nomads. Sadly, most of the world didn't care. OPEC had appealed to the UN several times, but no meaningful action had been undertaken. This grave situation would take an extraordinary leader to correct it. And, as she saw it, only one man had the necessary skills—Reuben Rogov.

With easy-flowing conversation seeming to speed up the clock exponentially, the van rolled to a stop at eleven thirty, and the autopilot announced, "You have arrived at your destination—Ford Park in Beaumont, Texas."

As they exited the van, Marisa spotted a sign over the entrance gate: *LAISSEZ LES BONS TEMPS ROULER.*

"Look, Izzy," she said, her voice rising excitedly. "It says, *Let the good times roll."*

"Can you read Cajun French?" Alden asked incredulously.

"No," Marisa said, "but it's close to how we say it in Portuguese, *Deixe os bons tempos rolar.* We say it on Carnival Tuesday."

"Mardi Gras," Izzy said, "or *Fat Tuesday."*

In front of the park, a half-dozen people carrying hand-lettered signs marched back and forth. One of the signs identified the protestors as *The Society for Prevention of Cruelty to Crustaceans,* while others stated their message:

ANIMALS HAVE CONSTITUTIONAL RIGHTS TOO

STOP BOILING CRAWFISH ALIVE—GO VEGAN

A steady stream of park visitors passed by the activists, some accepting leaflets and others ignoring them completely. Several people paused to chat briefly with the protestors before entering the park, an action that seemed odd since most who entered the park would be dining on crawfish within the hour. Seated in a golf cart nearby, two uniformed policemen watched the proceedings.

Marisa wasn't surprised at the protest. She'd seen similar ones in Rio representing every imaginable cause. Moreover, Darien was trying to convince her that deep-state politicians had deliberately divided the world into a thousand-piece jigsaw puzzle, making everybody a member of some minority group. Maybe he was right. If so, who could reassemble the puzzle to achieve unity? Again, it would take an extraordinary leader.

"I'm starving," Izzy said as they entered the park. "Let's eat before we look around."

"We'll have to eat at one of the long tables with everybody else," Alden said, "There won't be any tables for four people."

Darien pointed at a nearby table. "That one has plenty of room on this end," he said, "and it will be in the shade in a few minutes. Let's stake out our claim."

"I'll hold it for us," Marisa said. "Bring me a platter full." She started toward the table, which was covered with plastic sheeting to provide a surface from which to eat the boiled crawfish, a messy undertaking.

"I'm going to get mine fried," Izzy said, walking toward the serving lines with Darien and Alden. "Boiled crawfish are too gross for me."

"Didn't you dissect one in biology lab recently?" Alden asked.

"Yes, but I didn't eat it."

"Touché," Darien said. Laughing, they joined the lines of people waiting to get food.

A few minutes later, they were back at the table, enjoying a feast–crawfish, corn on the cob, new potatoes, boiled onions, and cold beer. At every table, conversation and laughter accompanied the food, making it evident that a crawfish boil was more than a dining occasion. It was also a social event.

Suddenly, the sound of accordions and guitars reverberated throughout the park, and everyone looked toward a temporary stage near the dining area.

"What kind of music is that?" Marisa asked.

"It's called *Zydeco*," Alden said. "It was invented in New Orleans, and it's illegal to have a crawfish boil without it."

"It's really peppy," Marisa said, tapping the table in rhythm with the beat.

"I've got a playlist with hundreds of songs similar to this one," Alden said. "I call it my Louisiana Collection. They're not all zydeco, but all have some connection to the state–songwriters, singers, or something else."

"Some of his songs are over 200 years old," Darien said.

Marisa's eyes widened. "No way!"

"It's a great list," Alden said. "I play it occasionally at the Cherry Tree."

The diners watched as the five-piece band warmed up. When the musicians were ready, an announcer walked to center stage and said, "*Mesdames et messieurs,* welcome to Beaumont, the Cajun capital of Texas. For your listening pleasure, today we have *Molly and the Mudbugs.*"

The announcer retreated, and Molly stepped through a slit in a yellow curtain at the rear of the stage. She wore burnt orange leotards and a waistcoat with sleeves portraying crawfish pincers. Strumming her guitar loudly as she strode forward, she shouted, "Hello, fun lovers."

The audience responded with, "Hello, Molly."

"Today, we're taking a trip in a time machine," Molly continued. "We're going to sing some songs from the early days of zydeco, starting with an ancient classic." She pointed toward her band and said, "Hit it, *mes amis.*"

The band struck up a lively rendition of *Jambalaya*, and Molly began to sing in Cajun French.

Amused at Molly's sleeves, Marisa leaned toward Darien and asked, "Do you say *pincers* or *pinchers?*"

Darien laughed softly. "We pronounce the *H.*"

"Let's get another round of beer and listen to Molly for a while," Alden said.

Everyone agreed enthusiastically with Alden's suggestion. After refilling their glasses, the conversation resumed.

Though they'd met only a few weeks ago, Marisa felt she'd always known Darien. He had a few eccentricities, but who didn't? She had some of her own and knew it. Yet, oddly, they didn't seem to clash with Darien's. Maybe the old saying, *opposites attract*, was true after all.

After considering the situation momentarily, she concluded that she was overplaying their relationship and daydreaming about something not likely to happen. As she attempted to push the thoughts aside, her iTab sounded a melodic ringtone, and a text message popped up. Shocked out of her introspection, she looked at the text, which read:

Marisa,

I've completed my passport application, but the system is backed up, and the State Department says the wait will be about three months. I apologize for not listening to you earlier, and I promise to be a better man when I get to the U.S.

Octavio

She stared at the message until Izzy asked, "What is it?"

Marisa held her iTab toward her sister. Izzy's eyes widened, and she said, "Is that good news or bad?"

"I'm not sure."

CHAPTER 11

The Beaumont crawfish boil was one of the most enjoyable trips Darien had ever taken. In addition, it kicked off a series of other adventures. Within six weeks, he and Marisa–with Alden and Izzy tagging along–went to the first three sites on their list, the Cockrell Butterfly Center, the Museum of Fine Arts, and Brazos Bend State Park. It was hard for Darien to believe he was getting paid to escort a beautiful woman around the Houston area. He fully expected to wake up and find that he'd been dreaming.

Despite the fun, a couple of things kept the trips from being perfect. The first one was Octavio. The reluctant-to-move artist was the elephant in the room–seldom mentioned but always present. Darien had seen enough to conclude the Marisa-Octavio connection was frayed to the breaking point. Octavio had demonstrated the uncanny knack of texting Marisa at the most inopportune time during every trip, and Darien was waiting for the day she would write him off as a lost cause. Still, he knew the relationship wouldn't be over until Marisa made the call. All he could do was bide his time, which he felt would come soon.

Something else could have been better too. While Darien enjoyed Alden and Izzy's company, he'd hoped they would see fit to skip a day trip now and then. But, at the moment, it didn't seem likely. Darien realized that Marisa thought the foursome arrangement negated the idea they were dating. From the beginning, she'd made it clear she was giving Octavio a chance to get his act together. Consequently, no matter how much fun they had on an excursion, Marisa counted it a business undertaking.

He picked up his iTab and pulled up the article he'd just finished writing.

> *The Cockrell Butterfly Center is a stunning three-story glass structure surrounding a 50-foot waterfall. This simulated tropical rainforest is filled with exotic plants and is home to various kinds of butterflies, including migratory Monarchs and their tropical relatives. In addition, the center features an interactive section where children can play games and visit a live insect zoo in the adjoining Brown Hall of Entomology.*

After deciding the write-up on the butterfly center was close to perfect, Darien went to the Museum of Fine Arts packet and began his review. One aspect of the trip still lingered in his mind—Marisa's fascination with the painting of Joan of Arc. At her request, they circled back through the room where it was on display, and she stared at it for several minutes. He liked the painting, too, but was surprised at how strongly it affected Marisa. Incredibly, she resembled the woman in Jules Bastien-Lepage's famous work. Maybe she felt like she was seeing her reflection in a mirror.

That afternoon, Darien began devising a plan to ask Marisa out in some manner that skirted the dating issue. Like a scene in a novel, it would require proper foreshadowing to sound reasonable. After tossing aside several half-baked ideas, he decided on a simple approach—he would suggest a trip to Freeport, his hometown. Marisa had asked about it several times, so it shouldn't seem like a bolt out of the blue. Within seconds, the complete plan materialized. First, he would show her the chemical manufacturing complex on which the city was founded. Afterward, they would go to Surfside Beach and eat at a seafood restaurant. Then, if it wasn't too cold, they might take a walk on the beach at San Luis Pass, the location with the whitest sand within a hundred miles of Houston.

Fortunately, a touch of foreshadowing was already in place. Several months ago, one of his friends, Jack Lawson, bought a restaurant in Freeport–the Beachfront Bar & Grill. Jack and Darien had been friends since kindergarten. They both played on Brazosport High School's basketball team the year they won the state championship, and Jack had recently sent Darien a generous gift card. So it seemed like a good plan. Well . . . at least good enough to try.

He called Marisa's number.

She answered on the first ring, and her picture materialized.

Hoping the quick answer was a good omen, Darien began by telling Marisa he'd completed two more chapters on the guide and was working on the Brazos Bend State Park file.

"I haven't finished selecting pictures for the park," Marisa said.

"Actually, that's not what I'm calling about."

"Oh? What's on your mind?"

Darien told her about his long-time friend buying the seafood restaurant and laid out his non-date invitation in a few short sentences.

Marisa laughed softly. "That's a clever piece of fiction!"

"Didn't I convince you it wouldn't be a date?"

"Not really."

"Why not?"

"Because it would be."

Darien sighed. "I know, but it was the best plan I could think up. I hope you're not upset at me for trying again."

"I'm not," Marisa said, shaking her head. "But you know my situation."

"Indeed, I do. You've told me several times."

"Thanks for asking me out, but I can't accept."

"I didn't see any harm in giving it a shot."

"*No harm—no foul*, as you basketball players say."

"Think about it some more," Darien said. "The offer will remain open indefinitely."

A ringtone sounded on Marisa's iTab. "I have to take a call," she said. "Talk to you later." Her picture faded away.

Though disappointed that his plan failed, Darien admired Marisa's loyalty. Even if the current Houston-Rio situation was leading to a breakup, it was clear she wouldn't get involved with anyone else before telling Octavio. Loyalty was a notable component of her psyche. Consequently, his fictionalized ploy was a dumb plan.

Still, he wasn't about to give up.

CHAPTER 12

I n November, the monthly Citizenship Meeting coincided with election day. In order to gain HUD credit for attending, housing unit residents were required to watch the election returns for at least two hours. Darien expected most to watch much longer; he certainly would. He'd looked forward to the occasion for weeks, as had almost everyone in the housing complex. The preliminary broadcast had begun at dawn on the IMAX screen in the auditorium, and the main program, Alphabet News' *Election Night Live*, would commence at 6:00 p.m. Darien, the only bona fide night owl in the Da Rosa-Thibideaux-Segura sextet, was anticipating an all-night stand unless the election was called early, which didn't seem likely according to recent polls.

Upon entering the balcony, the friends found four seats next to the front rail and two others directly behind them. As they always did, Rachel and Justin took the rear seats. Five of the six were excited. Justin, who hadn't voted, was attending only because the broadcast counted as a Citizenship Meeting. After exchanging greetings with those around them, they sat down and looked toward the IMAX screen, which was showing a front view of the White House. Night had fallen; however, high-intensity lights gave a daylight perspective to the scene and created a shimmering rainbow around the water fountain on the front lawn.

The camera pulled back to show the wrought-iron fence surrounding the White House. Black vans with heavily-tinted windows waited at intervals inside and outside the fence, and armed guards stood at parade rest near the vans. A crowd had gathered in the street, but a yellow *Do Not Cross* ribbon prevented them from approaching the fence. The crowd was vocal but orderly. Hand-held signs supported all three presidential candidates and their running mates: Rogov-Profeto, Ford-Cline, and Parker-Willis. While wondering why anyone would gather in front of the White House on election night, Darien studied the scene carefully, noting that about half of the signs supported Reuben Rogov.

Headlines began to scroll down the screen in front of the White House scene:

CAN ROGOV WIN WITHOUT A RUNOFF?

HOUSE AND SENATE UP FOR GRABS

PEACE PARTY EXPECTS TO CAPTURE SEVERAL GOVERNORSHIPS

Abruptly, the scene switched to Alphabet News headquarters in Times Square. Before focusing on the newsroom, the cameras made a panoramic sweep of the area. The *city that never sleeps* was wide awake and lit up in anticipation of the election. LED signs above the sidewalks flashed messages urging everyone to vote. The streets were full of pedestrians, and the mood was festive. If not for the fact that it was November 5, Darien would have thought the Big Apple was preparing to drop the ball at midnight on New Year's Eve.

At 6:00 p.m., the scene switched to Alphabet's newsroom, where the popular co-anchors, Angela Morales and Richard Frazier, were seated at the center of a crescent-shaped glass desk. A few years shy of fifty, the polished couple was the de facto template for news anchors throughout the county. This evening, an additional reporter sat at each end of the desk, and every member of the smartly-dressed quartet held an iTab.

The camera zoomed in on Richard. "Good evening, America," he said. "Thank you for joining Alphabet News for this special broadcast, *Election Night Live*. Tonight, Angela and I are joined by Christian Ellis and Monique Jackson. In addition, more than 100 anchors, correspondents, reporters, political analysts, and embeds will contribute from campaign headquarters, polling centers, and battleground states throughout the nation." He paused and glanced toward his co-anchor.

"BBC, CSPAN, PBS, Telemundo, and Univision will join Alphabet News tonight," Angela said. "More than 150 million early votes have been cast, suggesting this will be a record turnout. We will post the results on the map behind us. But, before results begin to come in, let's take a look at how the map is set up."

On cue, Christian touched the iTab in front of him. Instantly, the IMAX screen displayed a map of the contiguous forty-eight states with Alaska, Hawaii, Puerto Rico, and Cuba enclosed in a rectangular box beside it. All states were shown in shades of gray rather than the red-blue combination utilized in elections dominated by two parties.

"Today, our nation will elect numerous local, state, and federal officials," Christian said, "including the highest office of all, the President of the United States. While all races are important, the presidential election has dominated the headlines for months and will likely command most of our attention tonight.

"Electoral votes are shown on the map for each state. The total for all 52 states is 638; therefore, winning the presidency will require 320 votes. Current polls indicate a slight possibility that Rogov could win outright, but neither Ford nor Parker can do so; therefore, a runoff is likely. We will post each state's results as soon as—"

Richard held up a finger to interrupt Christian. "We've received word that Georgia's presidential race has been called," he said. "The winner is Isaac Ford, the incumbent. This puts the first 18 electoral votes in his column." While Richard was speaking, Georgia changed from gray to blue on the map.

A moment later, Alphabet called Ohio for Reuben Rogov, giving him 19 votes, and the Buckeye State turned green. Soon after Ohio, Virginia flashed red, signaling that its 19 votes had gone to Terry Parker. During the next thirty minutes, Darien and his companions watched intently as the map began to turn into a tricolored jigsaw puzzle.

Except for Florida, all states on the East Coast reported their results quickly. When 250 votes were tallied, Marisa leaned toward Darien and whispered, "So far, Mr. Rogov is well below the majority needed to avoid a runoff."

"The race has a long way to go," Darien said, immediately suspecting his comment sounded lame to Marisa, who was much more knowledgeable about the U.S. election process than he was.

"By my count, he'll have to carry California, Texas, and Florida to win outright," Marisa said, tapping her iTab.

"Do you think he can?"

"Florida and California are iffy."

The early calls ended, the waiting started, and the broadcast team began to mark time with miscellaneous election information. Finally, after a short foray into the history of the electoral college, Monique said, "We've just gotten some exit poll data from states in the Eastern Time Zone." She thumbed her iTab, and two charts appeared onscreen:

Is The Candidate Qualified?	Yes	No
Rogov	75	23
Ford	45	53
Parker	45	54

Is The Candidate Trustworthy?	Yes	No
Rogov	66	33
Ford	45	43
Parker	45	44

After pausing to give time for the audience to study the charts, Monique said, "We'll have some more exit poll data shortly." She looked toward Richard and asked, "While waiting, would you tell us what you see in these numbers?"

"For one thing, we're making history," Richard said. "This is the first presidential election with three viable candidates. Moreover, either of them could become the next President if neither wins a majority and Congress determines the winner."

"I believe the numbers suggest that Reuben Rogov has grass-roots support the polls failed to detect during the campaign," Angela said.

"If that's the case, why isn't he further ahead of his opponents in electoral votes?" Richard asked.

"You know how it is," Angela said. "Some people vote strictly along party lines, even when knowing the opposing candidate is a better choice."

Angela's answer struck a chord with Darien. The Segura family had voted a straight Independent ticket for years. As far as he knew, he was the first to break the mold. Though it initially bothered him, he was now comfortable with his decision. Incredibly, Rachel had admitted that Reuben Rogov was a stronger leader than Terry Parker, although she'd voted for Parker. He wondered how such a paradox would play out if the election ended in the House of Representatives. Would they care about what the people wanted, or would they attempt to gain power by aligning with the winner? The latter seemed much more likely.

"Let's go to Tessie Roberts, our correspondent in Florida," Richard said. "What do you have for us, Tess?"

The scene switched to a svelte thirty-something blonde standing in front of a crowd of vociferous young people barely old enough to vote. Many of them carried hand-lettered signs touting their choice for President. While all three candidates were represented, Reuben Rogov was the overwhelming choice.

"Hello, New York," Tessie said, flashing a perfect smile. "I'm in front of a Student Union Building at the University of Miami. Most of these students behind me are from out of state, but they're completely vested in this election. They see it as pivotal in their lives."

"What are their concerns?" Angela asked.

"Jobs, the dysfunctional education system, debt-free college, climate change, social justice–the usual list for people their age," Tessie said. "Practically everyone I spoke with mentioned the same things, and the consensus is that Reuben Rogov has a better chance of solving these problems than the other two candidates."

"It's not likely Mr. Rogov can win the presidency without a runoff unless he carries Florida," Richard said. "That being the case, do you have anything to report from the I-4 Corridor?"

"Nothing yet," Tessie said, "but I'll remind our viewers what the I-4 Corridor is and why it's so important. I-4 refers to *Interstate 4*, which runs from Tampa to Daytona Beach, a distance of 132 miles. Nearly 45% of Florida's voters live near this highway. This corridor has been critical in past presidential elections and will likely play a big part in the current one. We expect to have something soon from this important area."

As it turned out, *something soon* did not materialize. Instead, the broadcast team focused on congressional seats, governorships, and other offices for the next hour. Darien and his companions fidgeted in their chairs as the presidential contest lapsed into slow motion.

"Let's take a break and come back," Justin said, standing. "This waiting is boring."

"It would be more interesting if you'd voted," Alden said.

Ignoring his brother's jab, Justin said, "Would anybody care to join me for a Coke?"

Izzy stood. "I'll go with you." They stepped into the aisle leading toward the back of the balcony. Other viewers joined them as they walked through the seating area.

"I should have gone," Darien said. "I could use a cup of coffee and a restroom break."

"Me too," Marisa said, "but I'd hate to miss the call on the presidential election."

Two more hours passed, during which Texas and California were called for Mr. Rogov. Finally, just past midnight, the volume increased on the IMAX speakers, and Richard said,

"We're able to call Florida for Reuben Rogov. This victory puts 32 more votes in his column."

As Marisa stared at her iTab, Darien asked, "How does it look?"

"Not so good, even with the Florida win," Marisa said in a dejected voice. "The latest numbers show Parker ahead in Montana and Wyoming. The two states have only 11 votes together, but Mr. Rogov needs to win both to avoid a runoff."

About thirty minutes later, Alphabet News called Montana for Parker.

Immediately after the call, Richard said, "Our analysts have determined that the most votes Mr. Rogov can get are 319. A few states have not been called; however, we have sufficient exit poll data from them to make our projections." He looked toward his co-anchor and added, "Angela, give us the projected vote totals."

"According to our analysts, Mr. Rogov will end up with 319 votes–exactly half," Angela said. "Mr. Parker will get 171, and the incumbent, Mr. Ford, will get 148. Therefore, this presidential election will be decided by Congress. Would you explain how this process works, Richard?"

"According to the 12th Amendment, early in January, the newly-elected Congress will meet in joint session to verify the electoral vote count," Richard said. "If neither candidate has a majority, the House will elect the President by casting one vote per state, and the Senate will elect the Vice President by casting one vote per state. In both cases, a simple majority is needed to win. Due to separate votes in the House and Senate, the President and the Vice President could be elected from different parties."

Darien leaned toward Marisa. "Did you know that?"

"Yes, and it's scary."

CHAPTER 13

S eated in her work cubicle, Marisa flipped through an album of recently-taken photos on her iTab. She was selecting the best ones for the final chapter of *Top Ten Sites in the Houston Area* but was having difficulty concentrating. For the first time in her life, the political arena was vying for her attention, and she couldn't resist checking the news headlines every few minutes, though it was interfering with her work.

While selecting a picture of the San Jacinto Monument with the full moon hanging over it, Marisa's little finger (*accidentally?*) touched the *Breaking News* icon, and a new batch of headlines began to scroll across the screen:

NEWLY-ELECTED CONGRESS TO CONVENE ON JAN. 3, 2149

WHO WILL BE THE NEXT U.S. PRESIDENT?

PEACE PARTY SCORES NUMEROUS UPSETS

RADS AND INDEPENDENTS IN CHAOS

The same headlines had been repeated ad infinitum since the election a week ago, and Marisa had read the accompanying articles published by Alphabet News. Though rebroadcast by Alphabet's affiliates, formerly referred to as the *mainstream media*, the articles invariably retained the New York flavor. Once, Marisa had shunned such reporting; now, she was reading it avidly.

She clicked on the last headline, and the full article appeared. It began with a historical account of two former political parties, Republicans and Democrats, merging to form one party, the *Republican and Democrat Society*, i.e., the RADS. The writer speculated that such a merger was about to happen between the RADS and the Independents. If so, the newly-formed party would have the exact electoral vote count as the Peace Party. Such a situation could force Reuben Rogov to make some concessions in order to get elected by Congress.

As a student of U.S. history, Marisa knew the article was unrealistic. The RADS were devout progressives, and the Independents were equally devout conservatives–two immiscible doctrines. Both parties were more likely to support Mr. Rogov than to compromise with each other. For over a hundred years, the mindset of both parties had been *win-it-all-or-lose-it-all*. She'd begun to see them as dinosaurs. And, like dinosaurs, they were on the verge of extinction if they didn't change. Of course, unlike the dinosaurs, they had a choice. The question was, would they exercise it?

On a whim, Marisa googled *ConspiraciesRevealed,* Darien's go-to website for unusual slants on the news. She wasn't a subscriber and didn't intend to become one, but she'd seen numerous ads offering free trial subscriptions. The home page appeared and urged her to subscribe first and cancel later if unsatisfied. With flying fingers, she circumvented the pay-up-front pitch and reached the periodical's current issue.

The title of the lead article appeared:

Rogov, Parker, And Ford Hold Covert Meetings

ConspiraciesRevealed has discovered that about two dozen e-mails and text messages have been exchanged between Rogov, Parker, and Ford since the election. Their content is unknown; however, we know the three men exchanged them directly rather than through their staff. We did not initially view this as unusual, but now we believe these interchanges were employed to set up secret meetings between the presidential hopefuls.

Confidential sources report that clandestine meetings are occurring regularly. When confronted with this information, spokespersons for all three men denied such meetings were taking place.

Our most experienced political analysts are trying to make sense of this information. While it should be considered speculation at this point, the consensus of opinion is that Reuben Rogov is attempting to persuade one of the other candidates to release their electoral votes so he can win the election without congressional action. If he can accomplish this remarkable feat, his running mate, Mr. Profeto, will become Vice President when Mr. Rogov assumes the office of President. Otherwise, the nation's top two officers could come from different parties.

Marisa reread the article and leaned back in her chair, trying to reconcile the differences between Alphabet's viewpoint and the conspiracy publication. They were miles apart in their opinions, and one was wrong–possibly both.

With considerable effort, she pushed the political intrigue to the recesses of her mind and returned to the San Jacinto Monument chapter. Within a few minutes, she'd selected pictures of the reflecting pool, the Battleship Texas, and the picnic grounds where she and Darien had eaten lunch with Izzy and Alden. The project had been great fun, and she was sorry to see it end.

***

On Saturday morning, Marisa went to The Log Cabin. Exchanging greetings with friends as she passed by, she picked her way through the tables. The coffee shop had become a weekend office for her and Darien while working on the day trip project. Initially, they'd had trouble finding a good time to get together. He liked to work late at night, and she didn't. So, as a compromise, they agreed to meet on Saturday morning at nine o'clock, early enough that Darien was occasionally a few minutes late.

Contemplating the taste of hazelnut coffee accompanied by an apple fritter, Marisa took her place in a short line. Before she reached the counter, Darien entered the shop. She waved, and he joined her as she reached the head of the line. They exchanged small talk with the barista, Pablo Cruz, a friend who'd been one of Marisa's first Peace Party recruits. Pablo wore his political intensity on his sleeve along with his armband, a trait she was discovering within herself. Both fit the newly-coined term for an avid Rogov supporter—*Rogovite*.

Marisa placed her order while Darien studied the menu. A moment later, he ordered an apple Danish and a latte with a splash of vanilla. Both held out their iTabs, and Juan scanned the Log Cabin App on each. The apps blinked green, indicating acceptance of the payments, and they moved to the end of the bar to wait for their orders.

"Our office is vacant," Darien said, pointing toward a small alcove with a single booth. With pastries and coffee in hand, they crossed the room and sat down on the same side of the table.

"What did you think of the pictures I sent you?" Marisa said.

"They were perfect. I loved the shot of the full moon over the monument."

Marisa tapped her iTab and pulled up a picture of the picnic tables in the park. "What about this one?"

"I rewrote the description of that park several times."

Suppressing a chuckle, Marisa said, "Did you mention the swarm of giant mosquitos?"

They both laughed, and Darien said, "No, but I suggested it would be wise to bring a supply of insect repellant."

"Those were the biggest mosquitoes I ever saw."

"Of course they were. This is Texas."

An hour later, they finished the final chapter.

"When I upload this last chapter to Mom, the project will be complete," Marisa said wistfully. In the months they'd worked together, she'd grown used to having Darien as a writing partner, day trip companion, and friend. Though the activities they'd participated in could hardly be construed as dating, Octavio would be upset if he knew. Still, she felt pangs of regret that the project was over.

As if thinking along the same line, Darien caught Marisa by the hand. She turned to face him, and they gazed into each other's eyes. A few seconds later, she squeezed his hand and pulled away. They continued to look at one another in silence until a shrill ringtone sounded on their iTabs, breaking the spell.

"That was a bad time for a *Public Information Mandate,*" Darien said.

Simultaneously, they looked at their iTab screens, which held a brief message:

Update from HUD—The next monthly Citizenship Meeting is scheduled for December 5, 2148, at 7:00 p.m. CST. The program will feature President Isaac Ford speaking from the Oval Office. In addition to HUD-sponsored housing-unit participation, the broadcast will be transmitted to all smartphones, tablets, TVs, radios, and other devices capable of receiving radio wave transmissions.

With eyebrows raised, Marisa said, "What do you think Mr. Ford intends to speak about?"

"No doubt it will be something concerning the election."

After a round of political speculation, they left the Log Cabin.

The following week, the Brazilian Consulate published *Top Ten Sites in the Houston Area* on Amazon, offering the e-book free for a limited time. To Marisa's surprise, over 2500 copies were downloaded in three days, and twenty reviews posted with an average rating of 4.7 stars. She'd been relatively non-productive since her last meeting with Darien, not because the project was complete, but due to her growing concern about the outcome of the election. As she saw it, it would be nothing less than a political coup if anyone other than Reuben Rogov became President.

***

When the fifth of December arrived, Marisa and her companions went to the auditorium early and found seats on the balcony—four in front and two directly behind them, their standard seating arrangement. The IMAX screen showed an image of the White House with a bold-lettered news banner in front of it.

PRESIDENT FORD TO ADDRESS THE NATION
IN 10 MINUTES & 30 SECONDS

The banner scrolled by repeatedly, counting off the seconds with each journey across the screen. When the clock reached zero, a computerized voice said, "Attention, please. Stand by for a message from President Isaac Ford. Attention, please stand by."

The scene changed to the Oval Office. The President, wearing a blue suit and red tie, sat at a mahogany desk with the American flag and George Washington's picture hanging on the wall behind him. As the camera zoomed in, he glanced briefly at an iTab before looking into the camera.

"Good evening, my fellow Americans," Ford said. "Thank you for tuning in. I called this news conference to inform you of an important agreement between the three major political parties involved in the recent election."

A murmur rippled through the auditorium but stopped immediately when the President continued, "Let me repeat. The major parties have reached an unprecedented agreement, one nobody would have thought possible. During the past few weeks, Mr. Parker, Mr. Rogov, and I have met several times to discuss the future of our country. All three of us have America's best interests at heart, and we have reached a decision that we believe will help reunite our divided nation.

"Before disclosing our agreement, let's review the vote count of the recent election. As you recall, Mr. Rogov won

319 electoral votes, while Mr. Parker and I won 319 combined. These votes will be official once the Electors vote in December, but the meeting has yet to be scheduled due to the unusual nature of this election. Nevertheless, nonaligned election auditors have pored over the data thoroughly and concluded that an Electors' Meeting would result in a tie, thus passing the decision to Congress, as per the 12th Amendment.

"In addition, these same auditors have studied the makeup of the new Congress scheduled to be seated in January. Based on the number of House and Senate seats the Peace Party won, they have concluded that Mr. Rogov would win the presidency on the first ballot."

A roar rumbled throughout the auditorium for several minutes. When it subsided, Ford continued solemnly, "Over the last month, much to our surprise, Mr. Parker and I have received millions of e-mails and text messages requesting that we concede the election to Mr. Rogov. While this is an unusual request, we have decided to do so rather than carrying out a charade with a foregone conclusion."

Ford's last statement stunned the audience to silence. As they waited in expectation of his closing remarks, a door swung open, and Reuben Rogov stepped into the Oval Office. Everyone cheered wildly as he strode toward President Ford. With the thunderous applause resonating in the background, the two men shook hands.

When the din ran its course, Ford said, "Welcome to the White House, Mr. Rogov."

"Thank you, Mr. President," Rogov said. "You have made a great contribution to the cause of peace. Your patriotism will be long remembered, as will that of Mr. Parker."

After briefly expressing his thanks to the high-ranking RADS and Independents who orchestrated Ford and Parker's concessions, Rogov reiterated his intentions to bring peace through equality and then deferred to Ford.

When everyone realized nothing more was forthcoming from the President-elect, shouts of "Long live Reuben Rogov" reverberated through the auditorium.

With no hesitation, Marisa joined the chant.

CHAPTER 14

When the Citizenship Meeting ended, Izzy and Alden dashed to the rec room to play pool while everyone else went their separate ways. After visiting briefly with her mother and grandmother, Marisa went to her bedroom. She sat down on the edge of her bed to wait for a FaceTime call from Octavio, who'd texted early in the afternoon, saying he needed to discuss something face-to-face. She already knew what it would be–another passport setback. Delays due to government red tape had become his main talking point lately, practically his only one.

Six months had passed since Octavio first told her he would have his passport in three months. The time frame was easy to remember because his text put a damper on the crawfish boil in early June. About ninety days later, during a visit to the Johnson Space Center, Octavio sent another ill-timed text, essentially replaying the *three-month-delay* scenario. As far as Marisa was concerned, the second delay was strike two, and the next one would be strike three.

After considerable soul-searching, she realized it would be better if Octavio stayed in Rio. If he came to the U.S., there would be an Octavio-Darien conflict to resolve. Clearly, Darien was a better man, and she had developed strong feelings for him. Despite the ever-strengthening pull of politics on her life, she was seeing him in her future. Consequently, it was time to bid Octavio goodbye, though it would be difficult after so many years.

A few minutes later, her iTab chimed, and Octavio's avatar popped up. Marisa touched it, and a picture of Octavio appeared.

"Hello, Ipanema girl," he said flippantly.

Without waiting to hear more, Marisa said, "Please let me talk first."

Octavio's happy-go-lucky expression changed. "You must have something important to say."

"I do," Marisa said, her mouth so dry she could barely speak. "It's about our relationship."

"What about it?"

"I'm calling it quits—ending it forever as of today."

"Why would you do that?" Octavio asked, seemingly not grasping the finality of Marisa's words.

"It's not working," Marisa said. "Moreover, this long-distance relationship made me realize it never did work very well."

"It won't be long distance much longer. I'm nearly ready to come to Houston?"

"*Nearly ready*? What does that mean?"

"They said another month or two—maybe by the end of January."

"Octavio, it's over," Marisa said firmly. "I'm not going to wait for you any longer."

"I'm trying to get to the U.S. only because you're there."

"If that's the only reason, stop trying now."

"What are you saying?"

"Don't come on my account."

"I thought we had a mutual understanding."

"Maybe we did, but I'm ending it now."

"So . . . you're saying goodbye?"

"Yes, I am."

"What if I get my passport within the next few days?"

"If that happens, come to the U.S. if you still want to," Marisa said. "But, as I said, don't do it on my account."

After a brief pause, Octavio shrugged and said, "In that case, I'll probably stay here a while longer."

With a lump in her throat, Marisa said, "Goodbye, Octavio. *Deus esteja com você.*"

"I wish you the same. Goodbye," Octavio said, showing no signs of remorse.

As the call ended, a tear trickled down Marisa's cheek, not because she was sad the relationship had ended, but because she realized that Octavio had never loved her as much as he loved himself. She'd been in a no-win situation for years without being aware of it. Now that it was over, she wondered how she could have been so naïve. The long-distance relationship had been a disaster. Hopefully, she'd learned enough not to let such a thing happen to her again.

A few minutes later, Izzy came into the bedroom. In one sentence, Marisa told her about breaking up with Octavio.

Izzy sat down on the bed beside Marisa and put her arm around her. "Good for you," she said. "He was pretty much of a jerk."

"Even so, we had some good times together," Marisa said, not seeing any value in launching into a diatribe against her former boyfriend, especially since he was already receding in the rear-view mirror of her mind.

Izzy caught Marisa by the hand. "What are you going to do now?"

"About what?"

"About Darien."

"Don't rush me. It's only been five minutes since I broke up with Octavio."

"Then you've already wasted five minutes," Izzy said.

"I'll tell Darien about it tomorrow."

Izzy picked up Marisa's iTab and extended it toward her. "Text him immediately and accept his invitation to go to Freeport."

"It's too late to text anyone."

"Darien won't go to bed for three more hours."

Marisa pondered the situation as her revved-up sister waited in anticipation.

"Do it!" Izzy insisted.

After a moment of deep thought, Marisa accepted the iTab and texted: *Darien, is the invitation to Freeport still open?*

Ten seconds later, his answer appeared onscreen: *Absolutely! How about leaving the GW Saturday at 10:00?*

After Marisa confirmed Darien's suggested day and time, Izzy shouted, "Yes!" and hugged her so vigorously they fell backward on the bed while laughing giddily.

"Thanks, Cupid," Marisa said as they sat up. "One of your arrows found its mark."

"I always knew you and Darien were meant for each other," Izzy said. "It was obvious the first time we saw him in the auditorium, even though you ran away."

"As usual, you're over-analyzing the situation, Little Sister."

After speculating about the future for a few minutes, they went to bed.

An hour later, Marisa lay with her eyes closed but unable to fall asleep. Though her body was tired, her mind was restless.

Two separate issues were vying for her attention, Darien and the political arena. Recently, both had become critically important to her, and she wondered how she could fit them together. Fortunately, they would have an opportunity to discuss the subject during the upcoming visit to Freeport. If a relationship with Darien was meant to be, as Izzy proclaimed, the trip should get them off to a good start.

Tossing and turning, Marisa replayed President Ford's concession speech in her mind. Though a surprise to most voters, it was the right thing to do. Clearly, Reuben Rogov was the man for the job. Moreover, he'd made her feel special by squeezing her hand at the first Peace Party meeting. She didn't understand it, but her feelings for Mr. Rogov seemed like filial affection, and she was glad her first vote as an American citizen had been cast for him.

Across the room, Izzy snored softly. The sisters had chatted while getting ready for bed, and Izzy had fallen asleep the instant her head hit the pillow. Unable to do likewise, Marisa wrestled with her thoughts until, at long last, sleep began to overtake her. While slipping into unconsciousness, Marisa sensed movement and realized she was being whisked away–whether in mind or body, she couldn't tell.

When the sensation of movement ended, Marisa found herself standing on a street corner. Anxiously, she looked around. A few feet away, street signs identified the location as *1st St. NW* and *Peace Circle.* The traffic circle surrounded a white marble statue several stories high. Bordered by a garden ablaze with delicately-scented red roses, the figure glistened in the mid-morning sunlight. Though Marisa had never been to the location, it seemed familiar. She looked around for a definitive landmark and saw a domed building with numerous columns. Immediately, she recognized it as the U.S. Capitol Building and realized she was in Washington, D.C.

In wonderment, Marisa looked around and saw a historical marker next to the street sign. The marker held a brass plaque with the words, *Peace Monument*, in bold letters. Marisa sensed movement behind her and turned to see a small group of multi-ethnic people looking at the statue. The moment was surreal. She knew something of cosmic significance was unfolding but had no idea what it could be, though it involved her. Simultaneously, everyone looked toward Marisa, waiting for her to make a move. Turning back to the plaque, she saw a small button beneath the text and pushed it. A smooth computer voice began to speak.

"Good morning. Welcome to the U.S. Capitol. The Peace Monument before you is surrounded by a roundabout called the Peace Circle. This monument was originally known as the Civil War Sailor's Monument, but that name was changed due to the significance of peace to every citizen, military and civilian alike. This statue tells its story primarily through three classically robed female figures named Grief, History, and Peace. These figures interact in the following manner:

"On top of the monument, Grief holds her face against the shoulder of History and weeps in mourning. History holds a stylus and a tablet inscribed with the words. 'They died so that their country might live.' Beneath Grief and History, the other life-sized female figure, Victory, holds high a laurel wreath and an oak branch, which signify victory and strength. Below Victory, the god of war, Mars, and the god of the sea, Neptune, are depicted as infants.

"Peace faces the Capitol Building. At her feet, the symbols of peace and industry are displayed. Unfortunately, the dove,

signifying peace, is missing from the sculpture. It once nested upon a sheaf of wheat, along with a cornucopia and a sickle resting across a sword. Many have noted that the dove of peace, missing from this statue, is also missing in the real world. This, of course, raises the question: who can bring peace to the world? Ponder that question as you tour the capitol grounds and other sites of interest in and around the District of Columbia.

"Thank you for your attention. Enjoy your day."

When the recording ended, Marisa turned to discover all eyes fixed on her. For some unfathomable reason, she had become the leader of the small group. Trying to figure out what to do next, Marisa looked to her right and saw another street intersecting Peace Circle. Reflexively, she walked to the intersection. Without looking back, by the sound of footsteps on the pavement, she realized everyone was following her.

Multiple questions materialized in her mind, but no answers.

A moment later, she saw a street sign identifying the intersection as *1ˢᵗ St. NW* and *Pennsylvania Avenue.* Marisa knew the avenue led to the White House at 1600 Pennsylvania. Since she was standing on 1ˢᵗ Street, the White House would be sixteen blocks away. At that moment, she felt a strong urge to walk toward it and started along the sidewalk at a fast pace. Everyone fell in behind her like sheep following a shepherd.

A few minutes later, Marisa reached John Marshall Park and saw a sculpture, *The Chess Players,* which she recognized from her citizenship classes. About two dozen people were waiting on the sidewalk near the sculpture. Marisa approached, and they turned toward her. Then, without a word being spoken, they joined her entourage as she'd expected them to do.

As the march toward the White House continued, additional members joined at every street intersection, landmark, historical marker, and food court along Pennsylvania Avenue. Twenty minutes after leaving Peace Circle, the marchers numbered well over a hundred. Upon passing 13th Street, Marisa spotted a plaza crowded with ethnically-diverse people. Instinctively, she knew the people in the plaza were waiting for her.

A sign at the corner of the street read *Equality Plaza.*

When she saw the sign, Marisa realized The White House was not her destination—this plaza was. She had led a march from the Peace Statue to Equality Plaza, where a crowd awaited her arrival. Remarkably, the march linked *peace* and *equality*, the connection emphasized so strongly by Reuben Rogov in his acceptance speech. The symbolism was vivid and unmistakable. At that point, she understood why she'd been transported to the U.S. Capitol.

While Marisa stood at the corner of 13th Street and Pennsylvania Avenue, her trailing entourage split into two columns and walked on each side of her to join the crowd waiting in the plaza. Those who'd marched with her found a place to stand, and everyone turned simultaneously to face her. She knew this was a *now-or-never* moment, her time to make a definitive move. Moreover, Marisa understood why she was here. She had been called to deliver a message.

Doubting that anyone could hear her voice above the background noise, Marisa devised a simple pantomime to proclaim the message. Hastily, she took off her armband and waved it in the air. Then, she put it back on her left arm and patted it several times. As she waited with high expectations, many people produced folded armbands from pockets and handbags. Her sign language was working well. Within three minutes, virtually everyone in the crowd wore the logo of the Peace Party. All they needed was someone to lead them.

Feeling a surge of excitement, she clenched her right hand and raised it into the air.

Everyone in Equality Plaza mirrored her gesture.

"Peace through equality," Marisa shouted.

"Peace through equality," the crowd echoed in unison.

Marisa repeated the slogan a second time, as did her followers.

She repeated the slogan a third time, only to discover that her voice had changed drastically. Suddenly, it was weak and squeaky—hardly audible. This time, no one responded. Instead, they stood like zombies, motionless, with eyes vacant and unfocused. Reality was shifting before Marisa's eyes. Horrified, she watched as the people began to disappear. One by one, they faded out of existence like Cheshire cats. She stared at the empty plaza in stunned silence, trying to understand what was happening.

Her analysis was interrupted by a high-pitched voice. "Marisa, wake up. You're dreaming."

The voice was Izzy's. Marisa realized that her Washington, D.C. adventure had ended abruptly, and she was in bed. Maybe *back in her bed* was a better term, for she didn't consider the incident to be merely a dream. The out-of-body experience was too real to fit such a mundane description. She'd had thousands of dreams in her life, but nothing that compared to this.

"Wake up," Izzy repeated sharply.

Marisa opened her eyes slowly and looked around. Izzy was sitting on the edge of her bed, watching her intently. Marisa threw back the covers and swung her feet to the floor. As she sat up, the room spun momentarily. When it stopped, she regained her balance but felt groggy and somewhat disoriented.

"You were talking in your sleep," Izzy said.

Marisa rubbed her eyes. "What did I say?"

"Nothing I could understand, but you were barking commands like a Marine drill sergeant.

"I think I had a vision."

"A vision? Are you kidding?"

"No, I'm not."

"Tell me about it."

"I found myself standing in front of the Peace Statue near the U.S. Capitol Building."

"Maybe you were hallucinating," Izzy said. "We had a pretty heavy dinner."

"I truly believe it was a vision or some other kind of paranormal experience," Marisa said solemnly. "I led a march."

"Really? Where did you lead it?"

"From the Peace Statue to Equality Plaza."

Izzy raised her eyebrows. "I don't recall any place called Equality Plaza in Washington."

"It's that park across from the White House."

"If you're talking about the place where demonstrators gather," Izzy said, "it's called *Freedom Plaza*."

After pondering for a moment, Marisa realized that Izzy was right. "Well, it was Equality Plaza in my vision," she said, "and I have an idea Mr. Rogov will rename it after his inauguration."

"Your dream—uh, *vision*—must have been very convincing."

"It was a religious experience, a *calling*."

"What are you being called to do?"

"Move to Washington and work full time for the Peace Party."

"OMG!"

CHAPTER 15

Seated at his desk in pajamas, Darien looked over his shoulder and gave a voice command to the coffee maker. The machine responded with a soothing gurgle and, a minute later, announced, "Your coffee is ready." He picked up his iTab and went to the kitchen. Feeling somewhat at loose ends, he poured himself a large cup and sat down at the dinette table.

He sipped the strong black coffee while mulling over the previous day. Two events stood out–President Ford's concession and Marisa's late-night text message. The first would affect everybody in the country, the second only a handful.

Ford's concession seemed to indicate that many Americans who didn't vote for Reuben Rogov switched their loyalty to him shortly after the election, something unheard of in U.S. politics. Darien couldn't imagine how many e-mails, text messages, and phone calls it had taken to convince President Ford to support Mr. Rogov. As incredible as it was, all three major political parties now backed the new President-elect. In January, he would move into the White House with a strong mandate from voters and enough congressional backing to move forward as he saw fit.

By winning the U.S. Presidency while holding the Secretary General of the United Nations position, Mr. Rogov had become the most powerful man in the world by a wide margin. Undoubtedly, his near-absolute power would bring comfort to some people and stark terror to others. Darien, ever cautious, was not fully aligned with either camp, but he anticipated the next few months would tell which viewpoint was correct, if either.

And then, there was Marisa's text message—an incredible surprise. Darien couldn't help but give it more significance than the political situation. The striking Brazilian had caught his eye the first time he saw her. Moreover, it was obvious she was interested in him, though she dodged him initially and postponed the inevitable while waiting for Octavio. Her loyalty was admirable. She'd stuck by her indifferent boyfriend for ten months while he dilly-dallied in Rio. Though Marisa didn't mention any details of the breakup in her text, Darien anticipated hearing about it during the Freeport trip.

While contemplating his next move, his iTab pinged, and the words, *Incoming Message,* materialized onscreen. An icon popped up below the text—a hefty book with the words *Little Horn Literary Agency* emblazoned in gold across the front cover. This agency had rejected him only a few weeks ago, and he wasn't anticipating any further contact. Hoping the agency had had a change of heart, he touched the book icon, and it opened to reveal the message:

Dear Mr. Segura:

Recently, several imprints specializing in science fiction have contacted us in a search for original ideas, including those from new authors. Consequently, we have revised our policy regarding unpublished authors. After reconsidering your sci-fi novel, "The Photosynthesis Gene," I'm pleased to inform you that Little Horn will accept you as a client and will make every effort to market your work to one of the publishing houses in New York. Please review the attached contract or have your attorney do so. If it is acceptable, sign it digitally and return it immediately.

Regards, Immanuel Horn

Minutes later, Darien had a signed contract on his desktop. To his delight, the agent who would represent him was Immanuel Horn, the founder and principal shareholder of the well-known New York firm. Darien was surprised that Horn would take on an unknown sci-fi novelist. Most of his clients were chick lit authors, several of whom appeared frequently on the NYT best-selling list. If Horn couldn't sell his novel to one of New York's Big Five publishers, nobody could.

As he visualized *The Photosynthesis Gene* moving up the charts, his iTab pinged again. To his surprise, it displayed a picture of the Brazilian flag with *Marisa* written on it. He touched the icon, and Marisa's live image appeared onscreen.

"Good morning, Marisa," he said. Since he was still in rumpled pajamas and hadn't shaved or combed his hair, he was careful not to drag his little finger across the FaceTime App.

"Hi, Darien. Are you busy?"

"Certainly not too busy to talk to you," Darien said, detecting tension in Marisa's voice. He hoped she wasn't calling to cancel the Freeport trip. What a disaster that would be after he'd marked time for so long.

"I want to tell you about something that happened last night after we got home from the Citizenship Meeting."

Attempting to lighten the mood, Darien said, "I know one thing that happened–you agreed to go to Freeport with me tomorrow."

"Yes, I did," Marisa said, smiling. "And, after that, something else happened–something so bizarre I wanted to let you know as soon as you got up this morning."

"Would you like to meet somewhere?"

"I can't," Marisa said. "I'm at work, so I need to tell you over the phone."

"Okay, what's on your mind?"

Marisa described the dream-vision incident, repeatedly referring to it as a *calling*. In a state of shock, Darien listened without comment. After finishing the story, she added, "This morning as soon as I got to work, I requested a leave of absence from the consulate so I can move to Washington."

"No way!" Darien burst out, his voice rising and his heart sinking. "Tell me you're kidding,"

"I'm not," Marisa said calmly. "Moreover, the Consul General pulled some strings, and NatGov processed the request immediately. It was approved a few minutes ago. I'll be leaving early next week–Monday, if I can make all the arrangements in time."

"That soon?" Darien asked, stunned at the sudden turn of events. He'd never heard of NatGov moving so expeditiously. But, then, Homero Profeto, the Consul General, was one of the Vice President elect's first cousins. He'd probably extracted a favor from one of his high-level connections.

"This happened so fast I'm in shock myself," Marisa said. "It's not like me to make such a quick decision."

"What are you going to do in Washington?"

"I'll work with a newly-formed group called the Equality Team."

"You're sure about this calling?"

"Yes, I'm convinced this is the right move."

"How long do you plan to stay?" Darien asked, seeing a fervor in Marisa tantamount to religious conviction. When she said she'd been called, she meant it.

"At the moment, I don't know," Marisa said. "But it could be for the duration of Mr. Rogov's term in office, however long that may be."

"What does your family think of your sudden decision to move away?"

"Mom is okay with it," Marisa said, "but Zina–my grand-mother–insists I'm making a terrible mistake. Politics and politicians turn her off, and she's begging me to change my mind."

"What about Izzy?"

"I tried to get her to join the team, but she has an internship lined up here in Houston next semester, so there's no way she'd leave now. She's almost as strongly attached to this city as you are."

"I'm sorry you're leaving," Darien said, wondering if he and Marisa could make a long-distance relationship work. She might be reluctant to try again so soon after the drawn-out Octavio fiasco. And the concept hadn't worked very well for him and Lorelei either. Nevertheless, he was eager to try and hope for the best.

"We have a lot to discuss," Marisa said, "but I need to get back to work now."

"We'll have plenty of time to talk during our trip to Freeport."

"If the weather permits us to go," Marisa said. "Unfortunately, the forecasters are predicting snow and freezing rain tomorrow, so we may have to stay closer to home."

Darien took a deep breath. "Marisa," he said firmly, "after nearly a year of knowing each other, this will be our first real date. I've looked forward to it since the day we met, so we're going somewhere together tomorrow–just the two of us. If the weather keeps us from going any further than across the street to the Cherry Tree, that's where we'll go. Okay?"

"That sounds good to me. I'll see you in the morning."

CHAPTER 16

On Saturday morning, Darien awoke at 8:00 a.m., rather early for him. He'd had a restless night filled with weird dreams, most of which faded away when he opened his eyes. One dream, however, was unforgettable. It was about a snowstorm turning the Mediplex into a winter wonderland. After replaying it in his mind, he realized that last night's weather forecast had triggered it. The hyped-up meteorologists had predicted two inches of snow and made it sound like another ice age was imminent. Wondering what he would see, Darien swung his feet to the floor and went to his mini-balcony.

Hastily, he drew back the curtains and discovered the forecast was correct. The housing units and streets around them looked like a scene from *White Christmas*. He slid the door open and stepped outside. The air was frigid, 30º F according to the news screen atop the building next door. In the absence of a breeze, giant snowflakes floated down like dandelion puffs. He heard shouting and looked down to see a group of teenagers in a snowball fight, a rare sight in Houston.

The snowstorm would force him and Marisa to change their plans. Fortunately, they'd agreed not to let the weather prevent them from spending the day together. Since Freeport was out of the question, it was time to go to Plan B, the Cherry Tree.

He looked across the street. Not a single restaurant in the food court was open. Realizing the weather had destroyed both the primary and backup plans, Darien went into creative writer mode and pondered the situation. In fiction, the protagonist usually asked a friend to lend a helping hand, an approach worth trying in the current situation.

He went back inside, retrieved his iTab from the dinette table, and touched Alden's crawfish avatar. On the third ring, he answered, "Hey, Darien. What are you doing up so early?"

Darien told him about his date with Marisa and how they'd designated the Cherry Tree as their foul-weather backup plan. After telling the story in one breath, he asked, "Are you going to open the restaurant today?"

"Not officially," Alden said, "but I'm planning something unofficial."

"And what might that be?" Darien asked, suspecting he already knew.

"I have the owner's permission to take a few friends there for a private party," Alden said. "I'm thinking of you and Marisa, Izzy and me—just the four of us. What do you think of that plan?"

"I don't like it."

"Why not?"

"I've wanted to be alone with Marisa for a long time," Darien said, "and she's leaving next week. Could you let the two of us go by ourselves?"

Alden mumbled something inaudible under his breath.

"Will you do it?" Darien said insistently.

"You're asking a lot."

"I'm not asking—I'm begging."

With a sigh, Alden relented. "Okay, you can do it, but you'll owe me from now on."

"How do we get into the restaurant?"

"The lock recognizes my thumbprint or a keyboard password, *52-Mab-St*," Alden said. "The password has a couple of dashes, so I'll text it to you."

When the conversation ended, Darien called Marisa and told her about the arrangement he'd worked out with Alden. He sensed her excitement, and they agreed to meet at the Da Rosa condo at 10:30. He asked her to tell Izzy that she and Alden weren't invited to go with them. Hopefully, she would understand.

An hour later, he rang the Da Rosa's doorbell, and Marisa opened the door. To Darien's surprise, she looked like she'd stepped off a snowy slope in Colorado. She was wearing green ski pants with a matching parka and holding a pair of mittens in one hand. Marisa's family had followed her to the door. Her mother and grandmother stood directly behind her, with Izzy a step further back. All four women greeted Darien warmly. Izzy winked and gave a thumbs-up.

"Are you ready to go?" Darien asked.

Marisa smiled radiantly and said, "Absolutely." She kissed her grandmother on the cheek and stepped into the hallway.

Darien took Marisa by the arm, and they walked away. He didn't hear the door close, so he knew Izzy was still watching them–probably the other two women as well. Obviously, Marisa's family was pleased with the budding relationship. The family's blessings meant a lot to Darien, especially since the path he and Marisa were about to take wasn't along the Yellow Brick Road. Instead, if they ever got to Emerald City, it would be after a detour through Washington, D.C.

"Have fun," Izzy called as they turned the corner and headed toward the elevator.

A moment later, after donning their mittens, they stepped onto the snow-covered sidewalk in front of the housing unit. The traffic lights were out of service, and a lively crowd was gathering in the intersection. Winter attire covered the gamut from faded jeans to brightly colored ski outfits. Teenagers had already built several snowmen and were working on others. Rosy-cheeked preteens ran amok, yelling shrilly, and a woman pulled a toddler on a red sled with a spotted puppy trailing behind it.

"I'll bet you haven't seen anything like this before," Darien said.

"Actually, I have," Marisa said. "It snows in the southern part of Brazil."

They picked their way through the revelers and hurried to the Cherry Tree. Darien took off a mitten and entered the combination to the lock. He grasped the icy handle and pulled. The door didn't budge.

"I'm freezing," Marisa said, shivering and laughing simultaneously.

On Darien's second attempt, the door swung open, and they hurried inside. After locking the door, he turned toward Marisa, and they gazed into each other's eyes. Time stood still as they stared at one another.

Darien stepped toward Marisa and put his arms around her. With no hesitation, she leaned into him and returned his embrace. As she clung to Darien, he knew that she'd anticipated this moment as much as he had. He relaxed his arms enough to find her lips, and they shared their first kiss while standing inside the front door of the Cherry tree.

Abruptly, Marisa pulled back and started laughing.

"What's so funny?" Darien asked.

Marisa held up both hands to show him her mittens.

"I'm still wearing mine too," he said, and they laughed giddily.

"We're losing it."

"I lost it the first time I saw you," Darien said. They took off their mittens and parkas and hung them in a small closet with their iTabs. He took Marisa by the hand, and they started toward the kitchen.

"I have a surprise for you," Marisa said with a mysterious gleam in her eye.

"You've been full of surprises lately. What is it this time?"

"I'm going to cook lunch for you."

"What made you think of doing that?"

"Alden suggested it," Marisa said. "He called me shortly after you and I talked this morning."

"Are you a gourmet cook like your grandmother?"

"Zina taught me to cook, but I'm not nearly as good at it as she is," Marisa said. "So I decided on something simple, spaghetti and meat sauce—and a caprese salad, of course."

"That's one of my favorite meals."

"I know. Alden told me."

The small kitchen was arranged efficiently with refrigerators, a pantry, and cabinets along the wall opposite the stovetop and ovens. On many occasions, Darien had seen the Cherry Tree staff serve a house full of guests with no lost motion and minimal waiting time. But today, speed and efficiency were not the objectives. Instead, spending time with Marisa was all that mattered. Regardless of how delicious it might be, the meal was a corollary benefit.

As Marisa went to the pantry, Darien asked, "Can I help you find something?"

"No, thanks. Alden told me where everything is stored."

While Marisa was rummaging around, Darien went to a wine cooler and took out a bottle of champagne. After searching for champagne glasses unsuccessfully, he placed two small wine glasses on the counter beside the sink. He was still struggling with the cork when Marisa came out of the pantry carrying an armload of supplies. She walked up behind him as the cork popped.

"Hey," she said, her eyes widening. "What are you doing?"

He turned around. "Uh . . . I'm getting ready to propose a toast."

She placed everything on the counter and said, "Isn't it a little too early?"

Darien caught both of Marisa's hands and pulled her to him. She put her arms around him and lay her head on his shoulder. As if on cue, music began to play softly in the background.

Marisa leaned back. "What's going on?"

"That's Alden's Louisiana Collection," Darien said. "He must have programmed it to start at eleven o'clock."

The words of a song began, *I feel so bad I got a worried mind. I'm so lonesome all the time.*

"Do you know that song?" Marisa asked.

"It's called *Blue Bayou*. It's ancient but incredibly good."

Marisa caught Darien by the hand and said, "Let's dance."

He moved closer to her and put an arm around her waist. She placed a hand on his shoulder, and they began to spin slowly throughout their impromptu dance floor. As they danced to the rhythmic beat of the music, Marisa closed her eyes and lay her head against Darien's chest. At that instant, he knew there would never be anyone but her, regardless of the unusual circumstances they were facing.

When the song ended, Marisa raised her head and looked into Darien's eyes. Not wanting the moment to end, he pulled her closer, and they kissed as the next song, *Johnny Be Good*, began to play.

Marisa gazed at Darien inquisitively.

"That song's too fast for me," he said, turning to pick up the champagne bottle.

In a quick move, Marisa put a hand over the wine glasses. "We need to talk."

"We can talk while sipping champagne."

"Let's sip coffee instead."

"Don't you like champagne?"

"I do, but we have some difficult issues facing us," Marisa said. "I think we'd be better off discussing them under the influence of caffeine rather than under the influence of alcohol."

"Point well taken," Darien said, putting the cork back in the bottle.

Five minutes later, with coffee in hand, they selected a booth near the kitchen. Marisa sat down and slid over to make room for Darien. For a moment, they sipped their coffee without speaking. Music played softly in the background while Darien searched for a way to start the conversation about the long-distance relationship they were facing. Marisa's hesitance suggested that she was thinking about the same thing.

After looking at each other intently for a few seconds, Darien said the only thing that made sense, "I love you, Marisa."

"I love you too, but we're in a difficult situation."

Before Darien could reply, an emotional duet began to sing.

Marisa's eyes widened. "Did you hear those words?"

"I wasn't listening," Darien said, leaning toward her. "I was looking at you."

She pushed his shoulder. "Stop the music. Let's listen to that song from the beginning."

Darien slid off the bench and went to the electronics control panel near the pantry. "I've seen Alden do this a hundred times, so I should be able to do it," he said as he studied the touch-screen monitor. A moment later, he touched an icon, and the music stopped. When he looked around, Marisa was standing at his side.

Slipping an arm around his waist, she said, "Can you put the song's words on the TV screens?"

"We've had sing-alongs here, so it can be done if I can figure out how," Darien said. He touched a series of icons, and words appeared onscreen, but the music didn't restart.

As he was about to try again, Marisa said sharply, "Don't touch anything. Let's just read the words."

When he looked at the screen, Darien understood why Marisa was so excited. The verse read:

> *We've got to stop and think it over*
> *before we say we're in love.*
> *Are we right for each other?*
> *Can what we feel be lasting love?*

"Do you think this verse outlines our talking points?" Darien asked.

"It certainly does. Let's discuss it while we finish our coffee."

Once back in the booth, Darien said, "We can skip the first two lines. We've already said we're in love."

Marisa leaned toward Darien and kissed him lightly on the cheek. "Yes, we have, but what about the next line, *Are we right for each other?* Let's talk about that."

For the next few minutes, they discussed the dilemma facing them—Marisa was heading to Washington as a budding politician while Darien was staying in Houston as a science fiction author. The dialogue was lively yet amicable. Despite much talk about their future together, neither would consider giving up their vocation/avocation or the location where they intended to perform it. Though such an approach indicated they were putting their professions above their relationship, both denied it vehemently. And, regardless of contradictory evidence, they concluded they were right for each other.

"Have we settled everything?" Darien asked, knowing they hadn't come close.

"Not exactly. We'll work out the details as we go along."

Darien got up and caught Marisa by the hand. "The coffee didn't help solve our problems. So let's see what a glass of champagne will do."

She slid out of the booth and stood beside him. "Just one glass," she said. "Then, I'll start lunch."

An hour later, they sat down at the same booth to eat the meal Marisa had prepared. Darien's only contribution was the selection of a merlot from a Texas Hill Country winery. Other than that, as per her instructions, he'd stayed out of Marisa's way as she hurried back and forth. She didn't even let him set the table but indicated the dishwashing chores would be left entirely to him.

At the first bite, Darien said, "This is the best meat sauce I've ever tasted. You're a world-class cook."

"Nice try, but you still have to do the dishes."

"You're also gorgeous."

"The detergent is under the sink."

They laughed and continued eating. As they finished the meal, Darien was about to top off their wine glasses when the house phone began to blink rapidly, announcing an incoming call. Upon entering the kitchen, he'd put it on silent mode and occasionally checked the caller ID without answering. This time, however, he went to the phone to see who was calling.

The caller was Alden, and Darien felt obligated to answer.

He put the phone on speaker so Marisa could hear the conversation. "Hey, Alden. What's going on."

"I hope there's plenty of spaghetti left," Alden said. "Izzy and I will be there in ten minutes."

At that point, the phone went dead, and the song resumed:

> *We've got to stop and think it over*
> *before we say we're in love.*
> *Will this love last forever,*
> *Or someday cause us to part.*

Darien looked at Marisa and turned both palms upward in a helpless gesture.

Five minutes later, Alden and Izzy appeared and stayed until well past midnight.

CHAPTER 17

After eating half of his breakfast, Dr. Woodrow Throxmire placed the tray in the automatic recycling unit. The eggs reminded him of those served on the space station during his tour. He made a mental note to mention the subpar food to the condo's management. If it didn't improve, he might as well drop the meal service and eat at the Amazon Food Court down the street. The fast-food restaurants there still maintained their original identity, and he passed by them every morning.

Throxmire drained the last drop of coffee from his cup and placed it in the recycling unit with the breakfast tray. He touched the *Start* icon. A stainless-steel lid slipped into place with a click, and a conveyer belt whisked the dishes to a central dishwashing station in the main kitchen.

The condo was named *Lago Claro*, Spanish for *Clear Lake*. The high rise was among the most modern along the Texas Gulf Coast. Like others in incorporated areas, it came under the jurisdiction of HUD. However, Dr. Throxmire was outside of HUD's jurisdiction. He worked for Dr. Ignacio Allende, the Chief Medical Officer of the United States; consequently, he had a HUD variance, as did most government officials. As a result, he could live anywhere he wanted as long as he could afford the rent.

Dr. Throxmire was getting ready to make his *Highway 6 run*, a drive he'd made regularly for ten years. He'd programmed his car to take him to scheduled stops in five small towns along the Texas Highway–Alvin, Manvel, Arcola, Missouri City, and Sugar Land. Today, he would bypass the first four and go straight to Sugar Land to visit Amazon Senior Living No. 3. The facility was the farthest from Clear Lake but the most interesting location on his schedule. Some of the residents had accomplished remarkable scientific feats during their careers and enjoyed talking about them. When he wasn't in a rush, Throxmire provided an attentive ear, though he'd heard most of the stories several times.

He slung his backpack over his shoulder and entered the hallway. A retina scanner above the elevator door recognized him and said, "Good morning, Dr. Throxmire. Would you like your car brought to the front of the building?"

Throxmire affirmed that he would and approached the elevator. The door opened, and he stepped inside. As the glass capsule descended, he looked across Clear Lake. A thunderstorm brewing in the southwest had stifled early-morning sailing enthusiasts except for a few reckless adventurers running before the wind. Dozens of sailboats were anchored at the marina adjacent to the Lago Claro, and several people on the pier were battening down the hatches before the storm hit.

Though he liked the location, Throxmire wasn't impressed by the lake. His parents were originally from Colorado, but he was born in Venezuela. As a result, his first memories were of the South American countries where his parents worked—Venezuela, Guatemala, and Brazil. As a youth, Throxmire had visited many spectacular beaches, including Ipanema, his gold standard for any land-water interface. Clear Lake was plain by comparison, and no other beach he'd seen was comparable, including the ones in California, where he lived before moving to Texas.

Upon Throxmire's graduation from high school in Caracas, his family moved to Sausalito, California, and he attended UC Berkeley. In seven years, he earned a Master's degree in biochemistry and an MD in internal medicine. That was twenty-five years ago, and he'd worked in NatGov's healthcare services ever since. For the last ten years, he'd managed a team of doctors providing medical services to senior-living facilities. The job was tedious, but he never complained and believed his loyalty would be rewarded in due time.

For several years, Throxmire had hoped to leave the daily grind of caring for senior citizens and go into biochemical research. However, the job change would require some deft maneuvering by Dr. Allende's lieutenants because it would be a move away from NatGov's direct control into an area where their control was indirect. While it was theoretically possible for him to go out entirely on his own, Throxmire knew such a move would be foolhardy. The entire medical establishment was under NatGov's thumb, directly or indirectly. Of course, he'd never stated as much in public, nor would he, primarily because he was a beneficiary of the system. Still, having been a foot soldier for over a decade, Throxmire was ready to move up the ranks, and all of the pieces appeared to be in place.

Throxmire's loyalties were in a tug of war. In addition to his allegiance to NIAID and his personal ambitions, he had a strong bond with his patients. Most of those he would see today knew him as *Woody* or *Dr. Woody*. He was pleased that his patients accepted him as a friend. Furthermore, he didn't consider them pawns in a chess game, as some of his colleagues did as they struggled to move up the ladder of success.

As Throxmire stepped onto the sidewalk, a chilly gust of wind kicked up a cloud of dust and light debris. He fastened the middle button of his freshly-laundered white smock and joined a group of Lago Claro residents waiting for their cars. To his right, his car, a yellow sedan, was emerging from the parking garage with a covey of other personal cars. Most were brightly colored Mini-Micros, jellybean-shaped vehicles half the size of regular compacts. NatGov subsidized the ubiquitous Micros, but they lacked comfort, acceleration, and style. Throxmire disdained them and was glad he could afford something better.

Jockeying for position, the cars surged out of the garage and formed a small traffic jam in front of the Lago Claro. As the owners waited, the jam resolved itself, and the vehicles picked their way to the curb with Throxmire's sedan in the lead.

He tossed his backpack into the passenger seat and said, "Sugar Land," as he got in.

"Amazon Senior Living Number Three?" the autopilot asked.

"Yes. What's the current drive time?"

"Fifty-nine minutes."

The compact sedan eased into the traffic, found its way to Longshore Drive, and proceeded to the traffic light at Nasa Rd. 1. While waiting for a green light, Throxmire glanced at the headlines on the news screen atop the Amazon-Wells Fargo building. Several new headlines appeared:

ARAB/ISRAELI TALKS PROCEED AT MR. ROGOV'S REQUEST

DR. ALLENDE INDICATES PHOENIX-75 BATTLE
MAY NOT BE OVER

MARS COLONY PLANS TO DECLARE INDEPENDENCE SOON

He mulled over the last headline. The Mars colony had historical connections to Clear Lake. The Johnson Space Center was just up the highway, and the first seven astronauts had lived nearby. In junior high, while considering the possibility of becoming an astronaut, Throxmire memorized the men's names in alphabetical order: Carpenter, Cooper, Glen, Grissom, Shepherd, Shirra, and Slayton. After serving a stint on the space station, he felt a kinship with the seven men.

In like manner, Throxmire felt a similar kinship with several patients whom he would visit today, particularly Dr. Darien Segura. The elderly scientist was a friend despite being on the opposite side of the political spectrum. Likely, they would discuss various aspects of science today, and—as always—they would talk politics.

When his car swung onto Nasa Rd. 1, Throxmire's iTab sounded the ringtone of NAIAD's private channel, and a black hawk materialized onscreen. The icon identified the caller as Jason Falcon, his contact in Washington. Falcon was one of Ignacio Allende's top lieutenants and handled matters relating to jobs and other HR functions. From the beginning of his long tenure, Throxmire had never talked directly with Dr. Allende about his assignment. Instead, Allende gave orders through his lieutenants, who utilized the encrypted communication system. When Throxmire began working for NIAID, the method of conveying information struck him as bizarre. Now, after so many years, it seemed normal.

"Good morning, Dr. Throxmire," Falcon said. "Do you have a few minutes to talk?"

"Sure. I'm forty-five minutes from my first stop."

"Good. I called to let you know about an important vacancy that will occur shortly in the biotech field. We believe you're a perfect fit for the job."

Feeling an adrenalin rush, Throxmire asked. "Where will the job be located?"

"In Houston. The company is Vi-Tech."

"I'm familiar with that company. When do you expect the vacancy to occur?"

"Soon," Falcon said. "We need another board member to come over to our side before we can make the change. If it doesn't happen voluntarily, we'll call in a favor."

"Should I tell my patients to expect a new doctor soon?"

"Yes. Eldon Fletcher will be coming from Washington to replace you."

"I worked with Dr. Fletcher several years ago," Throxmire said. "He'll do a good job." Though he'd never mention it to Falcon, he suspected Fletcher was attempting to work his way into Ignacio Allende's inner circle. Perhaps he already had.

"There's something else you need to know," Falcon said. "Vi-Tech employs a virologist named Rachel Segura. She's the granddaughter of Dr. Darien Segura, your most famous patient."

"I've met Miss Segura at the facility where I'm going today. She's a nice young woman."

"Even so," Falcon said, "a potential problem exists that you need to be aware of. During the early days of the Phoenix-75 outbreak, Miss Segura's work on the virus's genetic makeup helped uncover some of its peculiarities. Recently, she completed another project and requested the opportunity to follow the chimeras as they moved through pathogenicity testing and into the vaccine development phase. As you know, Dr. Allende doesn't operate that way, so he denied her request."

"Does he ever make exceptions?"

"Never. He insists on maintaining complete secrecy."

"So . . . is Miss Segura a disgruntled employee?"

"I hope not," Falcon said, "and part of your job will be to see that she isn't."

Throxmire was puzzled. "Why are we focusing on her?"

"We need to keep her on our side."

"I still don't understand your point."

"Have you noticed that her eyes are different colors?"

"Yes, she has heterochromia."

"In addition, Miss Segura is a semi-identical twin," Falcon said. "That combination has produced several brilliant scientists in the Segura family. She will likely leave her mark on the world of science someday, and we want her to be in the NIAID fold when she does."

Stunned, Throxmire said, "I'm sure Miss Segura and I can work together."

"You have to," Falcon said firmly. "This Phoenix-75 saga isn't over yet."

CHAPTER 18

On Presidential Inauguration Day, Darien was greeted by a blast of cold wind and a flurry of snowflakes as he stepped onto the sidewalk. Eschewing the trek to the crosswalk, he sprinted across the street toward the Cherry Tree. The snowfall/Cherry Tree combination triggered a vivid memory of his date with Marisa six weeks earlier. After spending Saturday together, she spent Sunday with her family, and he joined them in the evening for a gourmet Brazilian dinner. Then, early Monday morning, he drove her to Bush Intercontinental Airport, where they said goodbye in front of the baggage kiosk. At that instant, he began counting the days, waiting for her to return.

The anticipated reunion had yet to occur.

Marisa had intended to return to Houston briefly during the holidays. Instead, on the spur of the moment, Frieda and Izzy went to Washington to check out her condo and visit the capital city. As a result of Marisa being gone, Darien ate a traditional Christmas dinner with his family and hung out with them on New Year's Day, watching parades and football games. Though he and Marisa had never spent a major holiday together, she was conspicuous by her absence.

Today, Darien would join a small group to watch Reuben Rogov's swearing-in ceremony. He was pleased Rachel had decided to attend. The two siblings had talked more about politics the past year than ever before. Though Rachel had voted a straight Independent ticket, Darien believed they were beginning to think more alike. After the election, she commented that Mr. Rogov ran a much better campaign than the other candidates. He wondered what Rachel would do if Rogov solved most of the country's long-standing problems during his first term. Maybe she would vote for him the next election.

One thing was certain—if the new President could change a Segura's mind, he could change anybody's.

He entered the Cherry Tree. As was usually the case, a crowd of patrons had gathered in the foyer. Many of those waiting to be seated were residents of the George Washington whom Darien knew. He exchanged greetings as he picked his way through the crowd and approached the front desk.

Seconds later, the hostess appeared and greeted Darien.

"Good morning, Heidi. Is Alden here yet?"

"No, but he reserved a booth in the back room," Heidi said, "and asked me to tell you that he'll be a few minutes late. He also said he has a surprise for you."

"Do you have any idea what he's talking about?"

Heidi shrugged. "Not a clue."

"Okay, thanks," Darien said. He turned to go and then looked back. "I'm in dire need of some caffeine. Please send me a large espresso."

"Will do."

Darien passed through the front dining area and entered the darkened back room. The Cherry Tree had adopted the dinner-theater concept for those wanting to watch Rogov's inauguration. The price of a reservation included lunch. As a result, serious inauguration watchers had occupied every booth and table except a large U-shaped booth with a *Reserved* sign on the table. Sliding into the booth, Darien watched the monitor as headlines scrolled down the screen.

FOOD SHORTAGE PREDICTED THIS SUMMER

PHOENIX-75 RESURGES IN CHINA

ISRAELI/ARAB TENSIONS MOUNT

EGYPTIAN ARMY CONDUCTS EXERCISES IN THE SINAI DESERT

U.S. AND RUSSIAN DRONES CLASH OVER SYRIA

TROOPS EXCHANGE FIRE AT IRAQ/IRAN BORDER

MEXICAN REFUGEES GATHER AT THE SOUTHERN BORDER

Behind the headlines, the camera showed an inaugural platform on the west steps of the U.S. Capitol Building. The stands were full, and people milled about in the aisles. The usual high-level politicos and dignitaries were in their places on the front row of seats, an indication the swearing-in ceremony would begin shortly.

On an impulse, Darien counted the scrolling headlines. There were seven—all bad. During his campaign, Reuben Rogov claimed that he was a problem solver, and Darien hoped he could perform as promised. He'd cast his lot with Mr. Rogov and the Peace Party and was finally wearing a party armband, as was almost everyone in the room.

Carrying a tray, Heidi approached the table and said, "Here's your coffee, Darien." She placed the espresso in front of him and retreated.

Darien picked up the steaming cup and fixed his eyes on the TV screen while waiting for the live broadcast to begin. He stared at the repeating headlines with hypnotic intensity, unable to understand why anyone would want to be President. The nation was in a state of emergency on every front, as was most of the world. Still, Rogov had sought the job and won it. Now, it was up to him to tackle the list of monumental problems that came with the office.

For no apparent reason, the rumble of conversation in the room dropped abruptly, jolting Darien from his headline-watching. He looked toward the entrance and saw five shadowy figures, evidently his group, entering the room.

Five?

He was expecting only four–Izzy, Alden, Rachel, and Justin. Perhaps the extra person was the surprise that Alden mentioned to Heidi. Due to the reduced lighting, Darien couldn't identify anyone in the group but could tell the extra person was a woman. The group started toward Darien, and the woman began to look like Marisa, which didn't make sense. She'd texted him yesterday afternoon without mentioning a trip to Houston. Surely, she would have told him.

A moment later, Darien recognized Marisa as the fifth person. He stood as she walked toward him. When they were a step apart, he reached toward her eagerly, and she extended her arms. After a long embrace, they kissed briefly.

"What are you doing in Houston?" Darien asked.

"Taking a short vacation, doing a little work, and surprising you."

"You're full of surprises," Darien said, shaking his head in disbelief. "How did you set this one up?"

"I didn't get this trip okayed until late yesterday afternoon," Marisa said. "When I finally did, I thought it would be fun to show up unannounced."

"How long are you going to stay?" Darien asked as everyone slid into the booth.

"Only four days," Marisa said. "It's sort of a mini-vacation, but my boss gave me a little work to do, so I can put the airfare on my expense account."

"What kind of work will you be doing?" Darien asked as he took Marisa's hand.

"I'm going to try to find a few people—preferably people I know—who would be interested in moving to Washington," Marisa said. "Now that the election is over, Mr. Rogov is going to make the Equality Team a permanent branch of government."

"You'll be a great recruiter," Darien said, surprised at how much Marisa had matured as a government operative in the short time she'd been away. Compared to her, the other five people at the table were political toddlers. He realized Marisa's zealotry was an aspect of her personality he'd have to adjust to, even if she moved back to Houston.

"I'll start my recruiting efforts with you," Marisa said, smiling as she looked around the table. "Would any of you like to discuss moving to Washington?"

Without hesitation, all of the potential recruits gave a negative shake of their heads, and Justin said, "Since I didn't vote, I'm probably not a good candidate."

Before Marisa could respond, the camera zoomed in on Alphabet News' lead announcers, Angela Morales and Richard Frazier.

"Good morning, America," Richard said. "Thank you for joining Alphabet News as we present Reuben Rogov's inauguration as the 66th President of the United States. No one can deny that Mr. Rogov has achieved a mandate. Moreover, with the Peace Party taking control of the House and Senate, he has ample support to move forward with his plans."

Richard paused. Without missing a beat, Angela said, "Since 1981, inauguration ceremonies usually occur in front of the United States Capitol facing the National Mall and the Washington Monument. That is the case today."

Heidi appeared with a tray of garden salads, and the meal began. With subdued voices, they chatted and ate while watching the preliminaries unfold onscreen. Most other occupants in the room did the same. Today's ceremony reminded Darien of the rally last spring at Amazon Field when Reuben Rogov first enthralled the country with his oratorical skills. Today, millions of Americans were waiting to hear more from him.

The room fell pin-drop quiet as the camera zoomed in on Reuben Rogov standing next to the Chief Justice of the Supreme Court. At the Justice's prompt, the President-elect repeated the words, "I do solemnly swear to faithfully execute the Office of President of the United States, and I will to the best of my ability, preserve, protect, and defend the Constitution of the United States, so help me God."

As the Chief Justice stepped away, leaving Mr. Rogov alone at the podium, the audience jumped to their feet and began applauding on the Capitol steps and in the Cherry Tree. After two minutes, Rogov held up a hand for silence. Obediently and in unison, everyone stopped clapping and sat down. The new President began his inaugural address in a rich, full-bodied voice.

"My fellow Americans, this peaceful transfer of power has occurred periodically in the United States for nearly 400 years. Today, with a simple oath, we will continue this tradition and begin a new administration. I am honored and humbled to stand here where many American Presidents before me have stood, and I appreciate your support.

"As you know, the main tenet of our party is *Peace through Equality.*

"When our nation was founded, our forefathers touted equality but embraced slavery—an inequality based strictly on skin color. This was a stark contradiction to the statement, *All men are created equal.* Over several centuries, our ancestors paid lip service to this concept; however, their actions did not bear out their words. Throughout the years, we have added other inequalities. As a result, today, the country is fractured along many lines, including color, religion, sex, age, education, social status, financial status, and other contrived benchmarks that past administrations have used to their advantage.

"I do not accept these manufactured divisions, nor will I allow them to continue during my presidency. I will work diligently to bring equality to every person in our nation. Sadly, the hopes and dreams of some Americans are still limited by their ancestry and the circumstances of their birth. This is unacceptable—the dream belongs to everyone.

"When the Peace party adopted the slogan, *Peace Through Equality*, we weren't thinking only of the United States. The entire world is in chaos, and much of the unrest is due to inequality. The citizens of many countries are victims of a caste system designed to prevent them from achieving equality. Moreover, some countries have deemed themselves superior to other countries, thus creating a kind of inequality that has led to countless wars.

"Many forms of inequality can be addressed within our country, but others must play out on the world stage. As your President, I will work with the United Nations as we strive to make every nation equal to its neighbors. We will confront these problems instead of passing them on to the next generation as so many others have done.

"Today, we begin our journey toward peace through equality."

The President paused, and pandemonium erupted in the viewing room, the first applause since the swearing-in ceremony. Until now, no one in the room had dared interrupt the elegant Reuben Rogov. Darien stood and cheered along with most others in the room. He was amazed at how easily Mr. Rogov had connected peace with equality and made the concept sound plausible.

After a moment's hesitation, Rachel stood without applauding.

Rogov raised a hand to silence the ovation. "The headlines you saw earlier are a list of problems that Vice President Profeto and I will address during our first one hundred days in office," he said. "Moreover, I anticipate solving all seven of them within three and a half years. If we are successful in doing so, Mr. Profeto and I will run for a second term. If we fail, we will not run again. As these headlines attest, few historical periods have been more challenging than the one currently facing us; however, we intend to press forward diligently on all fronts.

"Today, Phoenix-75 is threatening the world's grain supply; therefore, I will address this problem first. The virus' resurgence last year in China has already caused serious food shortages in the eastern hemisphere. We must solve this problem before the next growing season, which will start soon. To intensify our efforts against this menace, I am authorizing funding for a project designated *Operation Breadbasket*. Within a week, this funding will be made available to biotech companies, both large and small, that have demonstrated innovative R&D programs."

At the mention of funding to combat Phoenix-75, Darien's thoughts jumped to the financial problems facing Vi-tech. Justin's job was hanging by a thread, and he was concerned about Rachel's job as well. However, if the company could secure a NatGov grant, it would likely eliminate the necessity for job cuts. Mr. Rogov wasn't wasting any time. Darien was duly impressed.

During the next few minutes, the new President continued to discuss the highlighted list of crucial problems. As complex as the issues were, he insisted that he expected to find a solution to each of them. Mr. Rogov ended his speech, twenty-one minutes in length, with the phrase, "God bless you, God bless America, and God bless the world."

Upon Rogov's benediction, shouting and applause erupted throughout the room. Everyone, including Rachel, leaped to their feet again, and several people shouted, "Bravo."

Above the background clamor, a high-pitched voice shrieked, "Long live Reuben Rogov. Long live Reuben Rogov."

Papa's warning crept into Darien's mind, but it no longer seemed to have merit.

CHAPTER 19

A week later, with the Phoenix resurgence on her mind, Rachel entered the laboratory. She felt anxious, an unusual emotion for her. At his inauguration, President Rogov had announced that Operation Breadbasket funds would be available to selected companies within seven days. Time would run out in a few hours. But, as far as Rachel knew, Vi-Tech had not heard from NIAID.

To further complicate matters, immediately after Mr. Rogov initiated the program, Vi-Tech's CEO and Technical Director, Dr. Malachi Truman, announced his retirement. Most company employees thought the two events were connected, which seemed to be a reasonable assumption. Whatever the case, they would find out shortly. Dr. Truman had scheduled an *attendance-required* meeting at nine-thirty.

Rachel sat down at her desk and glanced at the clock on the wall. It read eight-thirty. Seemingly, it hadn't moved since she checked it last. She touched her iTab screen and retrieved a folder of Phoenix-75 lab notes. Mechanically, she scrolled through the files for a few minutes, then sighed and leaned back in her chair. For one of the few times in her life, she was having trouble concentrating.

At nine-fifteen, a shrill ringtone sounded on the company PA system.

"Attention, all Vi-Tech employees," a computer voice announced. "This is a reminder. A general meeting has been scheduled for this morning. All company personnel must report to the Technical Director's conference room at nine-thirty. This is not a drill. The meeting is mandatory."

As the announcement replayed, Rachel detected movement at her shoulder and looked around to see Justin approaching with a solemn look on his face. They exchanged subdued greetings and entered the hallway to join a group of colleagues walking toward the elevators. The normally-talkative scientists were in a blue funk, and the hall was unusually quiet. Rachel suspected that some of her cohorts had spent the weekend polishing their resumes.

They took an elevator to the tenth floor and entered the conference room which contained a rectangular table surrounded by beige chairs. Several rows of theater-style seats stood along the rear wall. Incoming arrivals, eschewing the chairs around the table, hurried toward the theater section. Dr. Truman was not in the room; however, his executive assistant, Janice Smith, stood near the podium at the head of the table.

Smith beckoned toward Rachel and Justin as they entered. They approached her, and she relayed Dr. Truman's instructions for them to sit near the podium. Mutely they took the seats indicated, and Rachel kept her eyes fixed on the door leading into the Technical Director's office.

Presently, the door opened, and two men emerged– Dr. Truman and Dr. Woodrow Throxmire. A murmur rippled through the room as they walked toward the head of the table. Immediately, Rachel understood what was happening. Dr. Throxmire was taking over as Vi-Tech's CEO and Technical Director. That was okay by her. At least she and Throxmire knew each other and had shared a few short conversations at Papa's senior living facility. And, though Throxmire was a staunch

Peace Party advocate, Papa counted him as a friend. She was comfortable with the change.

Throxmire looked toward Rachel and nodded before sitting down. He seemed perfectly at ease and wore a slight smile. Hopefully, his demeanor indicated that good news was in the offing. She glanced at Justin; his expression remained somber.

Truman stepped to the podium. He spoke briefly of his immediate retirement and expressed gratitude to everyone who'd been a member of Vi-Tech's workforce during his long tenure. The speech was short, to the point, and rather bland. He concluded by saying, "It's my pleasure to introduce Vi-Tech's next CEO and Technical Director, Dr. Woodrow Throxmire."

The two men traded places. Throxmire thanked Truman and looked around the room. "Good morning, everyone," he said. "I look forward to working with you. I'm sure you know that Vi-Tech has applied for funding via President Rogov's new program, Operation Breadbasket. For my first official act as your leader, it's my pleasure to announce that we have received a grant—"

Applause and cheers sounded throughout the room, interrupting Throxmire in mid-sentence. In a microsecond, the somber mood in the room changed to exultation. As the tension dissipated, Rachel turned toward Justin, and they exchanged high-fives.

Throxmire smiled and continued, "The grant is sufficient to provide job security for all of Vi-Tech's current staff into the foreseeable future."

Again, everyone in the room cheered.

When the applause subsided, Throxmire said, "I will assign a team to work on Operation Breadbasket immediately. Initially, the team will consist of two people. Others may be added from time to time. In addition, one of my immediate goals is to strengthen our ties with NatGov to get more opportunities like this one. For the time being, those of you not assigned to Breadbasket should continue working on your current projects. I will review all projects in progress and those in the planning stages to determine what changes are needed. If you would like to speak with me as we make this transition, contact Mrs. Smith for an appointment. Are there any questions?"

When no one responded, Throxmire gave a short pep talk and closed by saying, "This concludes the general meeting. Have a good day." He looked at Rachel and Justin and added, "Please wait. I'd like a word with you in private."

The two virologists remained seated as other personnel left the room. Dr. Truman returned to the adjoining office, and the new Technical Director sat down across the table from Rachel and Justin. After introducing himself to Justin, Throxmire turned to Rachel and said, "Nice to see you again, Miss Segura."

Rachel was minimalistic in her answer. "Hello, Dr. Throxmire."

"Congratulations, Miss Segura," Throxmire said. "Starting immediately, you are Vi-Tech's lead virologist on Operation Breadbasket, and Mr. Thibideaux will assist you. Incidentally, Dr. Ignatio Allende recommended that I assign this leadership role to you."

Rachel's eyebrows shot up. She was pleased but stunned. "That's quite a surprise. I've never had any contact with Dr. Allende whatsoever."

"To some degree, you have," Throxmire said. "When Dr. Truman sent Vi-Tech's application to NIAID, he included several research papers written by company biologists. Your master's thesis, *Altering Chimeras by DNA/RNA Splicing*, was one of the submissions. The best papers went up the chain of command to Dr. Allende. He singled you out, and I'm sure he did the same thing with researchers from other companies."

"How much will he be involved in the research?" Rachel asked, wondering if Allende was a micro-manager. As NIAID's top man, it seemed odd that he would take time to study all of the Breadbasket applications and read the papers accompanying them.

"He's involved a considerable amount at the moment," Throxmire said. "He has divided the research into three distinct parts. Vi-Tech's job—*your job, Miss Segura*—is to put together chimeras according to NIAID's specifications. For all practical purposes, this is a follow-up on the project you completed about a year ago."

"What happens after we produce the chimeras?" Rachel asked.

"Like before, we'll send the tailor-made viruses to NIAID," Throxmire said. "That's all we know at the moment. NIAID maintains a cloak of secrecy on all aspects of the project. So even as participants, we're on a *need-to-know* basis."

"That seems odd to me."

"I know, but Vi-Tech needs the work, so we'll proceed as directed."

Rachel nodded. "I understand."

Despite the secrecy, it was easy to deduce how NIAID was planning to orchestrate Operation Breadbasket. Upon receiving the newly-developed chimeras from Vi-Tech, they would forward them to other biotech companies to determine pathogenicity to animals and plants. Next, they would submit the most promising chimeras to additional companies for use in developing vaccines or immunotherapy agents. It was evident that NIAID intended to keep the project tied up in a neat bundle which they could control from *A* to *Z*. Rachel struggled to understand why they would keep participants from sharing their findings. The cloak-and-dagger approach seemed counterproductive but fit the modus operandi for which Allende was known.

"When will we start the project?" Rachel asked.

"As soon as we get the cultures," Throxmire said. "They're scheduled to arrive this afternoon."

"We'll get the equipment ready."

"I'll drop them off as soon as they come," Throxmire said, standing.

The elated virologists left the conference room and strode briskly toward the elevator. Some of their colleagues were chatting in a nearby doorway. As Rachel and Justin passed, everyone in the group gave a *thumbs-up* signal, and several said, "Congratulations, Rachel."

Once back in the lab, Rachel said, "Let's review the Phoenix-75 project we did last year. That should be a good place to start." They went to adjoining stools in front of the big screen monitor. With a series of hand signals, Rachel retrieved the data, and they began to pore over it molecule by molecule. She was confident that she and Justin could contribute significantly to Operation Breadbasket.

Still, the big question was, could they do it in time to avert the grain shortage threatening the world?

Early that afternoon, following a quick lunch, Rachel and Justin were back in front of the monitor when she sensed

movement from the corner of her eye. She looked around to see
Dr. Throxmire entering the lab carrying a small ice chest. He
wore a white lab jacket with W. THROXMIRE, MD, stitched
across the left pocket.

"Good afternoon, Doctor," Rachel said.

Throxmire put the ice chest on the lab bench adjoining the
monitor. "Here are the latest cultures," he said, "but before we
discuss the project, let's dispense with some formalities. Starting
now, I'll call you by your first names, and you're to call me
Woody or *Dr. Woody*, whichever you prefer. Okay?"

"Okay, Dr. Woody," Rachel said, aware the new CEO was
trying to make her feel comfortable. She appreciated his informal approach but thought that discarding *Doctor* from his title
was inappropriate at this early stage in their relationship. She
could do so later if things worked out. Better safe than sorry, as
Dr. Truman would say.

Throxmire looked at the 3D image on the screen. "Can you
zoom in on one of the RNA strands?"

"Of course," Rachel said. "What section would you like
to see?" She was somewhat surprised at Throxmire's question.
He seemed to be anticipating a little hands-on virology work,
although she knew the discipline was outside of his expertise.

"I read your master's thesis last week," Throxmire said, "and
I'd like to see the genes you modified to produce stable chimeras."

"This isn't the same variant," Rachel said, "but genes five and
six are virtually identical to the ones mentioned in my thesis."

At her command, the image on the screen expanded until
an RNA strand was visible. She started at one end of the molec-
ular chain and clicked the pointer stepwise to the fifth gene as
if instructing a college lab class. To her satisfaction, Throxmire
watched intently.

Rachel was enjoying the moment. She knew the new CEO wasn't questioning her work. Instead, he was trying to understand how she'd produced stability in such a volatile molecule. Other scientists had tried and failed, and some of those who'd criticized her technique initially had embraced it later, calling it a blend of science and art.

"I'm getting the picture," Throxmire said. "Rotate the image to the left a little,"

"Tell me what you're looking for," Rachel said, "and I'll point it out."

Abruptly, Throxmire turned toward Rachel and asked, "Do you enjoy teaching others these gene-splicing techniques?"

"Yes, I do. Currently, I'm teaching Justin," Rachel said, gratified that her new leader was showing interest in the work she loved.

"I'll be more direct," Throxmire said. "I have the opportunity to put two recently graduated virologists under your tutelage. Can you teach them your skills?"

Rachel nodded. "I'm sure I can, but it will take some time."

"They should be great trainees," Throxmire said. "Both graduated magna cum laude from Georgetown University."

"Georgetown?" Rachel echoed, taken aback by the Washington connection.

"Yes. They were hand-picked by Dr. Ignacio Allende."

"When does he want them to start?"

"Next week."

CHAPTER 20

Darien and the Thibideaux brothers left the housing unit on a perfect mid-September evening and headed toward the YMCA. As they passed the Amazon-Capitol One Bank, the news screen atop the building flashed, indicating that Alphabet News was posting new headlines. Reflexively, they glanced at the screen as a single banner materialized:

CROP SPRAY BEING TESTED AGAINST PHOENIX-75

"Operation Breadbasket rescued Vi-Tech," Justin said, "and I'm sure Rachel's work was the best submitted to NIAID."

"Don't sell yourself short," Darien said. "You helped her."

"She supplied the creativity," Justin said. "I helped only during the early phases of the project."

"She should have won a Nobel prize," Alden said. "Instead, Allende took the credit."

"That's true," Justin said with a nod. "Still, the project provided job security for the entire company, and I'm thankful for that."

"Do you know how long Lemke and Seth will be here?" Alden asked.

"They'll probably be leaving soon," Justin said. "They've been in Houston over eight months."

"Rachel told me she's taught them about all she can," Darien said. Though he didn't mention it for fear of downplaying Justin's ability, Rachel also told him the two men were exceptionally inventive and pushed the limit at every opportunity.

Last week, Lemke produced a chimera having only one spike, and Seth produced another with two hundred. Moreover, both variants were stable. In Darien's opinion, that was a final exam deserving an $A+$ grade.

"Let me ask you something about those guys," Alden said. "Can we count them as friends?"

"You're the people person," Darien said. "You tell us."

"Okay, I will," Alden said. "When I first met them, they were friendly and outgoing. They still are—at least, they *seem* that way. However, since our first conversation, I haven't learned much more about them. They have an invisible shield around them. I can get fairly close, but no closer."

"I feel that way too," Justin said, "but I thought it was because they displaced me as Rachel's assistant."

"What does Rachel think about them?" Alden asked.

"They treat her with great respect and deference," Darien said. "While at work, they call her *Teacher*, so her perspective isn't the same as ours. Since she's their mentor, she probably didn't expect to become close friends with them."

"She's my mentor too," Justin said, looking puzzled, "and we're close friends."

"It's not the same," Alden said. "You were friends before you became her assistant."

Dropping the subject, they walked on. As they approached the YMCA, Justin asked, "Who are we playing tonight?"

"The Red Dragons," Darien said.

"They'll probably win the league," Alden said. "We've never beaten them."

"We could beat them if you guys would score a few more points," Darien said.

"Yes sir, Captain," Alden said, clicking his heels together and saluting crisply.

***

Two hours later, they left the YMCA. Their team, the Mediplex Magicians, had been ahead of the Red Dragons at halftime but lost the game in the final minutes, as often happened. Though double-teamed constantly, Darien scored twenty-eight points. While at Baylor, he grew used to winning regularly, but that wasn't happening in the City Industrial League. Still, regardless of where he was playing, Darien played to win, though realizing someday he would have to accept the idea that basketball was *just a game.*

Upon reaching Holcombe Boulevard, the trio turned right and started toward the George Washington. The huge building, a half mile away, was being swallowed in evening shadows. Above it, the crescent moon glowed faintly, and Venus hung in the middle of a cluster of stars, presenting a rare celestial display. They marveled at the starry scene until the street lights came on causing it disappear.

When they reached the Cherry Tree, Alden said, "I'm starving."

"Me too," Darien said, "Let's run inside and grab a snack. We have plenty of time before the meeting starts."

They entered the restaurant. At Alden's instructions, the maître d' seated them at a booth in the back room. While waiting for a server to take their order, Darien's iTab buzzed, and the Little Horn Literary Agency's icon popped up along with the words, *Important Message From I. Horn.* His heart raced. Though he and Immanuel Horn had exchanged several texts and emails recently, this was the first one marked *Important.*

Eagerly, he touched the icon, and the message appeared:

Darien,

Congratulations! The Little Horn Agency is pleased to inform you that we have sold your novel, "The Photosynthesis Gene," to Pale Horse Publications. Pale Horse is a new brand created by the Hachette Book Group to market science fiction and fantasy by promising new authors. The offer just came in, and I wanted to let you know immediately, even though we have a few minor details to work out. I will follow up with you shortly. Again, congratulations.

Regards, I. Horn

"Yes!" Darien shouted, slamming his fist on the table so hard it startled his companions and caused nearby diners to cast a questioning look in his direction.

"Did you win the lottery?" Alden asked.

"Better than that, as far as I'm concerned," Darien said. He showed the message to his friends.

"Congratulations!" Justin said. "Dinner's on you."

"I'm thinking New York strip," Alden said. "The biggest one on the menu."

After eating, the three friends went to the balcony and claimed the seats Rachel and Izzy were saving for them.

The five-member cadre reminded Darien of how much he missed Marisa. They continued to text and FaceTime daily, and she'd made two quick trips to Houston since moving away. Even so, the long-distance relationship was challenging. Marisa had made Darien a part of her vocation/avocation by updating him regularly on various happenings in Washington. Moreover, she made no secret of her intention to draw him into politics. Earlier today, she'd given him a brief preview of the President's speech tonight. Try as he might, he couldn't comprehend the magnitude of her calling but knew it was real.

Below the balcony, the IMAX screen displayed a live shot of the White House Rose Garden with red and white roses blooming beside the walkway surrounding the rectangular grounds. A podium stood on the porch adjacent to the Oval Office. Reporters and photographers milled around on the steps and walkway, and high-ranking NatGov officials sat in folding chairs in the center of the garden. Radiant space heaters stood at strategic locations near the seating area, and a gentle breeze blew rose petals across the neatly-manicured lawn.

The Rose Garden scene dimmed as headlines scrolled down the IMAX screen:

PHOENIX-75 UPDATE

TEMPORARY CEASE-FIRE AT IRAQ/IRAN BORDER

U.S. AND RUSSIA DISCUSS SYRIAN INDEPENDENCE

EGYPT AND SAUDI ARABIA AGREE TO TALKS WITH ISRAEL

After several repetitions, the headlines disappeared, and the camera zoomed in on the door of the Oval Office. A moment later, the door opened, and Haley Cartwright, the President's Press Secretary, stepped out and strode to the podium. She laid her iTab on the stand and glanced at it before looking toward the main camera.

"Good evening, America," Cartwright began. "President Rogov instructed me to give you a brief report on the country's Key Economic Indicators, which provide a comprehensive, up-to-date picture of our economy. U.S. payrolls stand at 230 million, the highest figure since the Phoenix-75 pandemic. Next—"

"This is *1984-ish*," Justin said. "Nobody cares about those numbers."

"People with money care," Darien said.

During the next ten minutes, the secretary gave figures for the unemployment rate, gross domestic product, consumer spending, and a half-dozen other indicators. As she droned on, the friends whispered among themselves, as did everyone near them. Finally, the preliminaries were over, Cartwright retreated, and Reuben Rogov came out of his office and stepped to the podium.

A hush fell over the auditorium.

Darien glanced at his companions. Their eyes were fixed on the big screen as they waited for the President to begin. In the past, Darien and his friends paid very little attention during citizenship meetings, but things changed after Rogov's election. The new President had spoken at the January and February meetings, and he appeared to be planning to use the monthly programs as his primary vehicle for informing the populace. The first two speeches were outstanding. Even Papa listened to them without being overly critical, a miracle as Darien saw it.

President Rogov began, "Good evening, fellow citizens. Thank you for joining me." As always, he spoke without using a teleprompter, iTab, or notes.

"Under my leadership," Rogov continued, "the business of our great country is forging ahead, even though we face afflictions of monumental proportions. Today, we face economic and social problems that affect many Americans—especially struggling young workers and fixed-income retirees. Many problems–food shortages, disease, and job losses–were triggered by the recent resurgence of the Phoenix-75 virus. However, some of our ills are not attributable to the virus. Instead, they have come upon us over many years, and previous administrations have side-stepped them. It is time to confront them.

"At my inauguration, national news headlines listed seven major problems facing the United States and the rest of the world. Though not listed in the January headlines, we continue to face cyclical poverty, education disparities, racial reconciliation, access to healthcare, and other problems that I will address during my first term in office.

"You may be wondering if America can solve these problems.

"I am confident we can. But to do so, we must release the creative energy of every citizen. Whether in government or not, all of us must join this effort. The only solutions I will propose or accept are those that are fair and equitable to every citizen. Equality is the primary tenet of the Peace Party. No single American, or group of Americans, will be singled out to pay more than their fair share. We are in this together, and we will succeed together.

"Now, I will update you on the first issue.

"In January, the world was facing food shortages because Phoenix-75 had begun to attack wheat and corn. Even while facing other significant difficulties, this was America's most pressing problem. Though it affected other countries as well, the problem defaulted to the United States, as has happened repeatedly. Among all nations on Earth, only America could react in time to avert a worldwide famine, and we did so. Upon my inauguration, I initiated Operation Breadbasket, a project which Vice President Profeto coordinated very skillfully.

"Through a branch of NatGov known as NIAID, grants were made to dozens of biotech companies, and they went to work on this problem. As a result of this effort, a crop spray has been developed. This morning, I commissioned several large pharmaceutical companies to produce a spray-on vaccine in sufficient quantities to protect this year's grain crop. It will be available for application within days.

"Operation Breadbasket was a complete success. We will avert the predicted food shortage. At this point—"

Applause and cheers, both in the auditorium and the Rose Garden, drowned out Reuben Rogov in mid-sentence. Darien was amazed by the aura generated by the diminutive orator but knew it was real because he felt it himself. Despite fleeting doubts which occasionally surfaced when he recalled Papa's warnings, Darien numbered himself among the believers.

The President raised a hand for silence. Everyone in the Rose Garden and the auditorium complied, and he continued, "At this point, I will give you a short update on the other problems highlighted at my inauguration."

During the next fifteen minutes, Rogov delivered his report meticulously and confidently, stating that he expected to produce significant results early in his tenure. As an addendum to the confidence displayed by the new President, recent polls indicated that most Americans, including many RADS and Independents, believed he would be successful.

Listening intently, Darien noticed that Mr. Rogov mentioned Vice President Profeto frequently. In every case, he was quick to give credit to his second-in-command, something previous Presidents seldom did. In addition, Dr. Allende's name also came up regularly indicating the trio of leaders had solidified into a formidable team.

After commenting on each problem, Rogov said, "For your information, I have renamed a plaza near the White House. The park formerly known as Freedom Plaza will now be called Equality Plaza. This name reflects our party's goal of bringing peace through equality."

Darien was not surprised at the name change. Marisa had predicted it would happen.

When it seemed Mr. Rogov was about to conclude his speech on an optimistic note, his tone changed, and a look of concern sharpened his jawline.

"As your President," he said solemnly, "I have the privilege of delivering good news to you. Unfortunately, I also have the responsibility of informing you when a threat looms before our great nation.

"Now is one of those times.

"NatGov has detected the activity of an underground organization attempting to overthrow America."

A spontaneous low murmur interrupted Rogov for a few seconds, after which he continued, "According to preliminary findings, this junta operated two decades before being detected. As far as we can ascertain, it has no membership roll or official name. This terrorist organization has been popularized by conspiracy theory publications using the name, *Los Ignotos*, to identify it. While I do not condone such publications, I prefer to call the organization by a name; therefore, your government will also refer to it as Los Ignotos."

Darien was stunned at Rogov's words, not because he'd acknowledged the existence of the underground organization, but because his words echoed phrases from *ConspiraciesRevealed.* Though the President had denigrated the publication, he must have read it, and his reference bolstered the credibility of its content.

"My fellow citizens," Rogov continued solemnly, "your government needs your help. We believe Los Ignotos is poised to make a move soon; therefore, you must be vigilant at all times. Keep your eyes and ears open. If you see or hear any suspicious anti-American activity, report it immediately. The CIA has established a hotline for this purpose. Please add this number to your contact list.

"The number is 666-123-4567."

Rogov repeated the number and concluded his speech.

CHAPTER 21

Caffeinated and adrenalized, Rachel entered the lab on Monday morning with Justin at her heels.

Today, the two new graduates from Georgetown University would begin training under her supervision. As per Dr. Throxmire's instructions, she'd prepared a detailed course on RNA/DNA modification techniques. The tutorial was based primarily on her master's thesis and included some advanced methodology not presented in textbooks. Despite garnering much praise, the paper had also collected criticism from those who found the procedure difficult to master. However, the new graduates shouldn't fall into that category. They'd been hand-picked by Dr. Ignacio Allende. Surely the Director of NAIAD would send only the crème de la crème to Houston for an advanced genetics study.

The recruits, Lemke Grover and Seth Elam, moved into the Abraham Lincoln over the weekend. Even before settling into their new quarters, they contacted Rachel and invited her to a *get-acquainted* coffee with them on Saturday morning. Suspecting they were acting on Dr. Woody's instructions, she met them at the Log Cabin, and they sipped coffee and talked for over an hour. She enjoyed the visit. Both men were friendly and eager to start their training. They were about five years younger than Rachel and still slightly wet behind the ears, but both were plenty astute. She looked forward to teaching them.

Rachel and Justin entered the viewing room and sat down in front of the 3D monitor. She gave a series of hand signals, and the bank of LEDs on the control panel began to blink in various color combinations. A moment later, every light on the panel turned green and stopped blinking, indicating that the monitor, camera, and electron microscope were linked together and functioning correctly. She looked toward Justin and flashed a thumbs-up.

Immediately, she realized Justin was preoccupied. After working with him for two years, Rachel could read him like an open book. Lately, he'd begun to delve into conspiracy theories and was bringing his new-found interest to work with him. Knowing something unusual was on his mind, she decided to clear the air before the trainees arrived.

"What are you thinking about?" she asked.

"Dad heard from his brother in Europe last night," Justin said.

"What's he working on?"

"He's still trying to uncover information on Los Ignotos."

"Has he discovered anything new?" Rachel asked.

"He hasn't found any evidence to prove a cabal by that name exists."

"They're mentioned in the news all the time."

"That doesn't mean much these days," Justin said. "Maybe Rogov invented the name."

Justin's words surprised Rachel. Recent surveys showed that nearly all non-voters had begun to support Reuben Rogov, yet Justin was growing more critical of him. He was starting to sound like Papa—maybe worse. In fact, Papa had softened his anti-Rogov stance a little, as Rachel had done as well. While she was pondering the situation, her iTab pinged, and a text message from Dr. Throxmire appeared.

She glanced at the message and said, "Dr. Woody is bringing the new guys."

A moment later, Dr. Throxmire entered the viewing room with the young scientists in tow. Enthusiastically, they spoke to Rachel, and she introduced them to Justin, who had regained his concentration. Hopefully, working with the fired-up recruits would keep him focused.

After a brief conversation, Throxmire left the lab.

Rachel directed Lemke and Seth to the stools on each side of her. They took the places indicated, and Justin sat beside Seth. Rachel turned toward the foggy monitor and gave a hand signal. It came alive with bright colors. Vi-Tech's logo materialized and multiplied as it drifted across the screen.

"That's a clever screensaver," Lemke said.

"This first part of this lesson may be a little boring," Rachel said, "but I always start the same way I did as a student lab instructor. Nothing else works for me. But don't worry—we'll get past the elementary stuff quickly and move into something more challenging."

She signaled again, and the monitor divided into multiple cubes resembling tropical fish tanks. "As you know," she said, "viruses are not really cells, though many people call them cells. Instead, a virus particle is known as a *virion* and consists of a set of genes bundled in a protective shell called a *capsid*." Rachel knew the trainees had heard the virion definition numerous times, but she liked to start with the basics.

At another hand signal from Rachel, 3D images of virus cultures appeared in the two cubes directly in front of her. "Cube No. 1 contains the Pheonix-75 variant that began attacking grain crops last year," she said. "Cube No. 2 contains one of the chimeras Justin and I produced recently for NIAID. First, I want to show you what can be learned from a visual examination. After that, we'll look at some RNA fingerprints and other more complicated analyses."

As Justin and the trainees watched, Rachel manipulated the camera and selected a single virion in the first cube. Next, she increased the magnification and positioned the pointer on one of the protein spikes, moving it stepwise and naming each component as the pointer passed over it: "Spike glycoprotein, lipid membrane, E protein, M protein, RNA." Again, her approach was semi-OCD, but she didn't care. Over the years, it had proved to be effective.

Rachel selected a virion from the second cube to set up a *before and after* comparison. At her signal, the computer synchronized the images. At first glance, they seemed identical, yet one was the original Phoenix-75, and the other was its offspring, a chimera.

"Ignore the spikes," Rachel said. "The chimera has only 65. Look at the RNA and tell me what you see."

Lemke and Seth studied the images intently.

Rachel increased the magnification slightly. "Do you see anything different?"

"I see something!" Lemke said, excitement showing in his voice. "The uncoiled RNA in the chimera appears slightly shorter than the original."

"Bingo!" Justin chimed in. "We subtracted a few amino acids."

"I see it now," Seth said. "It's fairly obvious at this magnification."

"You're seeing the finished product in Cube No. 2," Rachel said. "My goal is to teach you how to examine a virus and figure out how to produce a chimera with a different number of spikes and stabilized RNA."

"That's what we came here to learn, Teacher," Seth said with a smile. "We're in your hands."

"How long do you think it will take us to master this process?" Lemke asked.

"Maybe as much as a year," Rachel said.

Both trainees' eyebrows shot up, but neither responded. Nevertheless, Rachel could tell they were expecting a much shorter stay in Houston.

The first week went by in a blur.

On Friday afternoon, she was shutting down the equipment when her iTab pinged, and Vi-Tech's icon appeared. She touched the spiked virus, and the words *TD's Office* appeared.

"Rachel," a voice said, "this is Janice. Dr. Throxmire would like for you to stop by his office this afternoon before you leave."

"I'll be right there," Rachel said, surprised by Dr. Woody's late Friday summons. He'd dropped by the lab several times during the week and had sung the praises of her teaching methods, so that couldn't be what he wanted to discuss. On the other hand, maybe he wanted to speed up the training. If so, she saw no reason not to. Both Lemke and Seth had exceeded Rachel's expectations the first week of their training.

After telling Justin to finish shutting down the equipment, she took the elevator to the tenth floor and entered the outer office of the Technical Director's suite. With a slight hand motion, Janice said, "Go on in."

At Dr. Throxmire's instructions, Rachel sat down in a chair across from him.

"How are the trainees doing?" Throxmire asked, leaning toward Rachel in an easy-going manner.

"They're both fast learners—some of the best I've ever taught."

"Good. Dr. Allende thought they would be."

Throxmire's demeanor changed slightly, and he continued, "Now, so you can concentrate more on training them, I'm going to transfer Justin to another lab."

Mentally, Rachel kicked herself for not seeing the move coming. Justin and the trainees had gotten in each other's way repeatedly during the week, so the transfer made sense. Even so, she was determined to see that Justin was treated fairly.

"Which lab will he be going to?" she asked.

"Cardiac tissue," Throxmire said. "Currently, they're short-handed."

"I'd like to have him back as my assistant when this short course is over," Rachel said, feeling she'd accumulated sufficient STEM capital at Vi-Tech to make the request.

"I don't have any problem with that," Throxmire said, standing.

As Rachel stood, Throxmire said, "How is Dr. Segura doing?"

"He's doing great. Thank you for asking."

"I'll run by to see him later this week. We've had some interesting conversations over the years."

Rachel started down the hall, thinking about the sudden turn of events at Vi-Tech. One thing stood out—Dr. Woody was more personable than Dr. Truman, making him easy to work with. Still, it was apparent that he intended to press her gently until the training course was complete. The reason was obvious—Dr. Allende was pressing him, probably not so gently.

This raised a question—*What did Allende have lined up for Seth and Lemke after they completed the training?*

CHAPTER 22

Izzy sat up in bed and adjusted the pillows to support her back. She signaled the wall-mounted TV, which came on as *Wheel of Fortune* began. The game show was the longest-running program in TV history and was still popular. Though Izzy loved it, she seldom had a chance to watch it live. However, she would do so today since she was staying home with a slight fever. iDoctor had diagnosed Izzy's problem as RSV, a mild upper respiratory infection, rather than Phoenix-75 as initially feared. The fever had already subsided, but it was too late to go to school. That made her plan for the day simple—stay in bed a while, watch TV, and spend some quality time with Zina.

As the music played loudly and multi-colored lights simulated a gigantic spinning wheel, the smartly-dressed host and hostess walked onstage and greeted the audience. Amid polite applause, three contestants took their places behind the curved desk in front of the wheel. The slim blonde hostess took her position beside the game board and waited while her cohort conducted a brief interview with each guest.

When the preliminaries were over, the host said, "We'll start with a toss-up for one thousand dollars. The category is *Around the condo.*"

With buzzers in hand, the contestants waited in anticipation as blank spaces appeared, forming two words with a dash between them.

"Robo-vacuum!" Izzy said before a letter appeared.

A soft knock sounded at the door, and Zina appeared carrying a tray. "I heard the TV, so I knew you were awake. How are you feeling?"

"I feel fine, but I'm going to stay in bed a while longer."

"I brought you some chicken noodle soup and a glass of orange juice," Zina said, placing the tray on the bedside table.

"Thanks, Zina," Izzy said, picking up the steaming bowl. "Pull up a chair and watch *Wheel* with me like you used to when I was little."

As Zina sat down, one of the contestants thumbed his buzzer and said, "Robo-vacuum."

"Right for one thousand dollars," the host said.

Izzy pointed toward the TV. "I beat you, dude!"

She turned toward her grandmother, who was looking at her instead of the TV. It was obvious she was thinking about something other than the game show. As they looked at each other, Izzy sensed that Zina wanted to talk about something important. She decided to pursue the issue while the vibes were positive.

Taking her grandmother's hand, Izzy said, "Is there something you want to talk about?"

"Yes there is, my dear–something you've wondered about for a long time. Before she left for work this morning, Frieda and I had a long talk and decided to tell you and Marisa everything we know about your father."

Izzy's heart leaped. "That's fantastic! When are you going to do it?"

"After discussing the pros and cons, we decided to do it today if Marisa has time to talk a few minutes. Would you contact her and see what her schedule is?"

"What about Mom?"

"She said she's available any time today. So, if Marisa is free, we'll link up with Frieda."

"I'll FaceTime her right now." Throwing the covers aside, Izzy swung her feet to the floor and picked up her iTab.

Marisa answered at the first ringtone. "Hey, Iz. Why are you still in your PJs?"

"I was feeling droopy this morning, but I'm okay now. Do you have time to talk?"

"I have a conference call in fifteen minutes, but I can talk until it starts."

Izzy rotated her tablet to show Zina on the screen. "Look who's here. She and Mom are going to tell us about Raymundo."

Marisa echoed Izzy's exclamation, "That's fantastic!"

"I'll get Mom linked up," Izzy said, thumbing her iTab.

Seconds later, Frieda's picture appeared, and Izzy said, "We're all here. Who's going to take the floor?"

"Go ahead, Mom," Frieda said. "This is still difficult for me to talk about."

"Okay, I'll tell the story," Zina said, "and you can join the discussion at the end."

No one proffered a comment, and Zina continued, "As you know, Raymundo was an adventurer and fortune seeker. Two of his cousins were the same way. We called them *The Three Musketeers*. The three men were constantly on the lookout for secret maps revealing the location of lost cities of gold, emerald or diamond mines, and buried treasure chests. They searched the jungles numerous times without success, but Raymundo always expected to hit pay dirt on his next attempt. Sadly, he never did.

"His final adventure occurred shortly after Izzy was born. Raymundo and his cousins found a hand-drawn map claiming to show the location of an emerald mine on a tributary of the Amazon. As always, they believed the map was genuine. After hastily assembling their jungle survival equipment, they left Rio and went to the river. Once there, they rented a small boat and traveled upstream for days. When they reached shallow water, they tied up the boat and continued their quest on foot.

"The map was a hoax. Instead of showing the location of an emerald mine, it led them to a headhunter village deep in the rainforest. Raymundo and his cousins were never seen again. Based on information obtained from other villages along the river, the three men were officially declared dead . . ."

Zina trailed off, and Izzy asked, "Where did they get the map?"

"At a flea market in Rio," Frieda said.

"*A flea market?*" Izzy exclaimed.

"Yes, and that should have been a red flag," Frieda said.

Mentally connecting the dots, Izzy said, "Somebody must have planted the map to set them up."

Frieda nodded. "We're sure that's the case."

"Did the government investigate their deaths?" Marisa asked.

"They did a brief investigation and sealed the file," Frieda said. "Several times, we asked them to reopen it, but they refused."

Izzy's eyebrows shot up. "Maybe someone in the government was involved."

"That's what we think," Frieda said.

Izzy pondered a moment and said, "Marisa, you're a NatGov official. Could you get the case reopened?"

"I doubt it."

"We shouldn't involve Marisa," Zina said. "It might cause problems for her."

"Is there anything we can do?" Izzy asked.

Zina shook her head. "In this case, I think it's best to let sleeping dogs lie."

Knowing there was nothing to be gained by continuing the discussion, Izzy made an effort to accept her grandmother's injunction. She was sure Zina had related all the facts about Raymundo, while keeping a rein on her suspicions. The unprovable allegation about government involvement was a subject for another day.

"Thanks for telling us about our father," Marisa said. "We'll rehash it the next time I come to Houston."

"You and Izzy needed to know about Raymundo," Frieda said as a teardrop trickled down her cheek. "But we didn't feel comfortable telling you the gory details when you were small children, so we kept putting it off. We waited much longer than we should have."

Izzy wrinkled her brow thoughtfully while processing the information about her father. The story closely paralleled one of the possibilities she and Marisa had discussed many times. She filed it away for a later review and decided to ask Zina the other long-standing ancestry question.

She squeezed Zina's hand. "Now that we know what happened to our father, please tell us about our grandfather?"

Zina shook her head. "I'm not at liberty to tell you at this time. As you know, I've not told Frieda the whole story."

"Marisa and I want to know more about him," Izzy said, "and so does Mom."

"I can't tell you until the time is right," Zina said with an air of finality.

Izzy sighed but didn't reply. She and Zina had reached this impasse several times before.

"I have to go," Marisa said as her picture faded away.

"I'll sign off too," Frieda said.

The call ended, and Zina patted Izzy's hand. "Let's watch the rest of *Wheel of Fortune* and see if we can solve the last puzzle before the contestants do."

With ancestry discussions verboten but not out of mind, Izzy looked toward the TV, albeit somewhat reluctantly.

The host said, "The category for the final puzzle is *A period of time.*"

With buzzers clenched in tight fingers, the contestants waited for words to materialize on the game board. Izzy stared at the screen as blank spaces appeared and formed two words, the first consisting of a single letter. After a few seconds, the letter *"M"* appeared at the beginning of the second word.

"A millennium!" Izzy said.

CHAPTER 23

Three years passed after Reuben Rogov's inauguration.
Many things changed during that time, but Houston's erratic mid-winter weather was not one of them. It had rained all morning, and the rain was turning into sleet. A razor-thin sheet of ice glazed the sidewalks, and most George Washington residents who didn't have to leave the unit were staying put. Darien and Alden were playing pool in the rec room, which was half full of people trying to find something interesting to do.

"Eight ball in the corner pocket for the win," Alden said, pointing with his cue stick.

"Not a chance," Darien said. "You can't get past the fifteen ball."

"I can if I put enough English on it," Alden said. Then, taking careful aim, he banked the cue ball off the rail. Spinning like a top, it glanced off the fifteen and ricocheted into the side pocket.

"You scratched!" Darien said, pumping his fist in the air. "That's three in a row for me."

In mock anger, Alden raised his cue stick over his head with both hands and brought it across his knee, pretending to break it. "I'm tired of shooting pool," he said. "How about a computer game?"

"Do you mean *Global Cooling on Mercury*?"

"What else?"

"Hey, pool sharks, what's going on?" a voice called. They turned to see Izzy approaching.

"We're just killing time," Alden said, "like everybody else in the room."

"This is a special day," Izzy said.

"What's special about it?" Alden asked.

"It's Reuben Rogov's third anniversary as President," Izzy said. "Marisa sent a text to remind me this morning." She looked toward Darien. "I'm sure she reminded you as well."

"Yes, several times," he said, nodding. "She also told me that Mr. Rogov plans to make an important announcement today." Marisa hadn't given him any hints about what Mr. Rogov would address, but he was virtually sure he knew. Undoubtedly, it would relate to one of the problems highlighted at his inauguration. Since that day, Darien had tracked and analyzed the President's actions like a game of *Clue*, and he'd discovered enough clues to have a good idea what was coming next.

During Mr. Rogov's first three years in office, he addressed six of the seven critical problems highlighted during his inaugural speech. All six were successful. His opponents—the handful that still existed—had difficulty finding fault with his approach to governance. Even Papa admitted the charismatic President was doing a good job. Some religious organizations believed God sent Reuben Rogov to right the wrongs of the world. Moreover, due to his unprecedented chain of successes, the concept was gaining traction. No one could deny that the President had worked miracles, not even the Seguras.

"How about a three-way game of pool?" Izzy said, interrupting Darien's political introspection.

"You and Alden go ahead and play," Darien said. "I'm going to get a Coke and some cheese crackers. Then, I'll take on the winner." He walked away, and Izzy began to rack up the balls.

On his way to the vending machines, Darien resumed his review of the President's inaugural *to-do* list.

Operation Breadbasket had alleviated Vi-Tech's problem and solved the first two problems on the inauguration-day list, the looming danger of food shortages and Phoenix-75's resurgence in China. By the end of Mr. Rogov's first year in office, the stubborn virus had faded into the background as the world's foremost problem, allowing the President to move to other issues.

A second Presidential initiative solved the next two problems on the list—the Israeli-Arab tension and Egypt's sword-rattling. Rogov, while acting as Secretary General of the United Nations and President of the United States, established a fund to start a massive hydroponics project in the Sinai Desert. Under his leadership, Israel, Jordan, Saudi Arabia, and Egypt signed a peace treaty and collectively agreed to operate the newly-created *Sinai Farm Coop*. The agreement occurred at the beginning of Mr. Rogov's second year in office, and the coop anticipated becoming Europe's primary supplier of bananas and citrus fruits within a few years.

Midway through Mr. Rogov's second year in office, he ordered the U.S. military to stop flying drones over Syrian air-space and demanded that Russia withdraw their drones as well. Due to the President's political clout—now acknowledged world-wide—Russia followed suit immediately and joined the United States in declaring Syria to be an independent nation. Thus, the 66th President solved the fifth problem on his inauguration-day list.

Immediately after his Syrian success, Mr. Rogov warned Iraq and Iran that their constant border skirmishes would no longer be tolerated. Though he didn't mention what punitive actions he might bring against them if they ignored his warning, leaders in both countries knew the eloquent potentate had enough backing to do anything he wanted. Consequently, they pulled their troops back, and the United Nations established a neutral zone along the border. With that action, Rogov solved the sixth problem on the list, and the Mideast was completely at peace for the first time in recorded history.

Today, only one of the seven original problems remained—the Mexican refugee crisis at the southern border. Darien was confident this problem would be the subject of Mr. Rogov's upcoming announcement.

The mystery was, what was he going to do about it?

A few minutes later, Darien returned to the pool table. But, before he could determine who was winning, his iTab vibrated, and a piercing ringtone sounded over the housing unit's PA system.

"Attention, please," a computerized voice said. "Stand by for a message from President Rogov. Attention, please stand by."

Everyone in the rec room looked toward the front of the room, where the monitor was coming to life.

Three circles of light—red, white, and blue—appeared on the screen and exploded into a shifting kaleidoscopic pattern. As the national anthem, *America the Beautiful,* played in the background, the fragments of light morphed into a live view of the American flag hanging on the rear wall of the Oval Office. The flag was surrounded by a gallery of sixty-six presidential portraits—from George Washington to Reuben Rogov. The latter was seated at a large mahogany desk with the pictures at his back.

President Rogov was wearing the traditional blue suit and red tie. Though diminutive in stature, the whole world listened when he spoke, including the RADS and Independents, who hadn't done so during the presidential campaign. The camera zoomed in on the President, who—as usual—was about to speak without notes.

With a faint smile, he looked into the camera and began, "Good evening, fellow Americans and other citizens of the world. Thank you for tuning in. I called this news conference to update you on a problem that Mr. Profeto and I have been working on since our inauguration, the refugees gathering at our southern border.

"The southern border issue has been mishandled repeatedly by former Presidents. Walls were built by one President and torn down by the next. The National Guard has been deployed and withdrawn multiple times. Some Presidents claimed the border was secure and simply ignored the problem. Even vigilantes have attempted to control the border from time to time. But, to date, no measure has been successful.

"It's easy to understand why poverty-stricken Mexicans and other Central Americans are seeking a better life in the United States. However, when they gather at the border, they provide cover for human traffickers, drug runners, foreign terrorists, and other criminals who are entering the country under the guise of asylum-seekers.

"The border situation is not solely the concern of the United States and Mexico. All of Central America is involved. Immigrants from all eight C.A. countries have crossed the border illegally for years. Therefore, acting in my dual capacities as Secretary General of The United Nations and President of the United States, I formed a special UN committee to analyze the problem and propose a solution. This committee, which I chaired, has been meeting for two years. We have worked diligently with the leaders of the countries involved. In addition, I met privately with all of the Presidents to assure them they will have my unwavering support throughout this transition and beyond. The process was complex and time-consuming, but we have completed it. The course of action we are instituting today will promote peace and equality throughout Central America, thereby alleviating the border problem. Indeed, it will change the world forever.

"Today, January 20, 2152, it is my pleasure to announce the formation of the *Federation of Central America.*"

Rogov paused and smiled. A roar of affirmation reverberated in the rec room.

A few seconds later, he held up a hand for silence and continued, "In alphabetical order, the newly-created Federation consists of Belize, Costa Rica, El Salvador, Guatemala, Honduras, Mexico, Nicaragua, and Panama. Each of these nations will be equivalent to a state in the U.S. Currently, they are drawing up a constitution similar to ours, and the national capital will be the city of Belmopan in Belize. This new nation will mirror the United States in many ways.

"These eight countries have abundant natural resources and a population willing to work. Under a unified banner, these new nation-states can provide better opportunities for their citizens, so they will no longer have to leave their countries to find a meaningful life. To jump-start a much-needed industrial revolution in the new Federation, I have commissioned forty U.S. corporations to form partnerships with C.A. businesses.

Since the United States and Mexico are closest to the problem, the Mexican President, Alfredo Garcia, and I have created twelve sister cities. Each U.S. city will work with its counterpart in Mexico to promote cultural and commercial exchange. Other details are being worked out.

"As many of you will recall, on inauguration day, I promised to solve the seven highlighted problems within three and a half years, and I have done so. Therefore, I am announcing my intention to run for a second term."

A round of cheers followed Rogov's last sentence, and shouts of "Long live Reuben Rogov" sounded throughout the rec room.

With a slight hand motion, the President quieted the exuberant crowd and continued, "Thank you for your support. It is my pleasure to serve America and the world. I look forward to continuing as your leader. We have accomplished much. Yet, even with our successes, the work is not finished. We must address other critical problems.

"Currently, the greatest threat to peace and equality is the underground junta, Los Ignotos. We have information that this cabal is about to launch terrorist attacks in several countries. Consequently, I am authorizing NatGov to root them out by any means. This effort will involve everyone and will cause difficulties in some instances, but it must be done. Please give me your cooperation as we move forward."

Rogov paused briefly before closing with his usual benediction, "Thank you for listening. God bless you, God bless America, and God bless the world."

The screen faded to black, and Darien mulled over the situation. As Mr. Rogov promised on his first day in office, he conquered the virus, brought peace to the Mideast, stared down Russia, and created a new country. No former President had done a tenth as much.

Yet, for some inexplicable reason, Darien felt that Rogov had used up his allotment of favorable outcomes.

If so, what would he do next?

CHAPTER 24

Darien swung his feet to the floor and sat on the edge of the bed. He was keenly aware that he'd been lollygagging too much lately and needed to do something to jump-start his creativity—maybe even change his writing schedule. In the past, he'd always produced his best work after 8:00 p.m. However, that wasn't happening at the moment. His creative muse had gone AWOL and hadn't reported for duty in two weeks. As a result, he'd produced less than a thousand words during that time. At such a snail's pace, it would take over three years to finish *The Telekinetic Dolphins*, his novel currently in progress. That was far too long.

In addition to his faltering productivity, his first novel, *The Photosynthesis Gene*, hadn't climbed the charts as he'd hoped. It was earning about three hundred dollars per month, hardly enough for him to request a condo upgrade from HUD. To make ends meet, he was still grading papers for an English professor at the University of Houston. What a tedious job. Darien had detected so many comma blunders, split infinitives, and run-on sentences that he was seeing them in his sleep. Though the part-time job kept his syntax sharp, he'd quit in a heartbeat if he could afford to.

Still seated on the bed, he looked toward the kitchenette and instructed the coffeemaker to make a large espresso. The machine beeped shrilly and said, "The coffee bin is empty."

Muttering under his breath, Darien put on his house shoes and went into the kitchenette. He opened the refrigerator and peered inside. The shelves contained a collection of well-aged jars–ketchup, mayonnaise, and mustard, along with an assortment of pickles and a jar of olives stuffed with almonds. Rummaging among the collection of nearly-empty jars, he discovered a sample packet of coffee, a new flavor recently debuted by Amazon-Kroger. Pleased at his find, he dumped the packet into the coffee maker and pushed the *Start* button. The inviting aroma of freshly-brewed coffee filled the room as the machine gurgled and produced a cup of dark steaming liquid. He picked up the cup and sat down at his tiny dinette table.

As Darien took his first sip, his iTab pinged and flashed an icon, a Brazilian flag with *Marisa* written across it–a FaceTime call. Their long-distance communication system had evolved into daily texts and FaceTime conversations. Marisa's work brought her to Houston regularly, but he longed for the day she would move back permanently. Still, since she now referred to Washington as *home*, he wasn't anticipating that it would happen soon.

He touched the icon, and Marisa's picture materialized onscreen. She was wearing a blue-gray suit resembling a military uniform. "Hello, Darien," she said, flashing a winsome smile. "How are things in Houston?"

"All is well but would be better if you were here."

"I can't come for several weeks. I'm too busy."

"What are you working on?"

"It's a new project," Marisa said. "I'm training Equality Team members, and I need your help."

"I'm still not interested in moving to Washington."

"I'm not trying to recruit you to come here," Marisa said, her voice taking on a business-like tone. "Two of my trainees have been assigned to the Mediplex area. They will be working on an Equality Survey, and I want them to start by interviewing people I know rather than strangers. Would you do me a favor and talk to them?"

Darien's caution shield slipped into place. "What's an Equality Survey?"

"We're looking for inequality in every area of life," Marisa said. "President Rogov abhors it and has vowed to root it out. He ordered this official survey to gather some preliminary information. It will cover a wide range of topics."

"Could you be more specific?"

"About what?"

"The range of topics."

"I know what you're thinking," Marisa said. "Yes, a few questions will be about books and other forms of the written word."

"Am I being singled out because I'm a writer?"

"Of course not," Marisa said, "but, as a writer, your opinion carries extra weight."

"What does Rogov intend to do with the book data after it's collected?"

"For one thing, he'll use it to help the Education Department make better textbook selections."

"What about books in general circulation?"

"He may address the problem of discriminatory books."

"That sounds like censorship to me."

"Mr. Rogov's main concern is equality. Any book that degrades others doesn't promote equality."

Darien's heart sank. He could never accept anything resembling censorship, but it seemed that whatever Reuben Rogov proposed, Marisa—and countless others—supported it. She was an avid politico, totally in tune with the President—a true Rogo-vite. As a result, politics had become his rival for her affection. Still, Marisa was doing her job, and he didn't want to overreact.

"Is inequality all they're concerned about?" he asked, push-ing aside his censorship questions.

"No, there's something else," Marisa said. "While in Hous-ton, they'll also be looking for activity by Los Ignotos."

Darien's eyebrows shot up. "*Los Ignotos?*"

"We believe there's a cell operating in the Mediplex area. You might be of help in locating it."

Stunned, Darien realized he was in a dilemma. He would have been glad to help locate a Los Ignotos cell if it didn't involve having a tête-à-tête with NatGov agents. Even so, he had to be careful not to appear anti-government. Or, even worse, sympathetic to Los Ignotos.

"So . . ." Marisa said. "Will you help me?"

"What happens if I say *no?*"

"You can say no to me," Marisa said. "But, if you do, someone you don't know will assign strangers to interview you. There's no reason to proceed in that manner. What I'm suggest-ing would be much easier for both of us."

Though Darien had nothing to hide, he hated being inter-rogated by strangers, even if they were part of Marisa's team. Still, what she wanted to do was better than the alternative.

"Okay," he said, shrugging in resignation, "send me a link to their calendar, and I'll pick a date and time for us to talk."

"We're not going to run the survey via the internet," Marisa said. "They'll come to your condo and interview you in person."

"This is the twenty-second century," Darien said, not trying to hide his frustration. "What's wrong with doing it electron-ically?"

"Recently, we evaluated several methods of running this survey," Marisa said. "Person-to-person is old school, but it worked best, so we're returning to it."

"I feel like a fly caught in a spider's web."

"*Darien!*"

"Well . . . I do."

"Don't worry. I'll tell the trainees about our relationship."

"That won't keep the survey from being official, will it?"

"No," Marisa said, "but let me emphasize an important fact—the surveyors are merely gathering information. That's all they're authorized to do."

With trepidation, Darien agreed on a time and date for the interview. As he feared, the political scene was changing rapidly, so having a rising star like Marisa in Washington might be a good thing. Still, their relationship had moved into uncharted waters.

A few minutes later, amid considerable angst, they expressed their love for each other and ended the call.

***

The following Wednesday, Darien's doorbell rang at 10:00 a.m., the time scheduled for the Equality Survey. He opened the door, and an early-twenties couple waited with iTabs in hand. Both had blond hair and blue eyes, and wore blue-gray suits *(uniforms?)* identical to the outfit worn by Marisa the previous week. Other than their attire, the young couple looked like typical George Washington residents.

"Mr. Darien Segura?" the man asked politely.

Darien's answer was minimalistic. "Yes."

The couple extended their iTabs toward Darien to show him their photo IDs. Even though he fully expected everything to be in order, he studied the documents carefully. To his surprise, the interviewers had the same last name, Hatfield. Their first names were Hannah and Haldon. Multiple questions popped into Darien's mind.

"We're twins," Hannah said, answering one of Darien's unspoken questions. "We know you are as well. That's one reason Miss Da Rosa selected us to interview you."

"May we come in?" Haldon asked.

Darien stepped to one side and motioned for the couple to enter. His mind was in a whirl. He knew Marisa had sent the well-mannered twins in an effort to make him feel comfortable during the interview. Even so, it was an official government action he disdained, and he resolved to keep up his guard during the process.

"Thank you," Hannah said as they stepped inside.

Darien led the duo to his office area. At his invitation, they seated themselves on the loveseat, and he sat down in his office chair. He swiveled toward the young couple, wondering what their opening salvo would be. Darien would have found the situation amusing if not for being in the crosshairs. The rookies before him seemed too young and polite to be NatGov agents. Despite Marisa's assurances, he'd pictured burly stormtroopers in black uniforms.

"Miss Da Rosa told us you're good friends," Hannah said.

"We are," Darien said, sticking with his plan to give brief answers to avoid inadvertently putting his foot in his mouth while the young zealots schmoozed him with small talk. If they wanted real information, they'd have to ask real questions. He wasn't about to volunteer anything.

"First, let's talk about your writing," Haldon said, still operating in *I'm-your-friend* mode.

"Which writing?" Darien said. "My published novel or the one I'm working on now?"

"The published one—*The Photosynthesis Gene*," Hannah said.

"What about it?"

"It contains discriminatory phrases," Hannah said.

"What phrases?"

"The ones you borrowed from another science fiction writer," Haldon said.

"Are you looking for a violation of copyright or equality laws?" Darien said with a touch of sarcasm in his voice.

"Only equality laws," Hannah said evenly.

"Specifically, you used the term *Cog* to refer to government officials and *Pure Saps*—or *Pursaps*—to refer to regular citizens," Haldon said.

"So?" Darien said, his voice rising. "Those terms are from a novel entitled *The Zap Gun*. It hasn't been banned by anybody as far as I know."

"I noticed that novel in your bookcase next to *Fahrenheit 451*," Haldon said, pointing toward it. "It's unusual to keep paperbacks in this age of e-books."

"Paperbacks are my hobby."

"Would you consider editing a few offensive phrases out of your novel and reissuing it?" Hannah asked.

"No," Darien said sharply. "Not unless I'm forced to."

"We don't have the authority to force you to do anything," Hanna said. "We're just gathering information."

"Still, this is something to keep in mind while working on *The Telepathic Dolphins*," Haldon said.

"It's *telekinetic,* not *telepathic*," Darien said, shocked that they knew anything about his work in progress.

"My mistake," Haldon said.

The conversation lulled briefly, and Darien tried to assimilate what was happening. Something he didn't understand was going on behind the scenes. He hadn't sold enough copies of *The Photosynthesis Gene* to cause much trouble, even if everyone who read it marched on Washington. It appeared NatGov was on the verge of restricting the use of certain words. The idea had been around for years and was gaining support. Recently, he'd read a *ConspiraciesRevealed* article discussing that method of censorship. The article was based on a quote by Philip K. Dick, *If you can control the meaning of words, you can control the people who must use the words.* Apparently, The idea had worked its way into the Equality Team's playbook.

"We're just trying to give you a heads up that might be helpful in the future," Hannah said.

"Let's move on to something else," Haldon said, "Los Ignotos."

When Darien offered no response, Hannah asked, "Have you noticed any subversive activity in and around this housing unit?"

"What kind of subversive activity are you talking about?"

"We've heard that a band of outsiders–non-residents–are trying to enlist residents to join a secret organization," Hannah said, "and we believe the organization is Los Ignotos."

"That's ridiculous," Darien snapped.

"President Rogov doesn't think so," Hannah said evenly.

"How would he know?" Darien said. "He doesn't live here."

"We're just trying to do our job," Haldon said, remaining calm and collected. "Marisa said you would help us."

"I haven't noticed any anti-American activity," Darien said, "if that's what you're asking."

"Maybe it never occurred to you to look for it," Hannah said.

"Some residents in this housing unit aren't members of any approved political party," Haldon said. "Unaffiliated people would be more likely to support Los Ignotos."

Knowing where the conversation was headed, Darien remained silent.

"For example, your friend—Justin Thibideaux," Hanna said. "What do you know about his political persuasion?"

"He's apolitical—never votes."

"That in itself is suspicious," Hanna said. "NatGov is not concerned with RADS, Independents, Socialists, Communists, or other duly-registered citizens. They all belong to official political parties. Those who don't support any party are the ones we're interested in. Such people might be supporting an illegal organization like Los Ignotos."

"That seems like quite a reach."

"You and Mr. Thibideaux have known each other a long time, haven't you?" Haldon said.

"Many years," Darien said. "Of all the people I know, he's the least likely to attempt to overthrow the government."

"That may be," Hannah said. "Still, unregistered citizens would be prime targets for Los Ignotos, so they need to be watched. One purpose for this visit is to find people we can trust to report any anti-American activity they observe."

"I know the CIA hotline number, 666-123-4567."

"Would you call it if there was a cause to do so?" Haldon asked.

Darien shook his head. "Don't expect me to spy on my friends. Furthermore, I've said all I intend to say, so I'm requesting you to leave now."

The twins glanced at each other and, to his surprise, stood in unison. "Thank you for your help, Mr. Segura," Hannah said as they started toward the door. Darien followed them and watched as they walked briskly down the hallway. Although the well-dressed twins epitomized etiquette and politeness, he suspected their appearance was a façade.

The thought, *Youth League,* popped into his mind.

CHAPTER 25

On Monday morning, Rachel entered the Starbucks adjoining Vi-Tech's lobby and picked her way through the crowd of early arrivals, many of whom were tapping at their iTabs while eating breakfast snacks. As was often the case in Mediplex coffee shops, most people in the room wore scrubs, lab coats, smocks, or other nondescript laboratory and hospital clothing. However, Rachel wore a yellow headband matching her iTab case. She didn't feel fully dressed without a splash of color, a characteristic shared by previous Rachels in the Segura family, according to Papa.

Rachel was now *Dr. Segura,* having earned her Ph.D. a year ago. Immediately after obtaining the degree, Dr. Throxmire promoted her to Assistant Technical Director over several coworkers with doctorates they'd held for several years. Since she was already Vi-Tech's *go-to* virologist, her fellow scientists readily accepted Rachel as one of their leaders. It probably also helped that they knew about the extraordinary accomplishments of her ancestors. Maybe they expected her to do something spectacular in the future and wanted to be on her team when she did. Whatever their reasons, they supported her, which was gratifying.

According to the company's organizational chart, Rachel was second in command. However, Dr. Woody was spending so much time in Washington that she was the de facto CEO/Technical Director. Her first year in the position had gone smoothly. Fortunately, she hadn't experienced any personnel problems, the main issue that often puts new leaders face-to-face with *The Peter Principle*. To some degree, though, the principal was currently being tested. She was in the process of making changes and trying to do it without ruffling feathers. The awkward situation involved Justin and Izzy. She'd already told Justin what she was planning to do. Today, she would tell Izzy.

The dilemma had evolved in an unusual manner. Six months ago, Izzy interned with Vi-Tech. While working on modifications of Phoenix-75, she proved to be a quick study, and Dr. Woody offered her a job upon finishing college. She had just graduated, so Rachel was putting the plan into effect.

Today would be Izzy's first day as a full-time Vi-Tech employee, and Rachel was going to give her an important assignment immediately.

Since she and Izzy were friends, Rachel thought an informal approach would be a good way to start. Consequently, she invited Izzy to share coffee and pastries before work. Though she felt that Dr. Woody trusted her completely, Rachel understood that her specialty was virology, not Human Resources; therefore, she was feeling her way along carefully.

Izzy was waiting for her beneath the *Place Order Here* sign. They hugged briefly and stepped to the counter.

The smiling twenty-something barista said, "Good morning, ladies. What would you like?"

Both Rachel and Izzy ordered tall lattes and scones. Minutes later, they picked up their orders and went to a small table in the corner of the room.

Once seated, Rachel said, "Welcome to Vi-Tech, Izzy. I'm going to assign you an important project immediately."

"The new Phoenix variant?"

"Yes. Last week, we received a large order from NAIAD, and they want us to produce a whole slate of chimeras."

"I assume you're going to lead the project."

"No, *you* are."

Izzy's eyebrows shot up. *"Me?"*

"Yes, you," Rachel said evenly. "Currently, I've got too many irons in the fire."

"What about Justin?"

"He'll be your assistant. I've already told him so."

"You're the boss," Izzy said, "but Justin has worked here so long that I would have expected it to be the other way around."

"This arrangement has nothing to do with time on the job," Rachel said. She didn't intend to explain that she was making Izzy the team leader because Justin wasn't the right choice to manage the project. Though he had the technical skills to do nearly anything, he didn't have the creativity required to lead a lab team. The deficiency surfaced when Rachel was training Dr. Allende's dynamic duo, Lemke Grover and Seth Elam. Even while puttering around like children, the Georgetown grads demonstrated tremendous originality. Now, they were back in Washington working on *who-knows-what* for Dr. Allende.

"Have you explained this arrangement to Justin?" Izzy said.

"Yes, and he's comfortable with it."

"Then, so am I," Izzy said with a nod.

"Good. Let's drink our coffee before it gets cold."

***

A week later, a new variant of Phoenix-75 struck the Houston area. The variant, *Kappa*, wasn't as deadly as its predecessors but was more contagious, especially among the elderly. Upon

Dr. Allende's recommendation, President Rogov issued another mask mandate and promised quick action to develop an updated booster. In addition, hospitals and senior living facilities began to institute stricter visitation rules. Most people had lost count of the times this had happened over the last few years.

Izzy, seated at her lab desk, thumbed her iTab. Nearby, Justin was preparing slides of the chimeras, the first batch created under her supervision. She'd instructed him to let her know when the slides were ready to examine. If the chimeras met NIAID's requirements, they would send them to Washington today. While waiting for Justin's signal, she pored over the Houston news websites, trying to detect a pattern in the virus uptick.

Immediately, an oddity jumped out. The number of new cases in Houston proper was reasonably stable, but cases in nearby communities had exploded over the weekend. To her surprise, Izzy knew every city and town mentioned in the Phoenix-75 update–Alvin, Manvel, Arcola, Missouri City, and Sugar Land. She and Alden had traveled through all of them with Marisa and Darien while they were working on the day trip guide for the Brazilian Consulate.

As she studied the list, she realized that every location suffering from a Phoenix uptick was along State Highway 6 south of the Houston city limits. Moreover, almost all new cases were in senior living facilities. Though not considering herself to be a *pandemic detective*, Izzy decided that she should contact Rachel immediately and let her know what she'd discovered.

Picking up her iTab, she typed, *I'd like to talk about today's Phoenix report when you get time.*

Seconds later, Rachel replied, *I'm down the hall. Be there in a sec.*

"Izzy, the slides are ready," Justin said.

"Go ahead and start the evaluation. Rachel is coming in a minute, and I need to talk to her before I look at them."

"I assume you want them classified as *satisfactory, questionable,* and *unsatisfactory?*"

"Yes. We'll reevaluate the questionable ones later."

Rachel entered the lab via a side door. After exchanging greetings with Izzy and Justin, she sat down on a stool near Izzy's desk and asked, "What's on your mind?"

In a single run-on sentence, Izzy recounted the Highway 6/Phoenix connection.

"I noticed that too," Rachel said, "and I have a theory regarding the virus surge in the facilities along that highway."

"What is it?"

"Dr. Eldon Fletcher and his staff must have been the carriers."

Izzy's eyes widened. "Really?"

"My guess is they accidentally spread the virus while making their rounds."

"How could that happen?"

"That's what we need to find out."

"Darien will say they did it on purpose."

"I know," Rachel said. "Anyway, I'm going to check into this mystery immediately."

"What do you intend to do?"

"I'm going to make a quick trip to Sugar Land and talk to Papa and his caregivers," Rachel said. "I'd like for you to come with me."

"Are you going to leave right now?"

"Yes."

"What about the chimeras we're working on?"

"Tell Justin to go as far as he can with them and wait until you get back." She glanced at the wall clock and added, "My brother should be awake now. He might like to join us."

While Izzy was giving Justin his instructions, Rachel called Darien. He answered on the first ring, accepted the invitation, and insisted on taking his car rather than a robo-cab.

Ten minutes later, Izzy and Rachel stepped onto the sidewalk as Darien's car arrived at the curb. After exchanging greetings, Izzy climbed into the cramped rear seat. Darien gave the autopilot the address for Amazon Senior Living No. 3 in Sugar Land, and they settled in for the twenty-minute ride.

"I've already got this mystery solved," Darien said before they reached the first traffic signal.

"We expected as much," Rachel said. "So, what's your theory."

"Dr. Fletcher deliberately infected residents in every senior living facility along Highway 6," Darien said emphatically. "Since he's their primary care doctor, it would be easy for him to do."

"Why would he do it?" Rachel asked.

"Because Ignacio Allende ordered him to."

"What would Allende gain by doing such a thing?"

"Control," Darien said. "Everything is about controlling the population."

Though difficult to do, Izzy decided to keep quiet. The Da Rosas and Seguras held a mixed bag of political beliefs. Rachel was an Independent, Marisa was a Rogovite, and Darien was somewhere between. She'd heard them argue for over three years without settling anything, and it was unlikely they ever would. Besides, she was beginning to wonder which side she was on.

Upon reaching the housing unit, the autopilot guided the car into a *Future Residents* slot. They got out and went inside. Izzy, who'd never been in a senior living facility, was surprised to see a dozen people standing around and a line forming at the reception desk. She and Darien stood on each side of Rachel as she got in the line.

Rachel reached the reception desk, and Olivia Torres–the long-time head nurse–smiled pleasantly and said, "Hello, Dr. Segura. It's good to see you again. I barely recognized you with that mask."

"Please continue calling me Rachel."

"I'll try," Olivia said. "Have you come to see Dr. Segura?"

"We want to see him, but we came primarily to investigate the latest Phoenix outbreak. Is there anything you can tell us that the morning news didn't report?"

Olivia's expression switched from outgoing to reserved, and she cast a furtive glance around the room. "Dr. Fletcher's staff has already completed an investigation," she said. "They plan to issue a statement later today."

"I assume they told you to say nothing until the report is released?" Rachel said, knowing Olivia would tell her everything if she got the chance.

Olivia nodded. "Yes, that's right."

"I understand," Rachel said. "Now, we'd like to see Papa."

"He's doing great," Olivia said, "but only one visitor at a time can go into his living quarters. And to do that, you'll have to wear the prescribed protection: smock, mask, gloves–the works."

Rachel turned to Darien. "Wait while I go in. Afterwards, you can go in if you want to."

"I'll wait in the car," Izzy said, turning to leave.

"I don't think I'll go in to see him today," Darien said. "I'll wait with Izzy."

"That's probably best," Rachel said. "It was a mistake to bring you here–I'm sorry." As Izzy and Darien left the building, she started toward the closet to get her protective gear.

Once in the car, Darien and Izzy drifted into a discussion about Marisa's commitment to politics. Neither could comprehend the *how and why* of Marisa's involvement; however, both realized she had become an active cog in the NatGov machinery. Due to his recent shift in direction, it was hard to guess what program Mr. Rogov would launch next. But, whatever it was, Marisa would likely have a part in it, and most Americans would support it. Clearly, the nation was still mesmerized by Reuben Rogov.

A few minutes later, Rachel returned to the car, and Izzy moved to the back seat.

Darien gave instructions to the autopilot and turned to Rachel, "Okay, let me guess," he said. "They told you Eldon Fletcher hasn't been anywhere near the housing unit during the last two weeks."

"Not exactly," Rachel said, suppressing a smile. "Last week, he visited every facility involved in the outbreak. A day later, he tested positive for Phoenix-75 and readily admitted to being the asymptomatic carrier. That will be the gist of the announcement later today."

Darien looked stunned, and Izzy asked, "How did you find out so much?"

"Olivia told me everything once we were out of earshot of the crowd in the lobby," Rachel said.

Izzy couldn't resist a friendly jibe. "Okay, Darien, where does that leave your theory?"

"It makes it better."

"No way!"

"Sure it does," Darien insisted. "What better way to spread the virus than to do it in plain sight and claim it was an accident."

Both women laughed, and Darien shrugged, apparently giving up for the time being.

"Olivia helped me take some samples," Rachel said. "I'm going to look at them as soon as we get back to the lab."

"What are you looking for?" Izzy said.

"I want to compare them to the NIAID samples we just received."

"I'll help you."

Upon arriving at the Mediplex, Darien dropped off his passengers in front of the Vi-Tech building as the quitting-time crowd poured onto the sidewalk. Izzy and Rachel exchanged hurried greetings with colleagues, but they brushed off all attempts to engage them in extended conversation. Instead of talking with cohorts, they wanted to find out ASAP if there was a connection between the samples from the senior living facility and the NIAID project.

They entered the lab, and Rachel handed Izzy three sample envelopes containing Q-tips. "Prepare slides from each of these while I program the equipment."

Izzy donned surgical gloves and took the samples to a germ-free hood made of transparent polycarbonate. Fifteen minutes later, after preparing a half-dozen slides and placing them in a viewing tray linked to the microscope, she signaled Rachel that everything was ready.

The two virologists left the sample preparation area and moved to the viewing area. They sat down before the monitor, and Rachel gave a hand signal. Images from their current NIAID project appeared on the left side of the screen. Then, at another hand flourish, the screen divided into two sections, and images of the senior living virus appeared on the right.

Transfixed, they stared at the screen.

"This is weird," Rachel said. "The housing unit samples bear little resemblance to the last virus NIAID sent us. I expected them to be identical or, at least, very similar."

"Could any of the chimeras we're producing be used to make a booster against the *kappa* variant?"

"I doubt it," Rachel said. "They're completely different."

In deep thought, the two women stared at the screen. Izzy imagined she could hear wheels turning inside Rachel's brain. She was fully aware that her mentor was a STEM genius who would leave her mark on the world someday—if not on this project, maybe the next one. She was pleased to have such a brilliant tutor.

Abruptly, Rachel said, "I thought of something else to look at."

"Good," Izzy said. "I've got brain freeze and can't think of anything worth mentioning."

Rachel gave the monitor a series of sign-language instructions, and dozens of icons appeared.

"What are you looking for?" Izzy asked.

"Slides of chimeras the Georgetown grads made near the end of their training," Rachel said, dragging the pointer over a stack of icons to separate them.

"What were they working on?"

"Nothing. They were just puttering around."

"Look!" Izzy said in a high-pitched voice. "There's an icon labeled *Lemke*,"

Rachel clicked on it, and the image of a virus appeared.

At first glance, it appeared identical to the samples from the senior housing unit.

CHAPTER 26

On Saturday morning, Darien and the Thibideaux brothers joined a crowd of Houston Astros fans seated before the monitor in the George Washington rec room. It was 11:00 a.m., ten minutes before the first pitch of a rare morning game. The Astros were in first place in the American League West, one game ahead of today's opponent, the Texas Rangers. In addition to league standings, the winner would also claim *Texas-bragging* rights. Consequently, today's game had attracted a host of avid fans and a few fair-weather fans like Darien.

At the back of the rec room, several groups of iTab gamers sat around small tables, and friends looked over their shoulders, cheering loudly from time to time. Most of them were competing in a *Global Cooling on Mercury* tournament and would pay little attention to the Astros. Alden, the best computer gamer Darien knew, had lost a close match a couple of hours ago and was still long-faced about it.

Suddenly, loud shouts erupted at one of the tables, and a *Global Cooling* contestant jumped up and waved both fists in the air celebrating a victory.

Darien glanced at Alden.

Alden shook his head in disbelief. "That's John Kelly," he said. "He couldn't beat me in a computer game if his life depended on it."

"Who beat you?"

"Somebody using a screen name," Alden said. "I'm sure he was a professional game developer who shouldn't have been allowed in the tournament."

"The baseball game is starting," Justin said.

At Justin's prompt, Darien and Alden turned their attention to the TV. The Astros' pitcher delivered his first pitch, and the Rangers' lead-off batter slammed it into the centerfield seats for a home run. Two hours later, at the bottom of the ninth, the score remained 1-0, and both teams had stranded numerous runners on base. Then, with two outs and a man on first, the Astros' designated hitter came to the plate and swung at the first two pitches, missing both.

As fans sat on the edge of their seats, the Rangers' pitcher wound up to deliver another pitch. Before he could do so, the monitor went blank, and a shrill ringtone indicated that a *Public Information Mandate* was overriding ESPN's broadcast. As everyone stared at the monitor, the scene switched to Alphabet News' headquarters in New York City, where co-anchors, Angela Morales and Richard Frazier, sat behind a crescent-shaped desk.

The camera zoomed in on Richard. "Good evening," he said, an unusually solemn tone lacing his voice. "Thank you for joining Alphabet News for this special report. About a half-hour ago, drones attacked religious shrines in several countries. Three sites were hit, and unsuccessful attempts were made on four others. We will have live reports from our foreign correspondents in a few minutes, but before we do, here's a summary of what we know. In the first attack, drones slammed into the Dome of the Rock in Jerusalem, exploding on contact and obliterating the Dome. Shortly after that, drones struck an

Islamic shrine in Mecca, and others struck the statue known as Christ the Redeemer in Rio de Janeiro. Damage is still being assessed at all three locations."

Using a tag-team approach, Richard stopped speaking, and Angela began. "The well-synchronized attacks are believed to be the work of Los Ignotos," she said. "Two attacks were directed against shrines of the Islamic faith and one against the Christian faith. No one knows whether that is significant or not, and nothing is known about the origin of the drones. They bore no markings; however, eyewitnesses say they materialized out of thin air. This suggests they were composed of stealth materials which are available in only a few countries.

"Now, let's go live to Jerusalem and get an update from Joseph Heineman, one of Alphabet's correspondents stationed there. Go ahead, Joseph."

The New York scene behind Angela and Richard was replaced by a live shot of the Western Wall with the correspondent standing before it wearing a *kippah*–a skullcap–over his salt-and-pepper hair. Behind him, men waited in a long line to approach the wall, and a crowd of women waited to the right of the men.

"Behind me, you can see the prayer vigil in progress," Heineman said. "Here in Jerusalem, that is an automatic response to a tragedy such as this.

"A few minutes ago, the officer in charge of the Temple Mount's first responders reported that fifty bodies have been recovered so far. In addition, about one hundred people were injured. These numbers are expected to rise as search and rescue efforts continue."

Heineman stopped abruptly, glanced at his iTab, and continued, "I have just been informed that a helicopter-mounted camera will give us a panoramic view of the Temple Mount at this time. Let's watch and see what we can learn from it."

The Western Wall scene was replaced by a video showing a massive heap of rubble that formed when the Dome of the Rock collapsed. No flames were visible, but wisps of steam rose as firefighters sprayed water on the hot debris that once had been the most exquisite Muslim shrine in the world. Several EMS teams rushed body-laden gurneys toward waiting ambulances as other first responders scurried to and fro. In addition to fire trucks and ambulances, a line of olive-drab jeeps and Humvees formed a perimeter around the Temple Mount. Israeli soldiers, wearing full-body armor and carrying laser rifles, stood with their backs toward the rock outcropping where the mosque had once stood. The menacing squad, resembling Clone Troopers from *Star Wars*, held a crowd at bay outside a yellow *Do Not Cross* ribbon encircling the mountaintop.

Darien was amazed at the near-instant response from the Israeli military and other first responders. But, since violence was common in Jerusalem, a rapid response was a way of life for those who lived there. Although it was a holy city to Christians, Jews, and Moslems, more wars had been fought at its gates than any other city during 4000 years of recorded history. Yet, oddly, part of its name, *salem,* meant *peace* in Hebrew.

After the camera completed a third sweep of the mountaintop, Heineman said, "That's all we have from Jerusalem at this time. Let's go back to New York."

"Thank you, Joseph," Angela said. "This just in—as we speak, the Security Council of the United Nations is being called into emergency session by Reuben Rogov. Immediately upon being informed of these high-tech attacks, Mr. Rogov advised all countries having well-known religious shrines to go on red alert and remain vigilant until further notice. Do you have any updates, Richard?"

"We have a preliminary report from Mecca—the holiest city in Islam," Richard said. "There is no Alphabet News correspondent in Mecca at the moment; however, two are on the way from Jeddah, about forty miles away. In the meantime, this is the view from a satellite camera."

The TV monitor showed an eye-in-the-sky view of a massive gray building forming a perimeter around a black building that lay in ruins.

"This large circular building is the Grand Mosque, the *Masjid al-Haram*," Richard said. "It is the world's largest mosque and is reputed to be the most expensive building in the world. It encircles the building known as the Kaaba, which means *the cube*. The Kaaba houses The Black Stone, considered by most scientists to be a meteorite but believed by Muslims to be of divine origin. The stone was set in the eastern corner of the Kaaba, where pilgrims could touch and kiss it. One or more drones flew into the building and exploded on contact, destroying it. Another hit the Grand Mosque, causing a large section of the roof to collapse. We have no report regarding the number of casualties but expect to have one soon."

As Richard spoke, the camera zoomed in on the chaotic scene playing out in the open area surrounding the remains of the Kaaba. A squad of first responders had already pulled more than a dozen bodies from the rubble and covered them with shrouds. Others were being carried away on stretchers. Men wearing olive drab uniforms and carrying AK-47s faced down a solemn-looking crowd standing around the circumference of the enclosure. A yellow firetruck waited outside the mosque, and firefighters stood ready with hoses. Sirens sounded as additional ambulances approached the scene. At first glance, the Mecca attack appeared to be a mirror image of the attack in Jerusalem.

"We'll bring you updates from Mecca as soon as our Saudi coworkers arrive on the scene," Angela said. "In the meantime, our Brazilian correspondent, Sofia Mendes, is standing by in Rio de Janeiro. Go ahead, Sophia."

Abruptly, the scene switched from Saudi Arabia to Brazil and showed a woman in her late thirties standing near a waterfall surrounded by lush green shrubs with orange flowers. Blue and yellow butterflies flitted around the flowers.

"Thank you, Angela," Sophia said. "I'm reporting from the Tijuca Forest, part of the Tijuca National Park. In a moment, I'll give a signal, and the camera will pull back from the park scene and focus on *Cristo Redentor*—Christ the Redeemer—the statue that was damaged by the drone attack.

"But first, some good news—no fatalities occurred in this bombing, even though several people sustained injuries from flying debris. The injured were taken to the hospital for treatment and observation, and we'll update you on their condition when information becomes available."

Sophia paused and gave a slight nod toward an unseen camera operator. A live shot of the statue replaced the verdant forest scene. Darien and most other viewers in the rec room gasped audibly when the picture of Christ the Redeemer appeared onscreen.

The statue's head was missing!

Sophia resumed her report. "This shot shows a panoramic view of *Cristo Redentor* at the top of Corcovado Mountain with

Sugarloaf Mountain and Guanabara Bay in the background. This magnificent statue watching over Rio has come to symbolize Brazil. In 2007, it was declared one of the winners in a worldwide poll to find the *New Seven Wonders of the World*. Before the damage, it was 98 feet tall. The outstretched arms, representing a cross, are 92 feet wide. Mass is held daily at 11:00 a.m. in a chapel at the base of the statue. I've been told that a crowd is gathering there now to pray for world peace. That's all I have from Rio at the moment. Back to you, Angela."

"Thank you, Sophia," Angela said. "Now, we'll take you to the United Nations headquarters here in New York City, where President Reuben Rogov is about to address the Security Council, the UN branch charged with ensuring international peace and security."

A wide-angle view of the UN Security Council chamber replaced the picture of Christ the Redeemer. An oak desk formed a nearly-complete circle near the center of the room, and ceiling lights above the desk traced its configuration. The front wall displayed a huge mural depicting a phoenix rising amid the ruins of war. Blue armchairs encircled the desk, and a row of matching pedestal chairs were attached to the floor behind them. A handful of people sat in theater-style seats at the back of the room, and others milled around aimlessly.

Reuben Rogov was not in sight.

Abruptly, the scene switched back to Alphabet's New York office, where Richard and Angela were frantically scrolling through pictures on their iTabs. Quickly turning toward the camera, Richard said, "We've been informed that President Rogov has entered the UN headquarters and will address the Security Council chamber in about five minutes. In the meantime, we have a condensed replay of the three damaged shrines."

"It appears Rogov is about to assume the Presidency of the Security Council," Darien said.

"Wouldn't that be a violation of the UN's bylaws?" Alden asked.

Darien shrugged. "Maybe, but who's to stop him from doing it?"

The scene on the TV monitor switched back to the Security Council chamber as Reuben Rogov entered the room via a door near the phoenix mural. As he approached the center of the circular desk, everyone seated around it jumped to their feet and stood at attention. Those milling around at the back of the room stopped in their tracks and faced the front of the chamber. Rogov strode confidently toward a podium on the desk. Upon reaching it, he picked up a gavel, struck the desk three times, and said, "Ladies and gentlemen, please be seated."

Everyone complied immediately. The room fell quiet, and all eyes turned toward Rogov.

"Citizens of the world," he said, "today, we have witnessed terrorist attacks on prominent religious shrines in three countries. Four other attacks were attempted but failed. Additional attempts will likely occur, so vigilance is required of everyone. The UN Security Council will not rest until we have apprehended and punished those responsible for these dastardly acts. We are initiating a coordinated effort with our branches in Geneva, Nairobi, Vienna, and The Hague. In addition, I will establish an anti-terrorist command center in one of these locations.

"Preliminary findings point an incriminating finger at the underground cabal, Los Ignotos, which is known to operate in ten to fifteen countries around the world, including locations in the Middle East and Europe, as well as North and South America. In Europe, cells are active in London, Hamburg, and Madrid. In the United States, New York, Los Angeles, and Houston are centers favored for recruitment, fundraising, and planning.

"Terrorist operatives train in lawless areas like Somalia and Yemen, as well as the mountainous area between Afghanistan and Pakistan. There have also been reports of training camps on one of the Indonesian islands."

"Over a year ago, I initiated a program to uncover local cells; however, the average citizen was reluctant to join the effort. Such timidity has served to embolden Los Ignotos and will no longer be tolerated. Due to today's unprecedented attacks, we must redouble our efforts, and we must work together."

After declaring all-out war against Los Ignotos, Rogov committed UN funds to rebuild the religious shrines and ended his address with, "Citizens of the world, may God bless you. Good afternoon."

The Security Council scene transitioned into the Astros postgame show. Nearly everyone in the rec room ignored it and huddled with friends to discuss the drone attacks and Rogov's response.

"He gave a lot of detailed information about Los Ignotos," Alden said, swiveling his chair around to form a triangle with Darien and Justin's chairs. "If NatGov knew that much about the organization, why couldn't they have prevented the attacks?"

"I believe Los Ignotos is a product of Rogov's imagination," Justin said emphatically.

"That would mean he's declaring war on a fictional organization," Alden said.

"What a great tool for controlling the masses," Justin said. "If it doesn't exist, it can't be destroyed. So, he can use it from now on."

"Is Zach still working as a freelance reporter in Europe?" Darien asked.

"He's there," Alden said, "but we never know exactly where. He travels under assumed names with multiple passports, so we have no way to contact him."

"He checks in with Mom or Dad occasionally if he can do it without revealing his location," Justin added.

"I wonder why he hasn't published a follow-up story about the helicopter crash in Spain," Darien said. "His associate who died in the crash was the first person to mention Los Ignotos."

Six months earlier, Darien would have thought it ridiculous to believe Los Ignotos was a figment of anyone's imagination. Now, he wasn't so sure. He'd read that a similar ruse was used early in the twenty-first century when Democrats and Republicans were separate parties. During that time, when one party was planning to commit an illegal act, they leaked bogus information claiming the other party had already committed the act. This technique was used repeatedly, especially during presidential elections and worked extremely well.

Alden and Justin's opinion about Los Ignotos being non-existent sounded feasible.

But, on the other hand, if they didn't launch today's attacks, who did?

CHAPTER 27

The IMAX screen came to life with an image of the American flag waving atop the White House as a trumpet solo played *America The Beautiful* in the background. A moment later, the flag faded away, and a news banner scrolled across the screen. Rather than the usual list of headlines displayed at Citizenship Meetings, there was only one–a shocker:

PRESIDENT TO RESTRICT CERTAIN PUBLICATIONS

Seated on the balcony with Alden and Justin, Darien felt a chill run down his spine, and his conspiracy-theory persona kicked into overdrive. Using the word *Restrict* in the headline instead of *Ban* or *Censor* didn't make it more palatable. Since taking office three years ago, the President had changed considerably, but the change had been so gradual that most Americans hadn't noticed. Consequently, his support was still strong.

During his tenure, the President had garnered sufficient power to do anything he wanted to. Darien wondered if book banning foreshadowed a NatGov department like the *Ministry of Truth* in George Orwell's masterpiece, *1984*. It would be a way to control the written word. Papa's prediction was beginning to loom large.

The troubling headline gave way to a live camera shot of the Rose Garden in front of the Oval Office. Though wilting in uncommonly hot weather, the red and white roses surrounding the rectangular garden were still colorful. A podium stood on the porch outside the office, and several reporters waited on the steps. A cadre of high-ranking officials sat in folding chairs near the steps, and a squad of black-uniformed guards stood nearby at parade rest.

The camera pulled back from the Oval Office and swept the perimeter of the garden. Immediately, Darien spotted an oddity—a green mechanical device standing on the walkway several yards from the seating area. At first glance, the out-of-place machine looked like a robot lawn mower, though it seemed unlikely that White House groundskeepers would leave a mower in plain sight when an important event was scheduled. Upon further scrutiny, the placement of the apparatus appeared to be deliberate rather than accidental, and a stunning fact struck Darien.

The device was a paper shredder!

Darien glanced at his companions. Even in the dim light, he could read question marks on their faces. As they waited expectantly, the door of the Oval Office opened, and Reuben Rogov appeared. He strode confidentially toward the podium, and the auditorium fell quiet.

The President began, "Good evening, world citizens. Thank you for joining me. As you have witnessed, I have addressed and solved several problems of epic proportions during my presidency. Some examples—Israel and her Arab neighbors signed a peace treaty, I negotiated an agreement with Russia whereby both countries withdrew from Syria, Operation Breadbasket averted a worldwide food shortage, and I created a new country."

Rogov paused briefly before resuming in a somber tone. "However, even with these and other successes, we still have afflictions to solve. Some of the ills we suffer are unrelated to diseases such as Phoenix-75 or hostilities between countries.

They have come upon us over many years, and previous administrations have sidestepped them or ignored them completely. Since I have promised to bring peace through equality, I will not avoid these inequalities.

"Today, I'm going to address inequalities brought about by the written word," Rogov said, pausing as a low murmur rumbled throughout the auditorium.

"Don't misunderstand me," the President continued. "I support all rights granted by the First Amendment. However, the right to free speech is not absolute. For example, everyone knows it's illegal to yell '*Fire!*' in a crowded theater.

"Though not clearly defined in the law in some cases, other aspects of free speech are also limited. Simply put, no citizen has the right to oppress other citizens through the irresponsible use of words. Derogatory language–both written and spoken–is equivalent to hate speech and has divided our country along many lines. As your chosen leader, I intend to bring equality to all citizens regardless of race, creed, color, religion, national origin, ancestry, marital state, parental status, or gender identity. Linguistic abuse constitutes a form of inequality, and I do not intend to ignore it."

Rogov paused briefly, before continuing, "I have instructed the Attorney General to clarify certain First Amendment rights which have been abused so egregiously that they now must be addressed. In addition, I have issued an executive order banning the possession of dozens of hate-mongering books that discriminate along the lines I pointed out a moment ago. My staff has developed an initial listing of these books and will add others. Surprisingly, some of these books were discovered recently in the White House, having been collected by previous Presidents and tucked into various nooks and crannies throughout the building. Tonight, they will be destroyed in your presence."

Rogov paused and gave a hand signal to a uniformed guard standing beside the door leading into the Oval Office. The man opened the door as the camera zoomed closer, revealing a two-wheeled handcart inside. The cart held hardback and paperback books in various sizes and colors. As Darien watched in near disbelief, the sturdy guard grasped the cart handles and pulled the load of neatly-stacked books across the porch to the shredder.

"Those books are on the banned list," Rogov said, pointing toward the cart. "All of them contain prejudicial themes, motifs, phrases, or words. Some of these publications were banned by California more than a century ago, and a few other states followed suit over the years. It is high time for NatGov to take the lead in eliminating these vile publications."

At President Rogov's signal, the guard near the shredder touched a switch. Whining shrilly, the device sprang to life. With every eye in the Rose Garden focused on him, the guard donned a face mask and began to toss books into the jaws of the shredder, a handful at a time. As book after book hit whirring teeth, the device shifted gears, and the high-pitched whine became a low rumble as millions of words were obliterated forever.

While the book shredding was in progress, Darien lay his iTab on one knee and googled *Books banned by California*. Several websites popped up, and he selected the one at the top of the screen. The list consisted of *To Kill a Mockingbird* by Harper Lee, *The Adventures of Huckleberry Finn* by Mark Twain, *Of Mice and Men* by John Steinbeck, *The Cay* by Theodore Taylor,

Roll of Thunder, Hear My Cry by Mildred Taylor, *Fahrenheit 451* by Ray Bradbury, and *The Zap Gun* by Philip K. Dick.

Darien stared at the list, trying to fathom the enormity of Rogov's dictatorial order. By the time he returned his attention to the IMAX screen, the shredding process was complete, and the stack of classic books was now three large bags of confetti. The guard stacked the bags on the walkway bordering the neatly-trimmed lawn and returned to his post near the Oval Office. No one stirred in the Rose Garden or the George Washington auditorium while waiting for Reuben Rogov to continue.

After a brief pause, Rogov looked toward the camera and said, "Fellow citizens, you have just witnessed the launching of a program that NatGov will implement throughout the country during the next few weeks. After my staff completes the list of banned books, a copy will be sent to everyone via iTab, and copies will be posted on public news screens nationwide. As a dutiful American citizen, you must consult the list and respond accordingly. Since we are dealing with both e-books and paper books, this program will consist of two parts.

"During the first phase, offensive e-books will be erased via a new app developed by the National Security Agency. I have ordered every company that provides Wi-Fi service to embed this app into all outgoing signals. This process will start immediately. Within the next few days, all inflammatory books will disappear from electronic devices, leaving other books intact. The erasure will occur automatically—there is nothing you have to do.

"However, the second phase—paper books—requires your cooperation. Although few such books are printed today, millions are still in existence. Therefore, I am calling on every

American to join me as we take this step toward eliminating prejudicial literature from our society. Within a few days, my office will develop a schedule for shredding this offensive literature. It will be a nationwide operation structured somewhat like a massive garbage collection. You will be notified of a date and time when a NatGov shredder will be in your neighborhood. Based on that schedule, you must bring all offensive books you own to be destroyed in public. This endeavor is another step toward granting equality to those Americans disenfranchised by the published word.

"Please cooperate so this project can be accomplished without the necessity of further governmental action."

After the lightly-veiled threat, the President concluded, "Citizens, it is a pleasure to serve you. Thank you for helping bring equality to all people. God bless you, God bless America, and God bless the world. Good evening."

The IMAX screen faded to black, and the lights came on as a cacophony of excited voices erupted in the auditorium.

***

Two weeks later, Darien sat at his desk staring at his bookcase. It was Saturday morning, the scheduled book-shredding day for the Mediplex area. One of NatGov's shredders was slated to be on-site within minutes. He wondered if the few residents who owned banned books would respond voluntarily to the executive order or if they would wait for NatGov to take *further governmental action* as Rogov had mentioned. To date, no follow-up action had been specified, but Mr. Rogov had become so powerful that an implied threat was probably sufficient.

To Darien's dismay, polls indicated that well over half of the population thought eliminating certain publications would help bring equality to everyone. Moreover, it seemed most Americans would support any program launched under the *peace through equality* banner. Rogov had intoxicated the nation with his stunning rhetoric. Clearly, he was the unparalleled master of groupthink.

If not for the Equality Team investigators having seen Darien's bookcase, he would have hidden the books in question and ignored the order. Unfortunately, Marisa's team, the Haldon twins, had seen his two banned books, even mentioning their titles before asking about Los Ignotos. For a brief time, he wondered if the Los Ignotos discussion was a red herring to detract him while the team looked around for books about to be banned. After some consideration, he tossed the idea aside. Such an approach would be useless as a standard interview technique because most people didn't collect paper books. And if they did, they wouldn't normally display them in plain sight as Darien did.

During the two weeks following Rogov's book-banning edict, Darien, Rachel, and the Thibeaux brothers had several lively discussions about the subject. Since Rachel and Justin possessed only e-books, no action was required by them. Like Darien, Alden was in a different situation. He had a small collection of paper books. One of them, *Huckleberry Finn*, was on the banned list; however, no Equality Team member knew he had it.

Surprisingly, the Hatfields interviewed Alden in the Cherry Tree and didn't mention anything about books. This made Darien think he'd been singled out because he was an author, regardless of Marisa's statement to the contrary. Apparently, in conjunction with the censoring of publications from the past,

NatGov was attempting to intimidate creators of future printed matter.

As he was mulling over the situation, Darien's iTab pinged and flashed a message:

Attention, George Washington and Abraham Lincoln residents.

A NatGov shredder is parked near the intersection of Morningside Drive and Dorrington Street. It will remain there for two hours. Please bring all banned books to that location for shredding and disposal.

Darien's iTab pinged again, and a crawfish icon popped up. He touched it and said, "Hey, Alden, what's on your mind?"

"Are you going through with your plan?"

"I'm still thinking about it. What about you?"

"I hid *Huckleberry Finn*. Only five or six people know I have it."

"Unfortunately, I can't do that," Darien said. "I was gullible enough to invite NatGov agents into my office."

"You have an excuse–a beautiful woman talked you into it."

"Still, I was an easy mark."

"You thought up a good plan," Alden said. "Go ahead and do it. Nobody will be the wiser."

"Okay, I will. Nothing ventured, nothing gained."

"Good for you!"

"Are you going to watch the book shredding?"

"Absolutely. Justin and I are loitering on the sidewalk near the front entrance. We'll wait for you."

"Okay–see you in ten minutes or so."

Darien turned toward the bookcase and removed four paperback books with identical dimensions. Two were recently banned books, *Fahrenheit 451* and *The Zap Gun,* by famous authors. The other two were *The Dar Lumbre Chronicles* and *The Alamogordo Connection*, by a virtually unknown author, Don Johnston.

Using a cheese knife as a tool, he carefully removed the book covers. When all four books were free of their bindings, he switched places with them, putting the banned novels in the covers of those which hadn't been banned and vice versa. When satisfied the fit was perfect, Darien removed each book, carefully daubed its spine with a touch of quick-drying glue, and put it back into the cover. To aid in drying the glue, he put the books in the microwave for thirty seconds.

Pleased at his plan, Darien smiled slyly. Hopefully, it was audacious enough to succeed. Hiding banned books in plain sight reminded him of an Edgar Allen Poe short story, *The Purloined Letter*, in which an important letter in a torn envelope was hung in a card rack by a dirty ribbon. Though the letter was right before their eyes, Paris police overlooked it because they expected it to be hidden. However, the famous amateur detective, C. Auguste Dupin, solved the mystery. Darien loved the story and admired Poe's incredible talent.

With the fake banned books in his hand, Darien left the housing unit to find Alden and Justin waiting for him on the sidewalk. Together they joined a small group ambling toward NatGov's shredder at the intersection. As they walked along, Alden greeted everyone near him by name. About half of them carried books, most only a few; however, several carried an armload. Darien was bewildered that only a few of those carrying books seemed troubled about what was happening. The charismatic President had seized power so incrementally most people hadn't noticed.

They approached the street corner and joined a loosely-organized line of people waiting to shred books. The massive shredder looked like a green garbage truck with a battery of security cameras mounted atop the cab. A uniformed guard stood behind the unit, and another sat casually in the driver's seat with the door open. Two black vans with heavily-tinted windows were parked near the intersection. The mouth of the shredding device housed a conveyor belt leading to a set of shiny steel teeth. As he moved forward slowly, Darien looked over the shoulders of those ahead of him as book after book disappeared into the waiting jaws of the green monster.

As he neared the front of the line, a duet of voices called, "Hey, Darien."

He turned to see Halden and Hannah Hatfield approaching through the milling crowd. Dressed in neat blue suits, they walked toward him at a fast clip, seemingly oblivious to other people around them. Darien muttered an expletive under his breath and raised the books higher so security cameras could get a clear shot of them. When he was about to give them a toss, he hesitated, reluctant to push ahead of the slow-moving man in front of him who looked longingly at each book before throwing it into the shredder.

Standing a few feet from Darien, Alden stepped toward the Hatfields and said, "Hello, guys, welcome back to Houston."

While the twins were distracted by Aden's greeting, Darien reached the head of the line and casually tossed his two books into the shredder. As they disintegrated into cellulose snowflakes, he turned toward the Hatfields and greeted them as if they were old friends. Both smiled cordially, and their facial expressions didn't reveal whether or not they realized Alden's greeting was a well-timed delaying tactic. Though young, the twins had a knack for concealing their game plan while extracting information from others, a trait which made them dangerous.

"Thank you for complying with Mr. Rogov's order," Haldon said.

"It's nice to see you again," Hannah said.

After a brief make-believe-friendly conversation with the Equality Team duo, Darien and his friends crossed the street and started toward the Cherry Tree with a group of other pedestrians. When they reached the restaurant entrance, a sizable group was waiting to be seated.

Alden sized up the crowd and said, "This is at least a thirty-minute wait."

"That's too long," Darien said. "Let's go somewhere else."

Justin pointed to the adjacent restaurant and said, "There's nobody at the Log Cabin's walk-up window. Let's get something to drink and sit on the benches under the awning."

"Good idea," Alden said. "The day is too nice to go inside."

A few minutes later, the friends were seated together, sipping coffee.

"Okay," Darien said, "let's analyze what we just saw." His conspiracy theory persona had shifted into hyperdrive.

"I saw a lot of people shredding classic books," Alden said solemnly.

"The thing that shocks me, "Darien said, "is that very few of them seemed to care. I would have expected a lot of resentment—maybe even a demonstration of some kind."

"Everybody has bought into Rogov's equality doctrine," Alden said. "All he has to do is mention equality, and most people will follow him blindly. He understands how to use mass psychology."

"Maybe biology offers a better explanation than psychology," Darien said.

"I know what you're going to say," Alden said, "but go ahead."

"Here's the scenario as I see it," Darien said. "If you put a frog in boiling water, it will leap out immediately, but if you put it in a pot filled with lukewarm water and gradually heat it, the frog will remain in the water until it boils to death."

Scoffing, Alden said, "That frog story is an urban legend."

"Maybe so," Darien said, "but it fits the current political situation perfectly. Rogov has made changes so gradually that we're in boiling water, and it may be too late to jump out."

The three friends fell silent and gazed at each other thoughtfully. Under normal circumstances, the boiling frog metaphor would have elicited a few chuckles.

Today, it didn't seem the least bit funny.

CHAPTER 28

For several days, Darien had been plagued by a feeling that unseen eyes were watching him. Moreover, there seemed to be an increase in the number of uncertain smiles and downcast eyes throughout the hallways of the George Washington. He wondered if his worrisome perceptions were real or paranoia caused by Rogov's book-shredding edict and his obsession with Los Ignotos. So far, no one had been reported for un-American activity, and life was going on as usual. On the other hand, the CIA contact number displayed on public news screens was a constant reminder that NatGov had increased surveillance.

His iTab buzzed, and a blue butterfly materialized–Izzy's avatar. He was surprised. Izzy hadn't contacted him directly more than a half-dozen times since they met, and in most of those instances, she was calling on behalf of Marisa. Something unusual was on her mind, or she wouldn't be calling him at ten o'clock in the morning.

He touched the icon. "Hey, Izzy. What's up?"

"Hello, Darien. Did I wake you?"

Darien pretended to stifle a yawn. "Of course not. I've been for up for ten minutes. What's going on?"

"I want to talk to you about something important when you have time."

"Now is a good time. Go ahead," Darien said, noting an unusually somber tone in Izzy's voice.

"I'd really like to talk in person," Izzy said. "Could you join me for lunch today?"

"Certainly," Darien said, his curiosity burning. "Where would you like to meet, and what time?"

"How about The Gryphon at eleven-thirty? I'll treat you to a gyro sandwich and a Coke."

"I won't pass up a deal like that. See you then."

"Thanks," Izzy said, ending the call.

The next hour dragged by as Darien tried to figure out what was bothering Izzy. Suspecting it was something that happened recently, he reviewed the most troubling occurrences of the year–Phoenix-75's resurgence, the book shredding, the Los Ignotos threat, and the attacks on religious shrines. The incidents were formidable, but he didn't know any more about them than Izzy did, so it seemed unlikely she'd want to discuss them with him.

After some consideration, he thought of another possibility–it could have something to do with Vi-Tech. Under Dr. Throxmire's leadership, The company was thriving; however, everything wasn't perfect. Rachel despised Allende's *need-to-know* method of operation. Maybe she was thinking about changing jobs. With her credentials, it would be easy to do. Universities all over the country were offering her professorships, none of which she'd considered as far as Darien knew.

And, though it seemed unlikely, there was a possibility that Rachel might take a job on Mars. Her semi-estranged boyfriend, Stephen, was trying to persuade her to go to the Red Planet with him, and the colony was looking for scientists. If she left Vi-Tech for any reason, the company would lose its best virologist. However, that wouldn't affect Izzy very much; her STEM star was on the rise.

Adding to the mystery, Izzy had picked a day when they could talk privately. Rachel was presenting a paper at a seminar in Dallas, and the Thibideaux brothers were in Baton Rouge attending an uncle's funeral. Consequently, Darien and Izzy would be alone together for the first time today.

He left the George Washington at 11:15. Upon reaching Holcombe Boulevard, he turned right and walked along the sidewalk bordering the wide street. Darien loved where he lived. Other than Marisa and his parents, everything he needed and most of those he loved were within a ten-block radius. However, the small-world setting was changing slowly due to the heavy hand of NatGov.

Ten minutes later, he reached The Gryphon to see Izzy approaching from the opposite direction. They met at the entrance, hugged briefly, and went inside. The hostess seated them immediately, and a teenage brunette wearing a *Shelly* nametag appeared at the table. After she took their orders and retreated, Darien looked toward Izzy, waiting for her to take the lead.

"I'm going to discuss my family," Izzy said, "and I want you to keep everything I tell you confidential."

"Okay, I will," Darien said, realizing he'd been wrong in assuming Izzy wanted to talk about current events or the situation at work. Instead, she was about to bring him into her inner circle by discussing a family issue.

"As we've told you," Izzy said, "Marisa and I know very little about our father and nothing about Mom's father—our grandfather. Zina hasn't told Mom anything about him either, and that's absolutely impossible for me to comprehend. After thinking about this mystery for years, I've come up with an idea I need to bounce off someone outside my family."

"I'm honored you chose me."

"It's obvious our grandfather was a prominent figure in some area," Izzy continued. "Otherwise, why all the secrecy? I've narrowed it down to three likely possibilities–a famous actor, a professional athlete, or a well-known politician."

"Which of the three professions do you think is the best fit?"

"A politician."

"Have you discussed this with Marisa?"

"Not what I'm about to tell you."

"Why not?"

"If our grandfather was a politician, she's following in his footsteps, and I don't want to put her on the spot or get her into trouble."

"Which politicians were prominent in Brazil around the time your mother was born?"

"The Profetos are at the top of the list. They were active in local, state, and national politics. In fact, they still are."

Darien's brows shot up. "So you suspect that one of the Profetos is your grandfather?"

"No other family fits as well as they do."

"Have you figured out which one it might be?"

Izzy shook her head. "No. Regardless of how hard I search, I can't find a thing. The trail is cold or has been covered deliberately."

"You should be careful about whom you mention this to," Darien said, "just in case the secrecy is being enforced by threats."

"I know. You're the only one I've told so far."

Shelly appeared and placed the gyros and Cokes on the table. They ate while discussing various absent-grandfather scenarios. After much talk and deliberation, Darien concluded that

Izzy's theory made sense. A politician–possibly a Profeto–fit the profile better than any other profession. However, they had no proof, and the information was dangerous, so they decided to keep their discussion to themselves for the time being.

"I can't stifle my curiosity any longer," Izzy said. "I'm going to put pressure on Zina until she tells the whole story."

"I hope it works."

"Thanks for letting me use you as a sounding board."

"Sorry I wasn't more help."

After finishing their sandwiches, they stood to leave, and Marisa said, "By the way, last night I dreamed that Marisa returned to Houston."

"I hope it was a premonition instead of a dream."

"Maybe it was. She and I believe that we exhibit ESP occasionally, just like you and Rachel."

"I'll keep my fingers crossed."

They left The Gryphon, and Izzy said, "See you at the Citizenship Meeting tonight."

"I'll meet you in the usual spot."

***

Six hours later, Darien and Izzy were seated on the balcony of the George Washington. The IMAX screen showed an image of the White House with a news banner in front of it:

PRESIDENT ROGOV TO DISCUSS
RESTORATION OF RELIGIOUS SHRINES

The banner scrolled by repeatedly as a clock at the corner of the screen began a thirty-second countdown. When the clock reached zero, a computerized voice said, "Attention, please.

Stand by for a message from President Reuben Rogov. Attention, please stand by."

The scene changed to the Oval Office. The President, wearing the usual blue suit and red tie, sat at his desk with the American flag and the presidential picture gallery behind him.

"Good evening, fellow Americans and citizens of the world," Rogov said. "Thank you for joining me tonight. I called this news conference to inform you about the projects I've authorized to restore the damaged religious shrines.

"However, before discussing the shrines, I have an important announcement concerning the scheduled presidential election. Currently, my approval rating stands at 83%. For this reason, after consulting with me, the RADS and Independents have decided not to field a candidate who has no possibility of winning. Therefore, even though it is unprecedented in American politics, there will be no election, and I will remain your President by acclamation."

Rogov paused as his last sentence sunk in. After a few seconds of stunned silence, the auditorium erupted with copious cheers mingled with a handful of boos. Instantly, Darien realized that Papa's prophecy was coming true right before their eyes. He and Izzy looked at each other in astonishment without uttering a word.

After the clamor subsided, Rogov continued, "Thank you for your support. Now, I will address restoration of the shrines. Acting as Attorney General of the United Nations, I have authorized a project to rebuild the shrines. I will fund this project by levying tariffs on all goods and services exchanged between UN members; therefore, every nation will contribute to the cause. This is the fairest way to raise funds, and I require your complete cooperation. We have to continue working together to bring peace and equality.

"The shrines are important to three religions—Christians, Jews, and Muslims. I'll give a brief history of each structure damaged in the attacks. This information will help you understand how I arrived at my decision.

"Let's begin with the statue of Christ the Redeemer in Rio de Janeiro. The statue is 98 feet tall and embraces the city with open arms 92 feet wide. All structural components were hauled up the mountain piece by piece and took years to assemble. It was completed in 1931 and is now considered one of the New Seven Wonders of the World. It is a magnificent statue and will be restored as soon as possible."

Rogov paused, and a picture of the statue appeared. The gleaming white structure was silhouetted against the cloudless sky, and several cranes worked in unison to move scaffolding into place.

"Next, let's consider Mecca," Rogov continued. "The Great Mosque of Mecca is the largest in the world. It is the site of a pilgrimage all Muslims must make at least once in their lives if possible. The Great Mosque encircles the Kaaba, a cubical structure. The Black Stone, revered by Muslims, was set in the eastern corner of the Kaaba at the time of the explosion. According to scholars, Islam started during the lifetime of Muhammad in the seventh century AD, as did the construction of mosques. Like the statue in Rio, this building will be restored completely."

Rogov paused again, and the scene switched to the Great Mosque. The debris had been removed, and armed guards stood at parade rest around the remains of the Kaaba.

"Lastly, we come to the Temple Mount," Rogov said, "but before I inform you of my decision, please listen closely as I summarize the 3000-year history of this site.

"Solomon's Temple was built on this rock outcropping around the tenth century BC. The Babylonians destroyed the temple in the fifth century BC, and many Jews were taken captive. Seventy years later, exiles returned and rebuilt the structure on a reduced scale. About four hundred years later, in 20 BC, Herod the Great began expanding the temple and restoring its original splendor. Herod's magnificent structure was demolished by the Romans in 70 AD, and Moslems built the Dome of the Rock on the site in the seventh century.

"A thorough study of Middle East history proves the original owner of this mountain was Israel. All subsequent nations who claimed ownership acquired it by force rather than by legal means. For this reason, I have decided to return the Temple Mount to Israel. Yesterday, Prime Minister Ehud Sharon informed me that The Temple Institute will begin construction of a Jewish temple immediately. UN funds will be available for this project as well.

"As previously mentioned, three prominent religions will benefit by these UN-funded restoration projects. Before authorizing funds, I ordered the religions to work together for the cause of peace. This morning, they formed a joint committee to work out a long-term plan of cooperation. I am an ex-officio member of this committee and will track their progress and assist as needed.

"For the first time since taking office, I am satisfied with my plan to project world peace into the distant future.

"Therefore, today, I am proclaiming 1000 years of peace."

CHAPTER 29

Darien approached The Fossil as Ima was unlocking the door.

"Hello, Bookworm," he said.

"Hi, Darien. Nice to see you. I thought you'd be in jail by now."

"For what?"

"Hiding banned books."

They laughed, but Darien decided not to tell Ima that he'd hidden two books, though he knew she wouldn't report him. They were birds of a feather–fervent bibliophiles–but she talked to a lot of people and might accidentally say too much. Why take a chance?

Motioning for Darien to follow her, Ima swung the door open and entered the shop.

"How many books did you have to shred?" she said as Darien joined her in the broad aisle between the display cases.

"Just two. What about you?"

"More than a hundred," Ima said. "They were worth several thousand dollars. A polite young couple helped me carry them to the shredder."

For the next few minutes, they discussed Rogov's book-banning edict. Both suspected they were on NatGov's potential problem list–Darien because he was a writer and Ima because she dealt in paper books. It seemed that NatGov disliked both.

"Are you looking for anything in particular?" Ima asked.

Darien shook his head, "Not really. Alden asked me to meet him here."

"What's he up to?"

"I don't know," Darien said. "I was shooting baskets at the Y when he called and asked me to meet him here. He was rather secretive."

As they were talking about Alden, he entered the shop. They exchanged greetings, and Ima retreated to her office.

Alden motioned toward the door. "Let's go outside." They said goodbye to Ima and left the bookstore.

"You're acting weird," Darien said as they walked along the sidewalk. "What's going on?"

"I want to tell you something," Alden said, "but I decided it best not to do it by telephone or in a restaurant."

"Why not?"

"I've heard the National Security Agency has begun to monitor personal phone calls," Alden said, "and they're certainly bugging restaurants. So meeting out here in the open is best."

"What's on your mind?"

"Zach has returned from Europe," Alden said. "He's at my parents' house and would like to talk to you."

"That's great! What does he want to talk about?"

"Collaborating on a book. Since NatGov has banned all conspiracy theory publications, he wants to write a novel."

"Science fiction?"

"I don't know," Alden said. "He'll have to tell you. When can you go to Beaumont with me?"

"How about right now?"

"Let's go."

"We'll take my car."

Less than two hours later, they arrived at the Golden Triangle, the housing unit where Alden and Justin's parents lived. Its name reflected the triangle formed by three cities–Beaumont, Orange, and Port Arthur. The unit was on the Sabine River, part of the border between Texas and Louisiana. Darien had fond memories of visiting the Thibideaux brothers when they were teenagers. They'd explored every inch of the river for miles in each direction and had shared many adventures along its banks.

They took the elevator to the fifth floor and rang the doorbell. Alden's mother opened the door with his father and Zach behind her. Darien knew Alden's parents as Dale and Grace; long ago, they'd told him to call them by their first names. They were exceptionally cordial, making it easy to see why Alden was a people person.

Grace hugged Darien and Alden in the hallway and said, "Come in, boys. It's good to see you." They stepped inside the condo, and the hugging resumed, accompanied by handshakes and high-fives.

After the lively greetings ran their course, Grace motioned toward the living area. "Sit over there, and I'll get you something to drink. We have iced tea, soft drinks, and beer. What would you like?"

Darien and Alden chose iced tea and went to the sofa. Dale and Zach, each holding a light beer, sat in recliners nearby. Grace retreated to the kitchen and returned a moment later with the tea. She sat down in a chair beside her husband, and all eyes turned toward Zach.

"It looks like I have the floor," he said.

Everyone nodded and leaned forward expectantly. Darien sensed that Alden and his parents were planning to listen instead of talk, a rare concession for a Thibideaux.

Zach looked toward Darien. "Thanks for coming. I'd like to discuss the possibility of co-writing a novel with you."

"Do you mean a science fiction novel?"

"No, but it would seem like sci-fi," Zach said. "I'd like for us to develop a storyline that exposes the deception NatGov is employing."

Darien's brows shot up. "You want to write a conspiracy theory novel?"

"Yes, but we couldn't call it that," Zach said. "The facts I've gathered would have to be turned into fiction."

"This is an unusual proposition," Darien said, "but I'm definitely interested."

"Great! I thought you'd be."

"What would you like to fictionalize?" Darien asked, anticipating something extraordinary. Zach had come up with some bizarre theories in the past, most with little or no evidence, yet his work was popular with conspiracy periodicals. He probably had something worth pursuing.

"What I say in this room shouldn't be repeated to anyone except our families," Zach said. "I think we should tell Justin and Rachel, but nobody else. I haven't told Dale and Grace yet, so everyone will hear the stories at the same time."

Everyone agreed to handle Zach's NatGov exposé with utmost care.

"Repeating the information that I'm about to reveal would put us on the government's hit list," Zach continued. "And, make no mistake—such a list exists. My friend, Juan Piedra, was on it, and you know what happened to him."

"Was it Los Ignotos?" Darien asked.

"Yes and no," Zach said. "When the drones took down the helicopter, that name hadn't been used to describe any secret organization. However, when conspiracy theory magazines reported that Juan's last words were Los Ignotos, Reuben Rogov began to use the name, though he knew no such organization existed. The real story is much stranger than fiction.

"Through much effort and personal risk, I obtained a copy of Juan's final radio transmission. High-tech experts specializing in linguistics have pored over it syllable by syllable. The recording contained a lot of static, but the experts believe his last word was *Ignacio* instead of Ignotos, and–"

"No way!" Darien burst out, his eyes wide. Then, in a quiet voice, he added, "Sorry I interrupted you."

"That's okay," Zach said. "Jump in any time you like. Anyway, you know where I'm heading with this story. I think if Juan had gotten the chance to say one more word, it would have been *Allende*."

"As you know, I'm a bona fide conspiracy theorist," Darien said, "but that's hard to believe."

"I know," Zach said. "Still, we're convinced the assassins were working for Ignacio Allende. Moreover, we think this organization existed for years before it was mistakenly called Los Ignotos, a name which suggests foreign terrorists. Rogov likes the name because it deflects attention away from the real culprits, a private hit squad assembled by Allende."

"What about the attacks on the religious shrines?" Darien asked, though knowing what Zach would say.

"We have evidence indicating they were responsible for those as well. Moreover, one of my associates has located a base in the badlands between Afghanistan and Pakistan. We believe the drones were launched from there."

"Rogov mentioned a paramilitary base in that area," Darien said, "but he claimed the troops training there were foreign terrorists."

"Many of them are," Zach said, "but they're on Allende's payroll. They're hiding the operation in plain sight by blaming others for an atrocity they intend to commit."

"Any idea why they would destroy the shrines?"

"It's part of a well-developed plan to control people," Zach said. "It's apparent that Allende, Rogov, and Profeto constitute a triumvirate. We believe they've been plotting to rule the world for over twenty years. Now, for all practical purposes, they're doing it. Allende probably originated the idea but had to wait until Rogov was ready to step into the spotlight. With his unique oratorial skills, he became the key player. Few rulers in history have had the ability to sway the masses the way Rogov does. He's one of a kind, which makes him extremely dangerous."

"How did you obtain this information?" Darien asked incredulously.

"I also belong to a secret operation with no name," Zach said, smiling slightly. "We're a highly organized group of undercover reporters working in a unique field—conspiracy theories. We utilize multiple identities and passports. In addition, we contact each other only by coded analog phones. One of our members assembles them, and we reprogram them daily."

"Then, how did Juan Piedra get caught?"

"He got careless."

"I can understand how you're able to remain incognito," Darien said, "but how did you find out so much secret infor-mation?"

"A few of our members are moles working for NatGov."

Darien shook his head. "This gets more bizarre by the second." The story was beyond anything he'd ever imagined, yet he was on the verge of accepting its veracity in toto. No one could make a conspiracy theory sound more real than Zach Thibideaux.

"Let's try to figure out a way to relay this information to the public," Zach said.

"I don't see how we could do it without getting killed," Darien said.

"That's what I want to discuss with you."

"I'm just a sci-fi author. This is above my pay grade."

"Maybe not, " Zach said. "I've thought about this a lot and have developed a rudimentary plan. We could try something other writers have used as plots. You once told me your favorite novel is *The Man In The High Castle.* What would you think of giving that approach a shot?"

"Are you suggesting we write a novel about a banned novel?" Darien asked.

"Something like that. Do you think we could do it?"

Darien shook his head. "Even if we could, NatGov would ban it immediately, so I don't see what it would accomplish."

"Okay, here's another one by the same author," Zach said. "It uses a more sophisticated approach. Remember *Radio Free Albemuth*? In that novel, government lies were exposed by embedding them as phrases in popular song lyrics."

"As I recall, the first time the protagonists heard the songs, they were breaking rocks in a concentration camp," Darien said. "That's probably what would happen to us."

"Well, maybe that wasn't a good idea either," Zach said, "but surely we can come up with something."

Darien looked toward Alden and his parents. "Any ideas?"

At that point, the dialogue evolved into a lively five-way conversation that went on for nearly an hour without producing a reasonable plan of action. When proffered initially, several ideas sounded tremendously inventive but failed under close scrutiny. The more they talked, the more they realized they couldn't come up with a plan that wouldn't put their lives in danger. Reluctantly, they decided not to attempt to present Zach's theories in a novel, and everyone fell silent and looked at each other.

After a bit, Alden said, "I think my idea of broadcasting the novel from Mars wins the prize."

"Maybe the booby prize," Darien said, breaking the tension.

Despite the lighter mood that swept the room, Darien realized they'd have to learn how to survive as citizens of a one-world government. Moreover, for the time being, he couldn't discuss Zach's stories with Marisa. There was no way she'd believe the drama unfolding on the world stage was orchestrated by a triumvirate headed by Reuben Rogov.

To further complicate the situation, before leaving Houston, Darien had told her that he and Alden were going to visit the Thibideauxs. Tonight, when he FaceTimed Marisa, she'd want to know everything they'd talked about. Sadly, he'd have to be evasive.

After a lively discussion about how the world was changing, Darien and Alden returned to Houston.

***

At 10:00 p.m., Darien made himself a glass of chocolate milk and sat down at his dinette table. With mild trepidation, he picked up his iTab and touched Marisa's avatar.

Her smiling face materialized at the first ringtone. "Hi, Darien. How was your visit to Beaumont?"

"It was great. You know how the Thibideauxs like to talk," Darien said, expecting a game of *twenty questions* to start immediately.

Instead, Marisa said, "I've got some exciting news to tell you."

"Great! What is it?"

"At my request, I've been transferred to Houston."

"Fantastic!" Darien said, realizing that Izzy's dream—and his as well—was going to come true. "When will the transfer take place?"

"In about a month."

"That's the best news I've heard since you left," Darien said. "Looks like we've beaten the odds."

Marisa nodded. "We certainly have, and there's something else I want you to know. I requested this transfer so we could spend more time together, and I promise not to put politics ahead of you again."

A lump formed in Darien's throat, preventing him from speaking aloud, but he managed to whisper, "Thank you, Marisa. I love you very much."

They talked for an hour. When they were about to log off, Marisa said, "As soon as we get the chance, let's visit your friend's restaurant in Freeport. We were supposed to have our first date there, but the weather changed our plans. So let's start over."

"I'll reset the time machine."

As Marisa's image faded, Darien pulled up Amazon-Tiffany's website and clicked on *Fine Jewelry*. A brilliant display of rings, earrings, bracelets, and necklaces appeared. Moving the pointer to *Precious Stones*, he selected the subheading *Diamonds*.

Engagement rings popped up.

CHAPTER 30

Stifling a yawn, Izzy slipped on a pink robe and went to the kitchen. She opened the refrigerator and peered inside. While trying to decide between orange juice and a cold latte, she heard a door creak and turned to see Frieda coming out of her bedroom.

"Hi, Mom. Did I wake you?"

"No," Frieda said, shaking her head. "My internal alarm woke me. I can't turn it off, even on Saturday."

"I was about to get something cold to drink."

"How about something hot instead?" Frieda said, joining Izzy in the kitchen. "I'm going to make coffee."

"Okay, I'll take a cup."

"Let's drink it on the balcony," Frieda said. "The weather is beautiful."

"Do you think Zina would like to join us?"

"We probably shouldn't wake her," Frieda said. "Last night, when we went to bed, she said she was totally exhausted. She hasn't been feeling well lately."

Moments later, with coffee in hand, they stepped onto the mini-balcony overlooking Morningside Drive and sat down in chairs so close together their knees almost touched. Below them, the Mediplex area was coming alive. A group of people wearing hospital scrubs waited at the Metro kiosk. Across the street, other early risers milled around in the food court. A clump of colorful mini-micros waited at the intersection, along with an ambulance and a fire truck. Sirens wailed in the distance. It was a typical Saturday morning in the fast-paced locality.

Frieda took a sip of coffee and asked, "What time did Darien come by for Marisa?"

"I don't know. He texted her instead of ringing the doorbell, so I didn't hear them leave."

"Her iTab is on the counter by the microwave," Frieda said. "It's not like her to forget it."

"She probably left it intentionally to avoid being disturbed at some inopportune time."

Frieda's brows shot up. "What are you suggesting?"

"I think Darien plans to propose to Marisa today."

"Really?" Frieda said, still showing surprise. "What makes you think so?"

"She transferred back to Houston to be with him, a move that could hurt her career. When Darien realizes that Marisa is finally putting him ahead of her political ambitions, he'll ask her to marry him."

Frieda smiled broadly. "I hope you're right. He's a good man, and I'd be pleased to have him as a son-in-law."

For the next few minutes, they talked about the relationship between the Da Rosas, Seguras, and Thibideauxs. As Izzy saw it, the three families had merged into a single unit with various interconnections. Marisa and Darien's love story set the standard. In addition, Alden had become Izzy's best friend—the brother she'd always wanted. Rachel was also a good friend, though she supervised both Izzy and Justin at Vi-Tech. At long last, Marisa's return to Houston made the sextet a possibility again. Hopefully, they could pick up where they left off, despite the changing political situation.

"Now that we're established in Texas, do you regret leaving Brazil?" Izzy asked.

Frieda shook her head. "Not really, but I miss my old friends in Rio, even though I have many new ones here."

"I'd like to see Ipanema and Copacabana again," Izzy said. "We've had some good times on Galveston's beaches, but they don't compare to Rio's."

"Another thing I miss is *Cristo Redentor* looking over the city."

"Me too," Izzy said. "Thankfully, the repairs are nearly finished. According to Alphabet News, the unveiling should take place any day now."

"They show updates regularly on TV, but you can't see anything," Frieda said. "The upper part of the statue is covered with . . . *uma fohla grande.*"

"A big sheet," Izzy said. "It's a drop cloth to keep debris from scattering everywhere."

"Mr. Rogov seems to be emphasizing the *Redentor* statue more than the other religious shrines."

"It's probably because they suffered damage that can't be repaired quickly," Izzy said. "Repairing the statue is much simpler."

Frieda tipped her head back and drained the last drop from her cup. "I need a refill," she said as she stood. "Would you like one?"

"Just a warmup."

"I'll check on Mom and get the coffee pot," Frieda said, pushing the curtain aside and entering the condo.

While waiting for Frieda to return, Izzy studied the scene below her. Despite the near-frantic activity, she loved it here. Houston was her home, and she hoped it always would be.

Suddenly, she heard a shout, "Izzy! Come here!"

She sprang from her chair and dashed inside to find her mother and grandmother in their shared bedroom. Zina lay corpse-like in her bed with one arm across her chest. In tears, Frieda knelt beside the bed and clung to Zina's other arm. Izzy rushed to the bedside and leaned over her pale grandmother, fearing that she had died during the night.

Sobbing, Frieda looked up. "Can you give her CPR?"

"Call 911–hurry!" Izzy said. "I'll see if she has a pulse." She took Zina's limp arm and gently placed a finger on her wrist. After an anxious moment, she detected a heartbeat, which was weak and irregular. Breathing a sigh, Izzy gave an affirmative nod toward Frieda, who was completing the 911 call.

"The EMS will be here in a few minutes," Frieda said. "Is there anything we can do for Mom while we wait?"

Izzy made the sign of the cross and said, "At this point, all I know to do is pray."

Frieda put her arms around Izzy, and they gazed at Zina in silent reverence. As they watched, she took a shallow breath, and her eyelids moved slightly.

"She's waking up!" Frieda said excitedly.

Zina opened her eyes and looked around the room slowly until her eyes rested on Izzy and Frieda. Time seemed to stand still as she stared at them without blinking. Presently, her lips twitched, but no words formed.

Fearing the worst, Izzy leaned over her supine grandmother. "Zina, can you hear me?"

With considerable effort, Zina rasped, "Yes, my dear," and tried to lift her head.

Calmer now, Frieda put her hand on Zina's shoulder. "Take it easy, Mom. Don't try to sit up. The ambulance will be here shortly."

Zina's voice strengthened slightly. "Put a pillow under my head."

"Lie still, Zina. You've been unconscious," Izzy said, suspecting her grandmother had suffered a heart attack or stroke.

"Raise my head a little," Zina said, struggling. "The time has come to tell you about your grandfather." Though only a whisper, her voice was emphatic. Obediently, they retrieved two pillows from the adjoining bed, put them beneath Zina's head, and waited expectantly.

"Can you call Marisa?" Zina asked, her voice barely audible. "She needs to hear what I have to say."

Remembering that Marisa had left her tablet behind, Izzy said, "I'll call Darien." She touched his avatar on her iTab. A moment later, after a dozen ringtones went unanswered, she left a brief message on his voicemail.

"They're on their way to the beach," she said. "We can't contact them right now."

"Did they go to Ipanema again?" Zina asked hoarsely.

Stunned, Izzy said, "They went to Freeport. We're in Houston. Remember?"

After a long pause, Zina said, "Oh . . . I remember now." She took a shallow breath and closed her eyes.

Frieda rubbed her mother's shoulder gently. "Wake up, Mom. We're waiting to hear your story."

Zina partially opened her eyes and said, "Frieda, your father was a politician."

"Who, Mom? Tell me now . . . please."

Ignoring Frieda's plea, Zina said, "He was a rising political star when we had an affair. I was only a waitress at the time, and he was married. When I told him I was pregnant, he wanted me to have an abortion, but I refused. He got furious at first, but I held my ground, and we worked out a compromise. For my silence, he used his influence to get me a sous chef job and, after that, the cooking show. And later, when—"

Frieda broke in. "Mom! What's his name?"

Undeterred by the interruption, Zina continued, "When you graduated from high school, your father rigged the lottery, and I won enough money to send you to college. The help he gave me was enough to keep us in the middle-income bracket but not enough to arouse anyone's suspicions. Moreover, an ominous threat accompanied his help. He swore he would cause serious trouble for me if I told anyone about him."

Zina paused and licked her dry lips.

"Please, Mom," Frieda begged. "Tell us his name."

"When you married Raymundo, I thought everything would change," Zina continued, "and they were different for a short time, but—"

In horror, Frieda interrupted again. "Did my father have anything to do with Raymundo's death?"

"I saw enough to realize that your husband was blackmailing your father," Zina said. "The situation resulted in the ruse about a lost emerald mine and set up Raymundo to be murdered."

"What an evil thing to do," Frieda said, weeping uncontrollably.

With tears trickling down her cheeks, Izzy put an arm around Frieda and drew her close. At this point, she understood why Zina had been reluctant to tell the story. It was too horrible to tell, especially to young children. Moreover, the information was dangerous to everyone who knew it. Even so, she was glad to hear the story after so many years of speculation.

Zina lay a bony hand on Frieda's arm. "Don't cry, my Dear," she said, her voice fading. "I'm nearly finished with my story—and my life as well. Over four years ago, your father arranged the Citizenship Exchange program so we could move to the United States. As far as I know, we were the only Brazilians to benefit from the program before it was canceled."

Straining intensely, she turned on her side as first responders burst into the condo.

Propped on one elbow, Zina looked directly into Frieda's eyes and whispered, "Your father is Reuben Rogov."

As Frieda and Izzy stood by the bed in stunned silence, two uniformed medical technicians rushed into the room. When they reached Zina's bedside, she went limp and fell back onto the pillows.

Seconds later, she let out a gurgling sound—the death rattle.

CHAPTER 31

Straining against their seatbelts, Darien and Marisa leaned toward each other and kissed as the red sedan exited Loop 610 via a ramp joining the Nolan Ryan Expressway. Once on the expressway, the car accelerated and merged with a bevy of briskly moving vehicles heading south. Even before returning from Washington, Marisa had suggested taking the trip to Freeport ASAP, an idea that thrilled Darien. As he saw it, they were getting a *do-over*. Hopefully, it would turn out well, despite the political winds swirling around them.

Before leaving the Mediplex area, Darien and Marisa ate a gourmet brunch at the Bayou Bistro. While dining on eggs benedict and sipping milk punch, they put together their agenda for the day. It included a stroll on the beach at San Luis Pass, a visit with Darien's parents, and–at long last–dinner at the Beachfront Bar & Grill. The final item would commemorate their first date, which took place at the Cherry Tree instead of the Freeport restaurant as originally planned.

During brunch, Darien and Marisa discussed various events that had occurred during Reuben Rogov's reign. Many of his political actions had directly affected their lives. Though difficult to do, Darien kept his promise not to repeat Zach's story about the origin of the term, Los Ignotos. It troubled him greatly to leave Marisa out of the loop, but despite their relationship, she worked for NatGov. He would tell her the bizarre story someday, but not today.

Darien's assessment of the President's first term had two distinct parts, three and a half years of unprecedented miracles followed by six months of questionable events. Though Marisa's viewpoint differed from his, they agreed that three recent incidents stood out: the Phoenix-75 resurgence, the shrine attacks, and the book ban. Despite much circumstantial evidence, Darien realized that neither the virus comeback nor the destruction of the shrines could be laid at the President's feet. Consequently, he didn't try to sell Marisa his theories concerning the events. If his suspicions were true, she would eventually find out.

There was one indisputable fact—the book shredding was entirely Rogov's undertaking. But, to Darien's dismay, most Americans supported the President's censorship edict. Even Marisa had no strong objections to it. Overall, the world continued to see Reuben Rogov as a promised deliverer. However, in tune with Papa's original thinking, Darien suspected the last six months foreshadowed serious tribulation in the future.

When Marisa returned to Houston, they vowed not to let anything separate them again. Moreover, he intended to ask her to marry him before the day ended, so regardless of what the future held, they would face it together. And, despite their differing political views, he knew Marisa truly loved him. Otherwise, she wouldn't have left her calling, Washington politics.

They passed a sign reading *Freeport 50 Miles.*

"We'll be at San Luis Pass in less than an hour," Marisa said excitedly. "I can hardly wait."

"Don't expect it to look like Rio's beaches."

Marisa leaned over and kissed Darien's cheek. "Who cares? We'll be together—that's what matters."

Suddenly, a shrill beep sounded, and multiple red lights blinked on the instrument panel. *"Warning! Computer error! Autopilot is in failure mode,"* a mechanical voice shrieked. *"Someone must take control. Warning, this is urgent!"*

Darien grabbed the steering wheel and jerked it to the left, barely in time to prevent his car from sideswiping a Metro bus. Unfortunately, his reflexive action caused him to oversteer. With tires squealing, the car skidded sideways onto the highway shoulder, which was under repair. As he fought to regain control, the left front fender clipped an orange barrel and sent it spinning onto the median. A split second later, after avoiding another line of barrels, he eased the car back onto the highway.

"Are you okay?" he asked, looking toward Marisa anxiously.

"I'm fine," Marisa said unsteadily. "Please keep your eyes on the road."

Darien repositioned his hands on the steering wheel. "I certainly intend to."

A few minutes later, they regained their composure and continued the conversation as the car zipped along under the cloudless sky.

Once outside the city limits, they reached a stretch of undeveloped land. The spring weather on the Texas Gulf Coast had included abundant rain in April, which brought flowers in May, as the old adage promised. As a result, both shoulders of the expressway were abloom with dandelions. And, beyond the shoulders, acres of pink buttercups, mingled with a few white ones, swayed in the gentle breeze.

"I didn't know Texas had such beautiful flowers," Marisa said. "We should have mentioned it in our day trip guide."

Though he didn't say so, the flowers were the most colorful Darien had ever seen along the expressway, and he'd traveled it hundreds of times.

Near Freeport, traffic slowed considerably, and public news screens above the expressway flashed red, indicating an important headline would be posted soon. They watched intently as a news banner materialized:

THE REDEEMER STATUE TO BE UNVEILED
TODAY AT 8:00 P.M. CST

"Fantastic!" Marisa exclaimed. "We'll watch during dinner."

At that point, Darien realized it would be better to wait until after the unveiling to ask Marisa to marry him. The ceremony would command everybody's attention, including his and Marisa's. He wouldn't try to compete with it. Besides, it should make an excellent lead-in to his proposal.

***

Shortly before sundown, Darien manually guided his small sedan into a lot beside the Beachfront Bar & Grill. The lot was nearly full of haphazardly parked vehicles, and additional cars eased along, searching for places to park. The motorized chaos reminded Darien of the bumper car ride at the State Fair in Dallas.

"There's a space," Marisa said, pointing.

"I was planning to get closer."

"If you take this one, we'll be able to get out when we decide to leave."

Not wanting to get blocked in, Darien followed Marisa's advice. A moment later, they were walking toward the restaurant hand in hand. As they strolled along the walkway, Darien mulled over everything that had happened so far during the day.

Except for the autopilot failure, the trip had been virtually perfect. They had sunbathed and beachcombed at San Luis Pass for a couple of hours as planned. Then, when a gusty wind sprang up and created a sandstorm, they moved on. Before leaving, they showered at a public bathhouse and changed clothes in preparation for their visit with Darien's parents, who lived a short distance from the beach.

Though Marisa had met the Seguras, they'd spent very little time together before today. The visit couldn't have gone better. Upon arrival at the condo, they went into the living room, and the conversation flowed freely. While they talked and sipped iced tea, Darien saw his parents fall in love with Marisa. As anticipated, when the visit was winding down, his mother urged them to stay for dinner. They declined the invitation multiple times while preparing to leave. When Marisa stepped into the hallway, Darien's mother caught his arm and pulled him back. She kissed him lightly on the cheek and whispered, "She's wonderful. Don't let her get away."

What a day.

And if all went as planned, the best was yet to come.

They entered the restaurant to find a crowd waiting in the lobby. Jack Lawson was at the front desk helping the maître d' with seating arrangements. "Hello, Darien," he said warmly. "Welcome to the Beachfront Bar & Grill." The two men hugged and patted each other on the back, after which Darien introduced Marisa.

Smiling, Jack looked at her and said, "Nice to meet you. I've been holding your reservation for three and a half years."

"Sorry I was late," Marisa quipped, laughing softly.

"Come with me," Jack said, motioning. "I've got a table set up for you. It's in a corner niche, but you'll have a good view of a TV when the President speaks." The trio picked their way through the busy room to a table holding a *Reserved* card. A bucket stand beside the table held a bottle of iced-down champagne, and two glasses were on the table next to a bouquet of long-stemmed red roses.

Significantly moved by his friend's thoughtfulness, Darien said. "I don't know what to say except *thank you very much*. This is incredible."

Jack picked up the bottle. Deftly, he removed the cork and poured two glasses without spilling a drop. Darien and Marisa clinked their glasses together and tasted the champagne while standing.

"The chef will bring you a tray of appetizers shortly," Jack said.

Darien pulled out Marisa's chair, and she sat down. When Darien was seated, he looked toward Jack and asked, "Do you have time to join us for a glass of champagne?"

"Not right now. Maybe later."

Jack walked away, and Marisa said, "It's about time for the Redeemer statue to be unveiled."

At the mention of time, Darien glanced at his iTab reflexively and, to his dismay, discovered that it was dead. "My tablet's not working," he said, recalling that Marisa had deliberately left hers at home.

Marisa's brows shot up questioningly. "Do you have any idea how long it's been out of order?"

Darien shook his head. "No, I don't. Maybe we should borrow a tablet from Jack and check in with Izzy."

"Let's wait until after the unveiling ceremony."

The chef appeared with a tray of fried calamari, miniature crab cakes, and bacon-wrapped scallops. As he placed the mouth-watering food on the table, a general-alert ringtone sounded, and the golf match on TV morphed into a picture of the Oval Office with Reuben Rogov seated behind his desk.

Without the usual preliminaries, the President began, "Good evening, world citizens. Thank you for joining me tonight. I called this meeting to update you about repairs being made on the religious shrines. As you may recall, upon my orders, the restoration projects began shortly after the attacks occurred. Moreover, as announced earlier today, one of the projects has been completed—the Redeemer statue overlooking Rio de Janeiro. Let's go to that location and watch the unveiling as an on-site reporter describes what we're seeing."

At the President's prompt, the scene switched to Rio, where spotlights bathed the glistening statue from top to bottom as darkness settled over the area. As had been the case since the repairs began, the statue's head was concealed by a sturdy cloth held in place by a framework of steel bars.

"This camera shot shows a view of the Redeemer statue atop Corcovado Mountain," an unseen female announcer said. "Sugarloaf Mountain and Guanabara Bay are in the background. As you can see, the walkway leading up to the statue is packed with people of all ages, as is the small courtyard surrounding its base. In addition, over a hundred thousand people have gathered in the national park near the statue. Some of them have been here eight hours or more, waiting to see this event in person."

Darien reached across the table and caught Marisa by the hand as they stared at the monitor.

"Watch closely," the announcer urged. "An operator is about to trip a switch to release the veil."

While the world held its breath, the veil split in two from top to bottom.

After a second of stunned silence, a discordant roar sounded in the Beachfront Bar & Grill and throughout the vast crowd assembled in Rio De Janeiro.

The statue's head no longer depicted Jesus Christ.

Instead, it depicted Reuben Rogov.

THE END

ABOUT THE AUTHOR
DON JOHNSTON

I was born in East Texas a long time ago and grew up with a sister and a brother.

When I was five years old, I found a tattered science book with several pages missing. The first intact page showed a monarch butterfly emerging from a chrysalis. That incident was the *ah-ha moment* that drew me into the world of science.

Upon completing high school, I joined the Air Force and served as a jungle survival instructor in Panama. While in Panama, I wrote a weekly gossip column for the base newspaper and won 2nd prize in a short story contest. After that, there was a 60-year gap in my creative writing. Following my military service, I enrolled in Stephen F. Austin State University and got married. After graduating with a degree in biology and chemistry, we moved to Houston where our only child, a son, was born.

After writing for three years in the Air Force, I didn't create any more fiction until I was eighty years old. My first novel, *The Dar Lumbre Chronicles* was published in 2018, and I've been writing ever since. *By Means of Peace* is my third novel, and the next one is simmering on the back burner.

Made in the USA
Monee, IL
12 November 2023